WARD ZERO

...the dead ward

by

LINDA HUBER

Ward Zero

All rights reserved.

Copyright © 2016 Linda Huber

The right of Linda Huber to be identified as the Author of this Work has been asserted by her in accordance with the Copyright Designs and Patents Act 1988.

Apart from any use permitted under UK copyright law, this publication may only be reproduced, stored or transmitted, in any form, or by any means, with the prior permission in writing of the author.

All characters appearing in this work are fictitious. Any resemblance to real persons, living or dead, is purely coincidental.

Acknowledgements

Very special thanks once again to my editor Debi Alper. Her help and encouragement with this book were, as always, invaluable. Thanks also to Julia Gibbs and Yvonne Betancourt for their proofreading and formatting skills, and to Debbie Bright of The Cover Collection for the cover artwork.

My sons Matthias and Pascal Huber have given me their time and also their patience as we worked through the production of this novel; I couldn't have managed without them. More thanks go to my cousin Fiona Ewers and my nephew Calum Rodger, for information about the themes in *Ward Zero* – it turned into a real family affair!

Bea Davenport and Debi Alper both helped me with the blurb – thanks, ladies, so much.

And to the many, many people who have supported me in so many ways, in real life and on social media – I hope I'm as much help to you as you are to me!

To my godmother, Doris

Linda Huber grew up in Glasgow, Scotland, where she trained as a physiotherapist. She spent ten years working with neurological patients, firstly in Glasgow and then in Switzerland. During this time she learned that different people have different ways of dealing with stress in their lives, and this knowledge still helps her today, in her writing.

Linda now lives in Arbon, Switzerland, where she works as a language teacher on the banks of beautiful Lake Constance. *Ward Zero* is her fifth novel.

Visit Linda at www.lindahuber.net
Follow her on Twitter@LindaHuber19

Also by Linda Huber

The Paradise Trees

The Cold Cold Sea

The Attic Room

Chosen Child

Prologue

Thursday, 20th July

He stared across the table in the crowded restaurant and his mouth went dry. Sarah. She was so lovely, smiling at him with shiny blonde hair just tipping her shoulders, and her blouse an exact match for the blue of her eyes. And now he would have to kill her too. It was too much to bear.

He reached for his glass, fighting to keep the 'I'm having the greatest time ever' expression fixed on his face. But her last remark had confirmed it – she knew way too much. And he, idiot that he was, had just made a monumental mistake. Sarah was busy with her fritters; she hadn't realised the significance of what he'd said. But she would, and the first thing she'd do was tell that bloody policeman. It was a risk he couldn't take. Time to switch his emotions off.

He took a deep breath, forcing himself to smile back. All he had to do was keep her busy thinking about other things, and after dessert he would suggest a quick coffee at home. His home. Once he had her safely locked up he could organise her death in peace and quiet. It shouldn't be too difficult – he'd already had a practice run.

When Sarah was gone too, he'd be safe.

If only he'd never gone to the hospital. He hadn't wanted things to end like this, not for one minute.

Chapter One

Two weeks earlier: Tuesday, 4th July

Sarah stepped into the arrivals hall at Manchester Airport. What a brilliant feeling – back on British soil for her first long break in two years. And she was ready for it. Teaching in Switzerland and travelling round Europe in the holidays had been exhausting, if exciting. And now – where was Mim?

A glance round the waiting crowd failed to locate her foster mother's strawberry-blonde head, and Sarah stood still. She hadn't spoken to Mim since last week, but they'd texted yesterday. At least... Sarah frowned. *She* had texted her new flight time and Mim had replied with a smiley, which, when you thought about it, wasn't typical. Mim had the gift of the gab even when she was texting.

'There you are! Sorry I'm late – I had to park at the back of beyond.'

Sarah spun round to see a short, very pregnant figure beaming up at her, dark curls damp on her brow. 'Rita! You're huge! Come here!'

A lump came into her throat as she hugged the other

woman, feeling the hardness of Rita's bump against her own body. Lucky Rita.

Rita hugged back. 'That's pregnancy for you. Come on, let's get out of this rabble.'

Sarah grabbed her case and turned towards the exit. 'You're on. But where's Mim?'

She couldn't imagine what could have kept Mim away from the airport when the two of them were supposed to be setting off on their long-anticipated tour of Yorkshire that very afternoon.

Rita took her free elbow. 'Ah. Now don't shoot the messenger, Sarah. It's not my fault. My darling mother insisted you weren't told until you'd arrived. Mim's in hospital. She had an emergency knee operation on Saturday and she's doing well.'

Sarah stopped dead. 'No! What happened?'

Rita shot her a sideways glance, the ghost of a smile on her face. 'She was biking home from the DIY store with a large tub of paint under one arm and didn't quite manage the turn into Allington Road. She collided with the fish van and her right knee was damaged so much the docs had to replace it. And the fish van, her bike, and the road were all left with an interesting new yellow pattern.'

Sarah closed her eyes in affectionate exasperation. It was such a Mim thing to do. 'Oh no, Rita, poor Mim. So what's the plan now?'

'Back to mine for coffee, then I guess you'll want to get down to Brockburn to see her.'

Sarah nodded, acknowledging the unease niggling in her gut. Her own experience of Brockburn General hadn't been the best. It was horrible to think of warm, energetic

Mim stuck in a hospital bed.

'Love to Mim! And call me tonight!'

'Will do. Thanks for the loan of your car.' Sarah waved as she drove off. Rain was streaming down the windscreen as she turned Rita's Opel towards the Manchester ring road, but by the time she reached Brockburn the sun had struggled through. For a moment her spirits lifted. It wasn't the prettiest town on earth, but even red brick looked better in sunshine. She took the short cut round the park then turned towards the east side of town, where Brockburn General had stood for a hundred years at least, and oh, Lord – was Mim okay?

The hospital was a sprawling collection of buildings flung up in different decades, most of them in depressing shades of grey. 'Colditz' was a good word to describe the place, and Sarah's mood plummeted, taking her back to the day of her grandmother's death. Black Tuesday. Blue-lighting up this road, sirens wailing, a paramedic pounding on Gran's chest and fourteen-year-old Sarah having hysterics on the seat beside him. Thinking about it still made the sweat break out.

Forcing down panic, Sarah flipped on the indicator. Nothing like that was happening today. She and Mim were going to turn Colditz into *The Great Escape*, weren't they?

The rehabilitation unit was a four-storey block at the back of the compound, beside maternity and opposite geriatrics, and Sarah parked as close to the main door as she could. A quick glance in the mirror confirmed her make-up was still in place and her hair no more chaotic than usual. She tucked her handbag under one arm and hurried across the car park. Two minutes more and she'd see with her own eyes how Mim was. She was being silly, worrying like this.

Glass doors slid open at her approach, and Sarah strode in before slowing down. The entrance area was busy and noisy, the cafeteria on the right providing an interesting olfactory challenge to the usual hospital smell, and the sounds of Wimbledon coming from a darkened TV room straight ahead. Sarah hurried towards the lifts. The wards here were named after rivers, but they had numbers too. Mim was in Clyde, aka Ward Seven, on the fourth floor. Sarah pressed the button. Going up...

The lift doors opened at the orthopaedic rehab floor and Sarah stepped out. A porter was waiting with an empty trolley, and she squeezed past with a muttered, 'Excuse me.'

He swung round and caught her elbow. 'Sarah? Sarah Martin? It is, isn't it?'

Sarah gaped at him. Tall, dark hair, thin face – handsome thin face, actually... Jack Morrison from Montgomery Road, way back when she'd lived with Gran, and golly, he'd changed since the days of teeth braces and school sweatshirts. 'Jack – goodness, it's been years! So you work here?'

He smiled, showing white, even teeth. 'I'm between proper jobs at the moment so I'm being a porter for the summer. What are *you* doing here?'

'Visiting my foster mum.' Sarah glanced at the clock on the wall behind him. She didn't have time for a long what-have-you-been-up-to conversation, even if he was the best-looking bloke she'd spoken to all year.

His face creased sympathetically. 'You had a hard time back then, didn't you?'

Sarah was touched. 'It was awful. But my foster family were – are – great. I'm fine. Are your parents still in Brockburn?'

'They've moved to a retirement complex down near the town centre. Unwillingly, I might add, but Dad's health... I've started doing up their old place. Not so easy – memories in every room.' His eyes were suddenly bleak.

Sarah bit her lip. Sensitive as well as good-looking, and he seemed to be having a hard time. Poor Jack. He was an only child, she remembered that, but oh, Mim was waiting...

His bleep saved the day. 'Sarah, I have to go, but why don't we have coffee sometime, catch up a bit?'

Relieved, she moved away. 'Great idea. Phone me at Mim's, huh? Miriam Dunbar, Allington Road.'

'I'll do that.' He touched one finger to his head and pushed his trolley into the lift. Sarah heard him whistle *The Song of the Clyde* as the lift started back down.

A young nurse directed her to room 145, and she opened the door with her heart in her mouth.

'Sarah, love! Come in and let me look at you!'

Mim was sitting beside a bed at the window, both legs resting on a footstool, and Sarah ran over to hug her. There was a long scrape on Mim's forehead and she was paler than usual, but her hair was shining and her lippie was on. She was wearing a tracksuit in her favourite turquoise, and the eyes fixed on Sarah were bright.

Sarah heaved a sigh. It was going to be all right. 'You bad woman, keeping all this from me. Now tell me how you are.'

Mim grimaced. 'Mediocre would be the best word, but it could have been a whole lot worse. As soon as I can bend my knee ninety degrees and straighten it enough to stand on safely, I can go home.' She dropped her voice. 'Which is more than can be said for some of the poor souls here. Rehab or not, it feels like an old folks' home, and I'm not ready for that.'

'Can you walk? Are you in pain?' Sarah settled down on the chair beside Mim's.

'I have elbow crutches, and I swallow every painkiller they bring me, but it is getting better. Now tell me about you. What's happening about the job?'

Sarah relaxed. Mim really did seem herself. 'The Zürich one is finished, but there's a vacancy for a primary teacher in the international school in Geneva this October, and I can have it if I want it. And oh, I don't know.'

'Why not?'

'Geneva's in the French part of Switzerland and my French isn't wonderful. And… you know. Andreas. I'll need to have a good hard think. I've to let them know by the end of this month.'

She glanced round the room as she spoke. It was pleasant enough for a hospital, with green-tinted blinds keeping the sun out, and a couple of flower prints on the opposite wall. The occupants of the other three beds were all elderly, and busy with visitors too.

A nurse appeared and parked a trolley beside Mim's

bed. 'Mr Lawrence is coming to inspect your knee. Let's get that dressing off.' She nodded to Sarah. 'You can stay if you want to.'

Sarah shook her head. She'd never been good with blood. 'I'll wait outside. I don't want to go all weak and wobbly on you.'

Mim stood up on her good leg and hopped over to the bed. 'Go and have a coffee, Sarah love. I'll try to persuade Mr Lawrence to let me home this week, now you're here to keep an eye on me. Wish me luck!'

'The very best. Tell him I'll do all I can,' said Sarah, kissing Mim warmly.

Petra Walker lifted the pile of post from the floor and closed the flat door behind her, her nose wrinkling. Pooh – Wilma'd been in hospital less than two weeks but the place smelled like a museum already. And it was only going to get worse. The new stroke on Saturday had knocked her poor grandmother for six all over again; she'd been semi-conscious or asleep most of the time ever since. Tears stung in Petra's eyes.

She leafed through the post – a letter from the bank, and a postcard of Malaga from Mrs Baker across the road's son Ray, that was nice of him. The rest was junk mail. Petra tossed it into the bin and slit the bank letter open with the bread knife, still on the worktop where Wilma'd last used it. God, how pathetic an old person's abandoned flat was.

And what the... Petra felt her eyes widen as she stared at the bank statement. This was a mistake, a joke – Wilma hadn't emptied her account last week, no way... But according to this there was exactly seventeen pounds and forty-seven pence left. Petra flung the letter on the table and scrabbled in her bag for her mobile. Bloody banks. Someone's head would roll for this. What had they done with Wilma's cash?

The voice on the phone was female and sounded about sixteen. 'I'm sorry, Mrs Walker, I can't give you that information.'

Petra's head reeled. They would have to get something sorted, power of attorney or whatever. How was she supposed to deal with this if they wouldn't talk to her?

'Please check the account. My grandmother's been in hospital for two weeks – she can't possibly have gone to the bank.'

Fingers clicked on a keyboard. 'The information you have on the statement appears to be correct. If –'

Petra broke the connection and stuffed the letter back into its envelope. She would go to the hospital right now. With any luck someone there'd be able to confirm that Wilma hadn't been to the bank. Although... there was a bank in the hospital now, and last week Wilma'd been able to get about and do things. Petra's heart sank. Surely Wilma didn't have all that money in her locker? The only way to find out was to ask, and maybe someone would be able to advise her what to do next about the stupid bank. Frustration fizzed up inside her.

The rehab unit was busy as usual, and Petra ran upstairs to Ward Five.

Nick the staff nurse was behind the computer at the nurses' station. 'All right, Mrs Walker?'

Petra slowed down. 'Is Wilma up to talking today?'

He shrugged. 'She was at lunchtime, but the physio tired her out. Have a look, though, she might be awake again.'

The door of Wilma's four-bed room was propped open. Petra approached the nearest bed, where her grandmother was leaning back on pillows, her mouth slack and eyes half-closed. Petra wiped away tears – the poor old thing looked like a real geriatric now.

'Gran! Wake up. Wilma!' Petra shook the floppy arm on the covers. There was no response. 'Gran – did you go to the bank? What happened to the money?'

'Wha...' Wilma's eyes rolled and she turned her head away.

'Tell me if you went to the bank! There's nothing left in your account – I need to know what to do about your rent. Wilma! Wake up, for God's sake, you have to –' Petra's voice echoed round the room. The other patients were staring now, and so were a couple of people in the corridor.

'Mrs Walker, stop. She can't talk when she's half-asleep. Come and tell me what's wrong.'

Trembling, Petra allowed the ward sister to lead her from the room.

He stood in the corridor, the hairs on his arms rising as he watched Vicky usher Mrs Walker into the visitors' room. No. How could she have found out already? A sickening wave of apprehension swept through him as realisation dawned. She'd have access to Wilma's post. He'd never have targeted the old witch if he'd known she was going to deteriorate like this. He needed his victims dopey enough to believe his story, but Wilma wasn't in charge of her life anymore. That was dangerous.

He crept up to the visitors' room, pretending to fiddle with his phone.

Vicky was speaking. '...thing to do is speak to Mr Paterson about it. He's the head administrator and he deals with complaints of all kinds. Are you sure it's not a bank mistake?'

'They said it was all okay. How can I get hold of Mr Paterson?'

'I'll call and make you an appointment, shall I?'

He stepped smartly from the doorway as Vicky emerged and hurried towards the nurses' station. She had what looked like an animated conversation on the phone, but he didn't dare go near enough to listen in, and all this manipulating his phone was making him conspicuous. He thrust it into his pocket and hurried along the corridor, an idea forming in his head.

Half an hour later he ducked into a deserted storeroom and called the admin secretary.

'This is... um, Evan in rehab Ward Five,' he said, making sure he sounded apologetic. 'Mrs Walker can't remember what time tomorrow her meeting with Mr Paterson is. She's a bit stressed at the moment.'

'Hang on,' said the secretary. 'Okay... He's not in tomorrow. Her meeting's on Thursday at three.'

'Thanks.' He rang off.

Sometime between now and Thursday at three, he was going to have to do something about Petra Walker. His stomach cramped.

The cafeteria was mobbed. Sarah collected coffee and digestives, and looked round for a table, her gaze stopping at a woman sitting by herself at the back of the room. She was wearing a low-cut black top under a short denim jacket, and was hunched over her coffee cup, looking cold as well as worried. That was... yes, that's right – that woman's daughter had been in foster care at Mim's two or three years ago.

Sarah hesitated, but the woman had seen her and stared back before giving a thin little smile and a nod.

Sarah went across. 'Do you mind if I sit here? You're Frankie's mum, aren't you? Mim Dunbar was my foster mother too.'

The woman pushed a hand through short hair dyed a vivid red, displaying four earrings studded in her ear. 'Help yourself. Sorry, I can't remember your name.'

Sarah sat down, trying not to touch the table top, which was unappetisingly sticky. 'Sarah Martin.'

The woman leaned back, her face dreary. 'Petra Walker. You visiting someone?'

'Mim. She had a knee replacement but I'm hoping to get her home soon. How's Frankie?'

The little girl's face slid into Sarah's head. Frankie had spent all summer with Mim the year she was eight, after Petra split up with her partner and then disappeared into a bottle. It had been a hard few weeks for them all.

The woman shrugged. 'Frankie's fine, but my gran isn't. She's in Ward Five, neuro rehab, and she's gone right down the tubes this past week. I've spent all bloody afternoon trying to find out where her money's disappeared off to. The silly old bat seems to have withdrawn most of her life savings last week and I can't think what she's done with all that cash. I mean in a hospital, for God's sake. And she's all but unconscious today so I can't even ask her about it.'

Sarah stared. She remembered Mim saying Petra's grandmother was a force to be reckoned with. 'You mean she went to the bank?'

Petra pulled out a packet of cigarettes, scowled at them and stuffed them back into her bag. 'No, she phoned them. There's a sub-branch in the hospital and apparently they'll come to you, for a fee. She could organise stuff like that last week, but she had another stroke on Saturday and they're talking about care homes now. It's a real bugger.'

Sarah was silent. Beside problems like these, her own worries seemed trivial. 'How old's your gran?'

Petra drained her cup. 'Eighty-seven. Three weeks ago she was doing her own housework, making jam and everything... I guess that's all finished. And what can I do? It's hard enough working and bringing up a kid alone – I never get a minute's break but someone comes along wanting something.'

'Maybe it's best to let other people take care of your gran now,' said Sarah gently. 'You can't do everything yourself.'

Petra scowled again. 'You're right there. But if she's

lost all that money there'll be nothing left to pay for the care home, will there? She'll end up stuck in a geriatric ward. I'd better get back. They were going to try and wake her for me. See you around.'

Sarah tried to sound positive. 'Good luck. Say hi to Frankie from me.'

It was a relief to be on her own again. Poor Petra. It must be awful, having to watch someone you love go downhill like that.

The lukewarm coffee turned bitter in Sarah's mouth. Would she and Rita be in a similar situation with Mim in twenty, thirty years' time? And what about when she was old? Rita had little Jamie and the coming baby to look out for her, but... Sarah put the cup down, her fingers shaking. What if she never had kids of her own? Oh, not as insurance for her old age, but – she did want her own family one day. And there was no sign of anybody even approaching Mr Right in her life at the moment – and her next birthday was the big three-oh.

A glance at the clock had her hurrying towards the lift. Stop being morbid, Sarah. Concentrate on Mim for now.

The expression on her foster mother's face was enough to banish all gloomy thoughts.

'I can come home on Thursday, if I can get up and down five stairs tomorrow!'

Sarah perched on the window ledge beside Mim's bed. 'You'd better do your exercises then, and get fit for whoever's going to test you!'

Mim immediately began to bend and straighten her knee. 'Sarah, it won't be a problem. This time on Thursday we'll be sitting in the garden sipping white wine – or

Prosecco, we can have a little party, and oh, hallelujah, I'll sleep so much better in my own home.'

It was after six when Sarah left the hospital. She'd watched Mim eat ham salad for her evening meal – 'The cold food's not bad, Sarah love, but anything that's supposed to be hot is so institutional it's inedible. I'm looking forward to a nice curry when I get home' – and walked up and down the corridor with her before leaving. Mim was pretty good on her crutches. It *was* going to be all right.

Driving along the main hospital thoroughfare, Sarah began to plan. She would turn the study into a downstairs bedroom for Mim for the first few weeks. And she'd better get some Prosecco in, too. A red-headed girl walking towards the main gate reminded Sarah of Petra Walker – poor soul, she wouldn't be planning her grandmother's homecoming any time soon.

Allington Road was a five-minute drive away, and the usual twin feelings of peace and pleasure settled into Sarah's head as she pulled up on the gravel in front of the red brick semi. Her time with Mim and Pop had been the making of her.

She'd arrived here late that terrible afternoon when Gran died, seven years almost to the day after her parents were killed in a car crash. A much-too-cheerful social worker had collected her at the hospital and taken her to Mim, and a vivid little scene was imprinted in Sarah's memory – Mim, opening the front door, taking one look at Sarah and pulling her into the longest bear hug ever. Sarah had emerged with a wet face and a warmed heart, knowing she'd be safe here.

The front door opened with its usual creak and she stepped into the hallway. The house fell silent around her, but it was a comfortable silence. You could tell children had lived here, little ghost children now, memories the old house carried in its core. Nostalgia brought tears to Sarah's eyes before common sense took over. Mim should sell this place and buy something smaller. There hadn't been many foster children in the two years since Pop's death – some cases were a two-person job.

She opened all the windows and raided the freezer. With a lasagne safely in the oven, Sarah sat in the kitchen scribbling a to-do list.

Food shopping. And she should go to the bank too, get her Swiss account organised for a longer stay here. Petra's disconsolate face flitted into Sarah's head and she frowned. She should have warned Mim to be careful about her cash in the hospital... Next, the cat. Caitlyn Mackie next door would have taken him in. And Mim's bed – but tomorrow would do for that, for everything, actually, except the cat. It would be good to have his company. Satisfied, Sarah poured a glass of Chianti and took it out to the back garden. Pop's bench was still in its place against the wall, catching the evening sunshine. Sarah sank down.

Sipping her wine, she relaxed tense limbs. Thank heavens today was nearly over. And help, she hadn't even had lunch, unless you counted hospital coffee and biscuits. This wine would go straight to her head.

'Sarah! Good to see you home!'

The voice came from the garden next door, and Sarah

opened her eyes to see a suntanned face under dark blonde curls beaming over the wall. 'Hi, Caitlyn. It's great to be back, though I wish it hadn't happened quite like this.'

Caitlyn nodded, her face sober again. 'How's Mim? I'm doing research for an article on hospitals at the moment. I must compare notes with her when she's home.'

Sarah lurched across the garden. The wine *had* gone straight to her head... Caitlyn was looking at her glass with raised eyebrows, and Sarah grinned back cheerfully.

'Mim's doing well. She'll be home on Thursday so I'll need to get the place organised. Want some wine? Oh – is Thomas with you?'

'Thanks, but I'm about to take the car to the garage to leave it for its service tomorrow. I'll get Thomas.'

Caitlyn trotted off and returned clutching Mim's overweight orange and white tomcat. Sarah accepted the furry bundle and fussed over him. There was nothing like cuddling a cat to make you feel better.

Caitlyn brushed cat hairs from her front. 'Let's catch up properly over a pizza soon. There's a brilliant new restaurant on Causey Street.'

Sarah dropped the cat, who stalked off and lay down in the sunshine by the back door. 'Great idea. Let me see what's happening with Mim first, then we'll make plans.'

Caitlyn turned back to the house. 'I'll come over and see Mim anyway, when she's home. Let me know if you need any help, Sarah.'

'Will do,' said Sarah. A catch-up with Caitlyn sounded good; she didn't have many friends left in the area. Jack Morrison's face swam into her head, and she grinned. And a catch-up with Jack would be – extremely interesting.

She returned to the kitchen to rescue the lasagne, Thomas running after her. Food, the news on telly and an early night seemed the best plan.

Three hours later she lay in bed, peace descending as she relaxed into the mattress. It was good to be back, even if things hadn't worked out as she'd expected. Thank heavens Mim was doing so well. It could easily have been so much worse.

But what a strange story that was about Petra Walker's grandmother and the money... Sarah shivered under the warm duvet. How she hated hospitals. But never mind – this time on Thursday, Mim would be safe back home.

Chapter Two

Wednesday, 5th July

Caitlyn set the coffee machine to make her first espresso of the day, then flipped the radio on. She wasn't used to silence in the mornings, but Tina and Mark were spending the summer on the Isle of Man with their father and his new wife, so she had the place to herself. A mixed blessing... but lots of me-time to make the most of.

She sipped her coffee, feeling her brain sharpen. Thank goodness for caffeine – investigative journalists needed their wits about them. *Consumer Critique* had commissioned her for a feature on wastage in hospitals and medical practices, and some of the information she'd turned up was hair-raising. In hospitals, for instance, up to half the food intended for the patients landed in the bin. Money makes the world go round, but no-one appeared to care when public money was poured down the drain – or into the bin – in health institutions.

The landline rang while she was loading her cup into the dishwasher, and she trotted down the hallway to the phone.

'Hi, Caitlyn, it's Sarah. Can I ask a favour? I want to

shift Mim's bed downstairs until she's fully operational, but it's a two-woman job.'

'Sure. See you in a sec.'

Caitlyn slid her feet into trainers and clambered over the low wall separating the two front gardens. The family next door had been a huge help to her during her divorce – especially Mim. It was nice to be able to do something in return. She banged on the front door and put her head round.

Sarah was in the hallway, a large cardboard box in her arms and a smudge of dust across her left cheek. She grinned at Caitlyn and jerked her head towards the back of the house. 'If we shift the bookcase, we can bring a single bed down to the study.'

Between them, they manhandled the bookcase up and the bed downstairs, then Caitlyn fetched the mattress while Sarah brought a little table from the living room for Mim's bedside lamp. In half an hour they had turned the study into a not unattractive bedroom.

'Sorted,' said Sarah, fluffing up the pillow. 'Come and have some blackcurrant cordial and tell me what the kids are doing nowadays.'

Caitlyn followed her through to the kitchen. 'Tina'll be off to secondary school after the hols, can you believe it? And Mark's his usual lazy self, but that's David's problem for the next couple of weeks.'

'So why aren't you taking the opportunity to spend three weeks sunning yourself in Greece?'

Caitlyn swirled her cordial round the glass. She'd asked herself the same question. 'I know. I should be. But – first summer away from me, you know. I wanted to be reachable.'

'Well, if you're ever fed up with your own company, pop over here. Mim'll be glad to see a fresh face now and then.'

'I will. Thanks, Sarah. So what's happening in your life?'

'Not a lot. I'm between jobs, and Andreas is history now. It was the old story – he traded me in for a younger model last Easter.'

'Scumbag.' They exchanged grins, and Caitlyn stood up to go. Time to get on with the research for her hospital article.

Sarah watched as Alexis the physio settled Mim back into a chair by her bed.

'Right, Miriam. The movement's pretty good. Have a rest for five and then we'll go on the stairs. That's the real test.' She handed Mim a glass of water and left.

'Think you'll manage five stairs?' said Sarah.

Mim glared at her. 'I will if it kills me. I want out of here.'

Sarah held back a smile. If Mim failed the stair test, fur would fly.

'I wonder how Frankie is,' said Mim suddenly.

Sarah had described the previous day's meeting with Petra, and to her dismay Mim was concerned. 'Frankie isn't the problem. It's the missing money.' She took the empty glass from Mim and set it on the locker.

'I know. But eleven's a tricky age, and if there's bad stuff going on... Petra might not cope, without her gran there for support.' Mim's voice was dejected, and Sarah patted her good knee.

'Frankie'll be fine. And here's Alexis, so you make sure you're fine too, on those stairs.'

To Sarah's relief Mim went up the five stairs with scarcely a wobble, muttering 'Old leg, new-leg-and-crutches,' as she mounted each step.

'Good,' said Alexis. 'Turn round slowly. Okay, ready to go down?'

Sarah held her breath. Going down was apparently more difficult than going up. Her expression tense, Mim negotiated her way back to ground level.

'Super!' said Alexis. 'As far as I'm concerned you can go home tomorrow after therapy. I'll set you up a course of outpatient physio three times a week. Are you going back to the ward now?'

Mim shook her head. 'I reckon I deserve a coffee. Come on, Sarah. We can have a peek into the TV room to see who gets through to the semi-finals at Wimbledon.'

Sarah followed as Mim crutched her way to the lifts. Downstairs, they found chairs in the TV room, where two athletic-looking young women with Russian names were thumping the ball around on the big wall screen.

'It'll be a while before I'm back at the tennis club,' said Mim, her voice gloomy.

Sarah gave her a little poke. 'No instant miracles, but hey – five stairs today, home tomorrow. It's all good.'

'I suppose so. I'll be glad to get out of here.'

Sarah followed her gaze to the old woman dozing in a wheelchair on Mim's other side. Her feet were swollen in hospital issue slippers, and a thin dribble of spit was working its way down her chin. She certainly wouldn't be going home this week.

Sarah stood up. 'I'll bring the coffee in here, shall I?'

She was reaching for her purse when Mim jerked upright in her chair. 'Frankie!'

Petra and Frankie were standing in the doorway, looking round the room. The small girl Sarah remembered had given way to a lanky child with mousy shoulder-length hair shrouding a glum expression, which brightened when she saw Mim.

Petra gripped Frankie's arm and pulled her across the room towards them.

'How are you, Petra?' said Mim. 'Sarah told me about your gran. Frankie darling, come and let me look at you properly.'

The girl reached down to return Mim's hug. 'I hoped we'd see you.'

Petra flashed them her thin smile. 'She's talked about nothing else since I told her I'd met Sarah.' She reached down to shake the shoulder of the old woman beside Mim. 'And this is my gran. Wilma! Heck, she's out for the count again. Why on earth did they leave her here? She should be upstairs.'

Sarah exchanged a glance with Mim. So this poor soul was the grandmother whose money was missing.

Petra plumped down in a nearby chair. 'I'm glad you're doing well, Mim. But it's a sad day when Gran sleeps through Wimbledon. Wilma! Wake up! Oh, what's the use?' Petra sounded close to tears, and Frankie's lips began to tremble.

Sarah hesitated, but Mim leapt into the breach. 'Why

don't you two join Sarah and me for coffee, and see if your gran's more awake afterwards?'

Five minutes later they were sitting in the cafeteria, Frankie with a large piece of chocolate cake in front of her.

'Eat that slowly or you'll be sick,' said Petra, her face grim. 'I don't know why I bought it – you'll get fat.'

Frankie shrugged, staring at the table top and twirling her hair.

Sarah stirred her coffee. 'No school this afternoon, Frankie?'

Frankie brightened immediately. 'It's closed today and tomorrow because so many people got scabies. I didn't get it so it's like a holiday.' She started on the chocolate cake.

Mim didn't miss a beat. 'Lucky girl. I'm sorry your gran's having problems, Petra.'

Petra's voice was rough with emotion. 'That last stroke has knocked her right off, but I so need to speak to her about the money. Those bloody posh banks are no help at all. I don't know what she was thinking, withdrawing all that cash. But she's been asleep or unconscious twenty hours a day since the weekend. If I thought I would end up like that I'd shoot myself.'

An uncomfortable silence fell and Sarah searched for something to break it. Petra shouldn't talk like that in front of her girl. The poor little thing was working her way through the chunk of cake, but whether or not she was enjoying it was anyone's guess.

'We can't plan the future,' Mim said at last. 'Sometimes things don't work out the way we'd like them to.'

Petra raised her eyes heavenwards. 'You can say that again. I've got an appointment with the hospital administrator tomorrow afternoon, anyway. We'll see if he can track down Wilma's savings because they were definitely real and I've got the bank statements to prove it. They should never have left all that money with her and if it doesn't turn up I'll sue. Frankie, if you've finished we'd better get back to Gran. Oh, for heaven's sake, look at you.' She brushed the child's front free of crumbs and turned to Sarah and Mim. 'Good luck. Maybe we'll see you again before you leave.'

Mim reached out and squeezed Frankie's hand. 'Pop up to Ward Seven if you come tomorrow. I'll be here till the afternoon.'

Sarah watched as the two trailed back towards the TV room. 'Petra has an – energetic – way of speaking.'

Mim pursed her lips. 'My mother would have called her 'a rough diamond'. Kind enough – she bought that chocolate cake without being asked – but a bit too direct. Mind you, she must be under a big strain. You can tell she cares about her gran.'

'Yes. Oh, Mim, I'm so glad you're okay!' Sarah reached across for a hug, and Mim hugged back.

'No problems here. Home tomorrow, then you and I are going to have the longest talk ever. I want to know what's causing that little frown line – and don't tell me it's my knee, because it's not.'

Sarah managed to laugh, but she could feel the lump rising in her throat. How very good it would be to get Mim away from the hospital. This time tomorrow...

Chapter Three

Thursday, 6th July

He cowered in his car, parked illegally by the main entrance to the hospital, his eyes glued to the nearby bus stop and sweat drenching his shirt. She must come, she must come... He had to stop her before she went to the administrator. If Ian Paterson started to sniff around it could all become very dangerous. The police might be involved, and if they started investigating they would find out that Wilma wasn't the only old dear to lose a large sum of money. Not all his victims had been in hospital, of course... His fingers drummed on the steering wheel. Glynis had. Oh God, they mustn't find Glynis. What a horror scenario that would be.

A number 25 bus drew up and disgorged a handful of unhappy hospital visitors fighting with umbrellas and – yes! There was Petra, and hell, she had the kid with her. He watched as they passed, huddled together under one umbrella. They were heading for rehab, so hopefully the girl would stay there with old Wilma. He would catch Petra on her way back down to the admin building.

His stomach was churning and he fumbled in his

pocket for a mint. It was all very well knowing that Wilma's stupid granddaughter was the biggest cow in creation, but that wouldn't help him with the real problem here – getting rid of her. The first part of the plan was fine. He would manage to lure her into the car, where the Taser he'd bought – just in case – at the start of the money project was waiting under his seat. One good zap and she'd be his. But once he'd got her locked up in the garage at home – what then? That was where his plan came to sudden end.

He turned the key in the ignition and the car jerked forwards. Now to park as near to rehab as he could, then he'd intercept Petra when she emerged again.

Rain was drumming ever harder on the car roof when he pulled up about twenty yards from the rehab entrance, but that was all to the good. Petra was unlikely to stand around wondering if she should accept a lift back to the other end of the hospital. Another horror scenario flashed into his head, making his heart pound. Supposing someone on Ward Five offered to drive her to the admin building? That wasn't impossible, and all he could do was hope it wouldn't happen.

He glanced at his watch. Any minute now...

Sweat broke out on his brow.

Petra dumped the bag of clean nighties on a chair. 'You sit here and wait for Gran. Though why they even bother bringing her to watch the tennis after physio's beyond me. If she starts snoring take her back upstairs, and I'll collect you there.'

Frankie flopped down without speaking and stared in the other direction, the picture of a sulky almost-teenager.

Petra tried to sound pleasant. 'I suppose she might be awake enough to talk to you. She always used to love Wimbledon.' Leaving Frankie picking her nails, Petra hurried towards the toilets beside the cafeteria. Better check her make-up before she left.

As soon as she stepped out the building she realised that touching up her face had been a waste of time. The rain, a steady downpour when they arrived at the hospital, was now an absolute monsoon, and thunder was grumbling in the distance. Petra's umbrella blew inside out the moment she put it up and she struggled to control it, wobbling on her heels. Hell, she should never have worn these shoes, but her waterproof ones were so crappy – she didn't want Mr Paterson to think she was Wilma's poor relation, desperate to get her hands on the money when the old girl snuffed it. Rain blew into her face and Petra felt like crying. What idiot designed this place, with the offices at the front near the bus stops, forcing visitors and patients alike to walk effing miles to and from the wards?

'Hi there!' The voice came from behind and she turned and peered into the car crawling along beside the pavement.

Thank goodness, someone was going to give her a lift.

'You're a life-saver,' she said, but the wind whipped her words away.

She dropped into the car and slammed the door. He reached under his seat, and shock took Petra's breath away. Shit, no! What the – Panic surged, and she twisted round to open the door.

But it was locked.

Fear swirled through him and his fingers slid on the yellow plastic as he fired the Taser. She twitched, the horror on her face mirroring his own expression when he realised – she wasn't unconscious! He fired the Taser a second time but again she only twitched like some electrocuted cartoon character, her eyes wide and fixed on his. There was no choice. He whacked the side of her head with the Taser as hard as he could, the sweat of sheer relief cold on his body when she slumped in the passenger seat, eyes closed.

Away, he had to get away from here. Thank God it was raining so hard. Even if anyone'd been out in this weather, the windows were awash and steamed up too – no-one could have witnessed what he'd done.

He gunned the car towards home. Six minutes, that was all it took to drive to the row of lock-ups behind his house, but it felt like forever and he swore as a lorry cut in front of him. Come on, *come on* – she mustn't wake up until he got her home.

His lock-up was a roomy, double compartment that had been Dad's workshop, at the end of the lane behind the house. The entire row was half-derelict; no-one kept a car there now. He ran to open the door then reversed inside, quick, quick, he was so nearly safe... He had made it.

Bile rose in his throat as he turned on the dim light

and slammed the heavy metal door down, leaving them cocooned in semi-darkness. But there was no time to be sick. Petra was making stupid little moaning noises as he pulled her from the car and dragged her to the side. Her hands, he should fix them first. He took one of the cable binders he'd laid out ready, but it was all he could do to slide the end into the tiny opening and he swore under his breath. His hands were shaking like a ninety-year-old's. At last he managed and tightened the binder round her wrists. Now her feet; that was easier. He grabbed the waiting length of blue nylon cord. And the gag... and the sack over her head.

He scrambled to his feet, staring at her, an anonymous bundle on the floor. She was immobilised and she hadn't woken up. Thank you, thank you. He could go home and calm down, and work out what to do. He had the shakes now; he couldn't keep his hands still... Up with the door again, down the lane, round the corner – and home. He was safe.

But what had he done, what had he done?

He had crossed a line and there was no going back. He ran to the bathroom and hung over the toilet bowl, his stomach heaving.

Sarah turned into the main hospital thoroughfare, Mim's raincoat and stout shoes in a bag on the passenger seat and the windscreen wipers going double time. Talk about Sod's law. The weather had been perfect ever since she'd arrived in the country, but now that they needed a dry day, on came the rain.

Mim was in the TV room with Frankie and Wilma, who was no more awake than the day before. Two young men were whacking the ball about the court; it appeared that Wimbledon was enjoying better weather than Brockburn.

Sarah crouched beside Mim's chair. 'All packed and ready to go?'

'Am I just!' said Mim, winking at Frankie.

The girl was slumped between Mim and Wilma, wearing a too-small blue tracksuit that hadn't been much protection against the rain, and chewing a strand of hair. She looked as if she'd rather be anywhere else than in a hospital TV room watching tennis with her great-grandmother. But she did smile back at Mim, Sarah noticed, and the hair was clean. Poor Frankie, it was an awkward time of life, with puberty on the horizon and the whole world suddenly different and awkward.

'Where's Petra?' asked Sarah.

Frankie pulled out her phone and glared at it. 'She went for her meeting with that administrator,' she said, her voice aggrieved. 'She's been gone for ages. And I hate tennis.'

Sarah laughed. 'Oh well. It's the finals at the weekend, then that's it for another year. And it could be worse, Frankie – it could be cricket.'

Frankie's eyes widened. 'S'pose,' she said, then grinned. 'Yeah – that would be much worse.'

Mim reached for her crutches. 'Sarah and I'll get my things and say goodbye upstairs, then we'll look in here before we leave. I'm sure your mum'll be back by that time.'

Sarah walked to the lifts beside Mim, noticing with

pleasure that the older woman was better on her feet than yesterday. It wasn't going to be a long convalescence, which was all to the good, because Mim wasn't a patient person.

The nurses fussed round as Mim collected her belongings, and Sarah chuckled to herself. Pop had always said Mim could charm the hind leg off a donkey. She'd ordered a huge box of chocolates for the staff, and they gathered in the corridor, waving and calling out good wishes as Mim and Sarah entered the lift.

'Everyone's favourite patient, that's you,' said Sarah, when the doors slid shut.

Mim raised her eyes heavenwards. 'Well, they've been very kind. And they have enough awkward sods to look after without me joining in. We'll check Petra's back, then home, James, with us! Oh, Sarah, I can hardly wait!'

To Sarah's dismay there was no sign of Petra in the TV room. The rain had reached London, and ball boys were pulling the court covering over the grass. Wilma was still dozing in her wheelchair, and Frankie was still chewing her hair. Impatience flared up inside Sarah. What was Petra thinking, leaving the child here all this time?

'No sign of Mum yet?' she said, seeing the tears in the girl's eyes.

'I wish I hadn't come,' said Frankie, scowling. 'This is so boring. She's not answering her phone so she must still be in the meeting. Can I go home?'

Mim sat down beside Frankie, her face concerned.

Sarah touched the girl's arm. 'I think you'd better wait. I'll see if I can find out what's going on. Who was Petra meeting?'

Frankie sniffed. 'Bloke called Mr Paterson.'

'Okay. You two wait here.'

Sarah hurried through the entrance hall. Someone in Wilma's ward would be the best person to ask. The lift took its time coming, and Sarah tapped her foot on the green linoleum. All she wanted was to get Mim home, but they couldn't desert poor Frankie.

Neuro rehab Ward Five was called Avon, and it had the same layout as the orthopaedic ward above. Sarah approached the desk as a blond male nurse emerged from a room behind it. He gave her a broad smile as he pinned on his badge. Staff Nurse Nick Wilson, read Sarah. Good. She explained briefly.

'Not back yet?' he said, frowning. 'That seems – odd. Ian Paterson doesn't usually go in for such marathon meetings with people's relatives. I'll give him a buzz for you.' He vanished back into the other room.

Sarah waited, aware that Jack Morrison had come up beside her. Golly, he was tall. She gave him a weak grin, feeling her heart rate increase as she caught a whiff of spicy aftershave. Wow. But that wasn't what she should be thinking here, was it? Come on, Sarah. Just find Petra, then get Mim home.

Jack's eyes were wide. 'Sarah! Is your foster mother in this ward now?'

Sarah explained again and he pulled a face.

'Gawd, poor kid. Um – how about making a date for that coffee?'

Sarah couldn't stop the grin spreading over her face. There was nothing she'd like more… 'How about the weekend? That would give me a day or two to settle Mim at home.'

'Sounds good. I'll call you.'

He gave her a quick salute and marched off down the corridor. Sarah watched him push the button for the lift, bobbing up and down on the balls of his feet while he waited. He caught her eye as the lift arrived and Sarah waved, hugging the warm feeling inside her. Maybe Mim's hospital stay was going to have a very interesting side effect...

Nick reappeared and spoke in a low voice. 'Um – Sarah, is it? There's something odd going on. Petra didn't show up for her meeting.'

Sarah could hardly believe her ears. 'Then where on earth is she? Her daughter's been waiting for hours in the TV room with Wilma. The poor kid's going bananas.'

Nick's face was blank. 'I'll come down with you and talk to them. It's time for Wilma to come up again anyway. Evan – I'm going downstairs. We seem to have mislaid Petra Walker. I'll bring Wilma back with me.'

The dark-haired nurse glared. 'Vicky's still at the head injury clinic.'

'So you're in charge. I won't be long.'

Nick turned towards the lift, and Sarah trotted along beside him. What could have happened? Even if Petra had decided for some reason not to go to the meeting, there was no excuse for leaving Frankie like that. Unless she'd been taken ill, or something.

Nick extracted Wilma from the busy TV room and manoeuvred her chair to a bench in the corner of the hallway. Mim and Frankie followed and sat down. Sarah balanced on the arm of the bench, noticing that Mim was

41

looking bright and fit, holding Frankie's hand. The girl's mouth was tight.

Nick woke Wilma very efficiently and bent till his head was level with hers. 'Your Petra didn't go to her meeting,' he said directly. 'Any idea where she could be?'

'Naaa,' said Wilma, her head lolling. A thread of spit escaped from her mouth.

Frankie looked round wildly. 'She did go! She left me in the TV room and said to wait for Gran, and she went! They brought Gran back at three and we've been waiting ever since!'

Sarah glanced at the clock above the lifts. It was nearly five. Petra had been gone for over two hours.

'Try phoning your mum again,' Nick said to Frankie.

Frankie tried first Petra's mobile and then their home number. When the second attempt failed she broke the connection and burst into noisy tears. Sarah pulled out a packet of tissues and handed one over, her eyes meeting Mim's over the girl's head.

Mim hugged Frankie. 'Oh, poor lovey. Maybe Mum remembered some bank papers or something she had to take to the meeting, and got tied up getting them. Why don't you come with Sarah and me, and wait at home with us?'

Frankie nodded, sniffing, but Nick looked aghast. 'I can't let you take Frankie just like –'

Sarah explained the relationship, and he raised his eyebrows. 'I see. But...'

'I'll call Mrs Jameson from Social Services. She can give permission.' Mim pulled her mobile out and made the connection. 'Sue, it's Mim Dunbar. Can you –'

Sarah cuddled Frankie, who was sobbing quietly now. Mim finished her explanation and listened for a moment before passing the phone to Nick.

'Okay... Right... I'll do that. Thanks.' He handed it back, his expression still bemused, then grinned at Sarah.

'Is that what's called being in the right place at the right time? Okay, if Frankie agrees she can go with you.'

Frankie was staring at Wilma, who had fallen asleep again. Sarah's heart went out to the girl. What a horrible situation. She of all people knew what it was like to feel abandoned.

'Let's get going, ladies,' she said, trying to sound matter-of-fact. 'Frankie, could you help me with Mim's things, please?'

Dejection all over her face, Frankie lifted one of Mim's bags.

Sarah tried to sound encouraging. 'A couple of hours can seem like half a lifetime when you're waiting. I'm sure your mum'll turn up soon.'

Brave words, she thought – but something must have happened to make Petra abandon her meeting and leave her daughter all this time. Communication wasn't difficult nowadays no matter what was going on.

Sarah left Frankie and Mim by the door while she ran to fetch the car, great fat raindrops soaking through her jacket straightaway. It wasn't the kind of day to go anywhere unless you had to. So where on earth was Petra?

Bent over the kitchen table, all he could hear was his own

breathing – loud and shaky, to go with his old-man hands – and the rain battering on the kitchen window. Dark disbelief was swirling round his head. Everything that could have gone wrong with his glorious get-rich-quick plan had done exactly that. What was he supposed to do now? He had bloody abducted a woman.

The memory of the struggle in the car made him retch anew, and he stumbled across the room and spat into the shiny brightness of his lovely new sink. He would never know how he'd managed to go back to work and look normal for the rest of the afternoon. And it wasn't over yet; this was his evening break. He still had a couple of hours late shift to go.

Unbelievable, how it had all gone so wrong. It wasn't the first time he'd put his old lady plan into action; it had worked perfectly four times before Petra's grandmother. Four times when no-one suspected a thing and all the lovely money was his. All he wanted was enough cash to make a beautiful home. He'd never had a nice home... He wasn't a violent person. A sob burst from his throat.

His plans hadn't stretched this far; getting Petra out of circulation had been the main objective. Okay, he'd done that.

He thumped the table top in frustration – he couldn't think straight when he was this uptight. He needed time, but that was exactly what he didn't have. People used the garage lane as a short cut to the station – suppose Petra managed to moan loudly enough to attract attention? Unlikely right this minute with the rain still pissing down, but it wouldn't rain forever. He needed her unconscious, or...

...asleep. Brilliant – Mum's old sleeping pills were still upstairs. Almost crying with relief, he floundered up the stairs and yanked the packet from the bathroom cupboard. Yes, yes – twelve pills, that would do very nicely.

There was no sound from the lock-up as he approached, the pills in one hand and a bottle of water in his jacket pocket. He stood in the lane, listening. Was she still alive? But she must be. He opened the door, slid inside, and pulled it shut again. This time, he'd brought a powerful torch to help the dim light on the ceiling, and he played it round the lock-up. Christ, this was like something out of a horror movie. Bare concrete walls darkened by years of grime and exhaust fumes, untidy shelves of anonymous tins and jars up one side – and a body huddling centre stage.

Petra's chest was heaving so she was definitely alive and something told him she was awake, too – and afraid. Choking back his own fear, he knelt and checked her bonds. Good. Now for the pills.

She twisted her head away as he lifted the sack just enough to push a pill into her mouth, past the gag. A slosh of water and the pill was down. He stared at the foil pack. If... if he gave her them all, she would die... and no-one would find out about the money. Old Wilma was on the way out too. He pushed another pill into her mouth and she fought against him, wriggling and pulling her head away, making stupid little whimpering noises. He forced the bottle into her mouth and tilted it. To his horror she choked, coughing and retching, her lips turning blue in the light of the torch on the floor beside him. He jerked back; no, no, how disgusting – he couldn't do this. Retching along with her, he covered her face again and backed towards the door, hands covering his mouth as he watched her struggle to breathe. What a coward he was. He couldn't even give a helpless woman a few pills. He leaned against the door, sipping the water and waiting for Petra to fall asleep.

Ten minutes later her breathing was steady and deep.

Sarah parked as close to the front door as possible and hurried round to help Mim out.

'Up you get, and in you go,' she said, holding an umbrella above Mim's head and grasping the older woman's elbow with her free hand. The Fiat was low; it was a struggle to extract Mim. They should have thought about that before Rita reclaimed her Opel yesterday.

Frankie emerged from the back and collected Mim's bags without being asked. Sarah smiled over her shoulder. 'Thanks, Frankie. Come on in.'

The child looked shattered, and Sarah could sympathise. That feeling of helplessness after being abandoned was something she remembered all too well. Her anger that Gran had left her alone in the world had mingled with grief first, and then guilt because she was angry. It all added up to the worst, the loneliest feeling possible. It was just wrong of Petra, deserting her poor daughter like this. Unless... but if she'd had some kind of accident on the way to her meeting, wouldn't they have heard about it by now?

'Oh, Sarah, you don't know how glad I am to be home,'

said Mim, stepping carefully over the door mat. 'Come on, Frankie love. You'll see a few changes since you were with us.'

Frankie shuffled inside, and Sarah glanced at Mim. The biggest change since Frankie's time here was that Pop wasn't around now. She followed the girl into the living room. Frankie was staring at Pop's photo on the bookcase, and Sarah hugged her. 'We miss Pop, of course, but – it was his time to go.'

Frankie nodded, and Sarah felt she'd said enough. To a child, sixty-four was a ripe old age, and Frankie hadn't known Pop long enough to grieve for him.

Mim was in the doorway. 'Where's the little table?'

'In your new study-bedroom. Go and have a look. Frankie can take your stuff through while I make us a cuppa.' Sarah sighed. The bottle of Prosecco chilling in the fridge was no longer appropriate; they could hardly celebrate with Frankie sitting there worried out of her wits. Nick had said he would make some inquiries at the hospital and find out if anyone had seen Petra, but if she didn't show up soon they'd have to phone the police.

Mim and Frankie joined her in the kitchen, and Sarah was glad to see a touch more colour in the girl's cheeks. The best thing was to distract her until Nick phoned.

Sarah shook a packet of biscuits into the tin. 'Not that you deserve chocolate digestives after what you did, you bad thing,' she said severely to Mim. 'Has she told you how she bust her knee, Frankie?'

Mim rose to the challenge and managed to make Frankie laugh with the story of the fateful bike ride home from the DIY store. 'So goodness knows when

47

the downstairs loo'll get its coat of paint,' she finished, reaching for her mug.

Frankie gazed round the kitchen. 'I'd forgotten what a big house this is,' she said, and Sarah wondered what the girl's own home was like.

'We needed it big for all you lot,' said Mim.

Frankie stared at Sarah. 'Were you fostered here too?'

Sarah nodded. 'It was well before your time. I lived with my gran before, but when she died there wasn't anyone else. So I came to Mim and Pop.'

'What happened to your parents?' Frankie's eyes were wide.

Sarah bit her lip. They were back to talking about dead people. So much for keeping things upbeat.

'They died in a car crash when I was very small,' she said briskly, putting the mugs in the dishwasher. 'I don't remember much about them. Why don't you help Mim unpack while I organise some grub? I'm sure Nick'll track your mum down soon. Your mobile's on, isn't it?'

Frankie checked, her expression gloomy again, then followed Mim into the study. Sarah pulled a packet of burgers from the freezer and put three in the microwave to defrost while she washed a lettuce, listening to Mim pointing out the photos of various foster children that were sprinkled around the study.

Frankie picked her way through half a burger before putting her knife and fork down. 'I want my mum.' Her voice was thick.

Sarah reached for her mobile. They should call Nick now. If the police were going to be involved it should happen sooner rather than later. 'I know, lovey. This is rotten for you. Is your dad around, Frankie? No? Right, I'll call Nick, and we'll see what he thinks. You could clear up here, maybe? Mim'll remind you where things go.'

Sarah took her phone through to the living room and shut the door behind her. It might be better if Frankie didn't overhear this conversation.

She should have asked Nick for a mobile number, Sarah realised as she waited for the hospital switchboard to answer. She asked to be put through to rehab Ward Five, and waited on, listening to canned music this time.

The voice that eventually answered the phone was brusque. 'Neuro five, staff nurse Evan Carter.' It was the dark-haired nurse from that afternoon.

Sarah gave her name and asked for Nick.

'He's busy with a patient. Do you want to leave a message?'

Sarah made a face. An overworked, bad-tempered nurse relaying a message wasn't ideal. But then the line crackled and Nick's voice sounded in her ear.

'Good, I was about to call you. Someone saw Petra fixing her hair in the ladies' loo down at the cafeteria around three o'clock, but that's all. She didn't arrive in the admin building. There's a reception desk on the ground floor there and the secretary's adamant about it. Petra's not answering her phone, and she's not in A&E because I checked there too. With a child involved I think we have to phone the police. Shall I do that, as she disappeared from here?'

Sarah's heart sank. 'Yes please. What on earth's happened to her?'

'Lord knows. She could have gone anywhere after she

left rehab. I'll get onto the cops now, and call you back.'

'Tell them –' Sarah hesitated. Mim would certainly insist on keeping Frankie, if the need arose, even though she wasn't functioning like a normal foster mother. 'Tell them Frankie can stay here for a day or two if necessary.'

She put the phone down and rubbed her cheek. Something very odd must have happened to Petra. She might have had problems in the past, but you could see she cared about her girl.

Uneasiness churned in Sarah's stomach as she went back to the kitchen. It was such a big thing, calling the police in. There didn't seem any way she could give Frankie this news without alarming her. They were admitting that Petra really had vanished.

Frankie, however, saw things differently. 'Oh good – they'll soon find her, won't they?' she said, her face brightening. 'I mean, they've got radios and stuff and dogs to search for people, haven't they?'

'I guess so,' said Sarah, trying not to show her anxiety. 'We'll wait until Nick calls back. Look, the rain's stopped. Why don't you go and see if Thomas is in the garden? I'm sure he'll recognise you.'

Frankie vanished through the back door, and Sarah told Mim about her conversation with Nick.

'Of course she must stay, if it comes to that,' said Mim immediately. 'I suppose Petra couldn't have gone somewhere to collect something, had an accident and been taken to a different hospital?'

'Brockburn General's the only accident and emergency hospital round here, isn't it? But that's something the police'll be able to find out.'

Mim looked sober. 'Sarah – Petra lost the plot when her partner left her back then, but she was devastated when Frankie was placed here. It was the start of getting her life back. I'm sure she'd never do anything that would mean losing her child again.'

The landline rang ten minutes later. Sarah was half expecting it to be the police, but Nick's deep voice greeted her once again.

'Just to let you know the cops'll be coming round to see you soon. They were pretty non-committal, but they've sent someone to check Petra's flat and they'll contact Social Services about Frankie. Oh, and we haven't said more to Wilma. No point worrying her before we know what's going on.'

Sarah blinked, startled. Could Petra be lying at home unconscious? They should have thought of that as soon as they realised she was missing. Sarah relayed the conversation back to Mim, who banged her fist on the table.

'I wish I was fit and able to help properly. All this sitting in the kitchen is getting right up my nose already.'

Sarah stepped out the back door. Frankie was hunched on the bench outside, Thomas clutched on her lap. Sarah dried a piece of seat with a tissue and perched beside the girl.

'He's a big smoocher, isn't he?'

Frankie scratched round Thomas's ears. 'I've always wanted a cat but Mum says it wouldn't work. We're on the third floor.'

'Yes, that makes it difficult,' said Sarah. 'Frankie, the police are coming round soon. I expect they'll have some questions about where your mum might have gone.'

Frankie's voice was petulant. 'How should I know that?'

Sarah heard the doorbell ring inside. She pulled Frankie to her feet, rudely ejecting Thomas. 'That'll be them now. Come on.'

To Sarah's initial consternation Mim was already at the front door. But then, the physio had said exercise was good for her. Sarah put a hand on Frankie's shoulder as they went into the living room behind two police officers, an older man and a young woman, as well as Mrs Jameson from social services.

'Hello, Sarah,' said Mrs Jameson warmly. 'I hear you're home for a few weeks.'

'Just until Mim's biking round again,' said Sarah. 'We timed it rather well, all things considered.'

'You did. This is Sergeant Harry West and PC Mandy Craven.'

The senior officer must have been about forty, with thick dark hair and no expression at all on his face. Sarah could feel Frankie trembling beside her on the sofa, and reached for the girl's hand. Sergeant West summarised what Nick had told him, then spoke directly to Frankie.

'We've had a look in your flat, and your mum isn't at home. Did she mention any other meeting, or appointments she had today? No? Do you know what she was planning to do after her meeting at the hospital?'

Frankie shook her head.

'Does she have any special friends she goes out with in the evenings? Any boyfriends, man-friends? Any favourite nightclubs or restaurants you know about?'

Frankie was one big head-shake. Taken aback, Sarah hugged the girl's thin shoulders. Couldn't the man be a little more sympathetic? And why all the questions about nightclubs and man-friends when Petra had disappeared on her way to meet the hospital administrator? The sergeant's next question returned them to Brockburn General, however.

'Can you tell me what this hospital meeting was about?'

'Business,' whispered Frankie, glaring at the floor. 'Gran lost some money in the hospital and Mum's trying to find it.'

'She told me about that,' said Sarah, and went on to outline what Petra had said.

The sergeant looked thoughtful. 'We'll look into that too. He turned back to Frankie. 'Tell me, how old are you now, Frankie?'

'Nearly twelve,' said Frankie, sticking her chin out.

Mrs Jameson leaned forwards in her chair. Her voice was gentle. 'We can see you're old enough to understand, but the thing is, Frankie, it's against the law to leave a child your age alone all this time. And this isn't the first time it's happened. You know my colleague was called in by your neighbour twice last year.'

A little shock ran through Sarah. So that was the why of the questions. Poor Frankie.

'But there was nothing wrong!' cried Frankie. 'Mum was at a dance, both times, that's all! I was fine at home!'

Mrs Jameson gave Mim and Sarah a meaningful look, and turned back to the girl. 'Well, we'll have to find you a temporary home until we know what's going on.'

53

Mim leaned forwards. 'She's got one right here.'

The social worker looked relieved. 'That would seem best, if you're sure it's not too much for you. We'll know more tomorrow, so we'll leave the paperwork until then.'

'But – aren't you going out looking for Mum?' cried Frankie, staring wildly at the two police officers. 'She might be lost, or hurt, or – anything!'

Sergeant West stood up. 'We'll be looking, don't worry. But it's odds-on your mum'll turn up when she's ready.'

Sarah accompanied the three visitors to the front door, her mind in a whirl. She couldn't share the sergeant's confidence. If Petra had been planning to go out clubbing she would hardly have left her daughter in a hospital TV room. That was asking for trouble.

A little worm of apprehension twisted in Sarah's middle as she watched the police car drive off. Maybe something bad *had* happened to Petra.

She was about to go back inside when Caitlyn jogged round the corner into Allington Drive. Sarah went down the path to meet her by the gate. It might be as well to let their neighbour know what was happening.

Caitlyn's face was alarmed. 'Sarah, is everything all right? I saw the police car.'

'It's a fostering thing. One of Mim's previous kids is back because her mum's gone AWOL. Come in and say hello to Mim.'

She led Caitlyn into the living room, where Mim was on the sofa, her leg on a cushion on the coffee table.

There was no sign of Frankie.

Caitlyn went to kiss Mim's cheek. 'Good to see you home and looking so well. But what's with the fostering, Mim? You're not exactly at your fittest.'

Mim pulled a wry face. 'I couldn't say no – remember Frankie? She's not in a good place at the moment.'

Sarah craned her neck to see into the kitchen.

'It's all right, she's outside with the cat,' said Mim. 'Why don't you two go and make coffee? I'm parched and Caitlyn looks like she could do with something to drink.'

In the kitchen, Sarah set the machine burbling and filled Caitlyn in on what had happened that afternoon.

Caitlyn leaned against the worktop, sipping a glass of water. 'Poor kiddy. She must be worried sick.'

'The police seem to think Petra's gone off somewhere, so they're not exactly rushing around with bloodhounds,' said Sarah grimly. 'She's done something similar a couple of times before, apparently.'

'She must be completely unfeeling. Heck, Frankie can't be any older than my Tina.'

Sarah frowned. 'She's not unfeeling, just not your typical earth-mother type. It could all get a bit messy, and Mim's afraid we'll have tears half the night with her stuck downstairs.'

Caitlyn put her glass into the sink. 'Do you suppose this Petra tried to get to the admin building via the tunnel system in the cellars, and collapsed, or something? It's pretty rabbit-warrenish down there. I told you I've been researching an article on hospital kitchens? The other day they took me to see round the storage areas etcetera, and some of these are in the cellar. Bits of the place look

55

like a hundred years ago.'

Sarah stood still. What a horrible idea. 'But the general public couldn't get down there, could they?'

'I don't think there's anything actually stopping you going down the stairs and through into the tunnel system. It's not the kind of thing most people would do, but... that was quite some rain this afternoon.'

Sarah put the coffee jug on the tray. 'And she'd want to arrive at her meeting as dry as possible. I wonder if anyone's checked that. I'll call the nurse who's been helping us, he'd know.'

She made the connection, and Nick's voice boomed in her ear.

'Sarah! Great to hear from you.'

Heavens, thought Sarah. Does he think it's a social call? She outlined Caitlyn's idea.

'Okay – I'll make sure someone checks that, though I don't think it's likely.'

'That'll set our minds at rest. Thanks, Nick.' She was about to end the call when he spoke again, his voice breathless now.

'Sarah – let's go for coffee sometime? I think we'd have a lot to say to each other – how about it?'

Astounded, Sarah searched for something to say, aware that Caitlyn was staring at her.

'Oh, um, great, let's think about it when things've settled down, huh? Bye.'

She ended the call and grinned at Caitlyn. 'He's going to check the cellars. And he asked me out – I think! It was a definite suggestion that a coffee sometime would be fun, anyway. That's the second invitation since I arrived here. And I thought it was going to be an unromantic summer.'

She lifted the coffee tray and started back to the living room. Another invitation from a good-looking man. Exactly what her self-confidence needed.

It wasn't until she was lying in bed that night that another train of thought started. Why on earth should Nick think they had 'a lot to say to each other'? All they'd ever talked about was Frankie and her family, and she hadn't given him any grounds to think she might be interested in him. Could he have another reason for wanting to stay in touch with her – and Frankie?

He was right there in Ward Five, nearly every day. Maybe he knew more about Wilma's missing money than he was letting on.

Chapter Four

Friday, 7th July

Sarah was pottering around in her bedroom after midnight when she heard footsteps padding to the bathroom, and put her head round the door. 'Okay?' she whispered, and Frankie nodded. The girl's face was tranquil, so Sarah left her to it. At ten past four, however, she woke to the sound of muffled sobs in the room next door.

Sarah grabbed her bathrobe and hurried through. 'Oh, sweetheart, everything feels worse in the night when you can't sleep. Tomorrow we'll be able to do more about finding your mum, and you know Mim and I'll help you all we can.'

She sat on the bed, rubbing Frankie's back. Gradually, the sobs died away, and the child fell asleep. Sarah left quietly. Poor scrap. It was all very well saying things like that, but in reality there was little they *could* do. They could phone the police and hear what was going on, phone the ward and ask how Wilma was, visit the old lady... and that was it. And in the middle of it all was Mim with her wonky knee, needing peace and quiet to get her strength back.

Sarah sighed, then smiled wryly. On the other hand, peace and quiet and Mim didn't go together. Mim would make her own decisions about how much she was involved in Frankie's affairs, and if Sarah knew her foster mother, it would be right up to her neck. Mim was Mama Lion when it came to her foster kids.

Frankie was up and dressed in her blue tracksuit when Sarah came out of the shower on Friday morning. The girl's face was pale, but there were no signs of last night's tears. Sarah hugged her, remembering how often Mim had hugged little Sarah in the first days after Gran's death. A hug was worth a hundred words, Mim said. No more, no less. And Frankie's tense little body did relax for a second.

Sarah kept an arm round the child as they went downstairs. 'Let's get you some breakfast. Frankie, which school do you go to? I'll give them a call that you won't be in today. And we'll phone Mr West at nine and see what's going on.'

'Mosshill Primary. And it's Sergeant West,' said Frankie, and Sarah pulled a face.

'Bit of a mouthful, isn't it? Let's demote him when he's not around to hear us.'

A smile flashed over Frankie's face and was gone in an instant. She watched as Sarah frothed up milk for cappuccino. 'I tried my Mum's phone again.'

Sarah chose her words carefully. 'I think Petra must have lost her mobile. If she still had it she'd have called you.'

Frankie scowled, and descended into a bowl of cornflakes. Sarah stood by the toaster, sipping her coffee.

If Petra had merely been out on the town she'd have texted Frankie by now at the very least. It was becoming more and more evident that she either didn't want to be found, or else something had happened to her – or her phone.

'Morning, girls. Is that coffee?'

Sarah turned to see Mim standing with her crutches in the doorway, fully dressed in a pair of rust-coloured trousers and a cream blouse. 'Oh, Mim love – I thought you were still asleep. I was going to help you up to the shower.'

'I had a cat's lick and a promise in the downstairs loo at six, and I've done all my exercises too,' said Mim virtuously, sitting down beside Frankie. 'But you could make me some toast. We'll see what's happening today, and plan my ablutions accordingly. Did you sleep much, Frankie?'

Frankie pushed her bowl away. 'I want my mum,' she whispered, two tears trickling down her cheeks, and Mim hugged her. The same bear hug Sarah remembered so well.

'I know, lovey. Sergeant West might have more news soon.'

Sarah placed a mug of coffee in front of Mim. 'I'll phone him now. Frankie, you can make Mim's toast.'

Mim's eyes met hers, and Sarah grimaced over Frankie's head. Mim was fearing the worst, Sarah could tell.

She went through to the living room to phone in private. A quick call to tell the school Frankie would be absent until further notice, and Sarah was punching out

Harry West's number.

His voice on the phone was brisk. 'I'm afraid there's still no news of Petra's whereabouts.'

'Right,' said Sarah, her heart sinking. 'But I need something to tell Frankie. I wondered about going with her to her home – she needs to pick up some clothes and so on. And she might notice something that could help find her mother.'

The idea had sprung to mind as she was talking, but it was a good one, thought Sarah. It could well be that Petra had left some sort of clue at home.

Harry West was speaking again. 'There was nothing as far as we could see, but we're going back there in an hour to investigate the missing money connection. You could bring Frankie then for her things.'

It didn't sound as if the police had looked very thoroughly yesterday, and Sarah felt even more depressed. How could they be so sure Petra had vanished voluntarily? She wasn't the most attentive mother, okay, but she was missing and someone needed to be looking for her.

Harry was still speaking. 'We'll come and report progress later today too. Can we say half past four in Mrs Dunbar's home?'

'Fine. But – isn't there a chance Petra'll be found by that time?'

There was a long pause before he spoke again, and Sarah gripped her phone, feeling it tremble against her ear. Did he know something they didn't? That wasn't impossible.

'There's no way to know for sure,' he said eventually.

'It would be best not to tell Frankie everything's going to be all right, in case it isn't.'

'I understand,' said Sarah dismally. 'I'll see you later. Thanks.'

She put the phone down and sat for a moment, her shoulders drooping. Should she have mentioned those vague suspicions she'd had last night about Nick? But that's all they were, suspicions. And the police would be interviewing the ward staff soon, surely – she could leave it to them.

And how was she supposed to put this 'new' information together in a way that wouldn't send poor Frankie straight into the depths of despair? At least it was going to be a busy day. The more there was to do, the less time the girl would have to brood.

'No real news yet, Frankie, but the police are going to your flat to look for clues,' she said, joining the other two at the kitchen table and trying to sound encouraging. 'We can go there in an hour and collect some stuff for you, and we'll hear the latest there. Mim, how about if Frankie and I do that, then we'll pick you up and we can all visit Wilma?'

'Yeah,' said Frankie, sounding more or less normal. 'We're on the third floor and sometimes the lift's off.' A moment later, however, she turned to Sarah with big eyes. 'What did you mean, "no real news yet"?'

For a moment Sarah felt like crying. There was no reassurance she could give the child, but she had to say something that didn't sound completely hopeless.

'It means they haven't found your mum in any of the places they've searched so far. You know, restaurants and hospitals. So they're still very busy looking for her. They're going to come and see us at half four and they'll tell us more then, unless of course they find her before that. Try not to worry, Frankie.'

Everything was black, pitch black, and there was a terrible pain somewhere close by, but Petra couldn't localise it because her head was buzzing like it would explode any second. She must have been taken ill, but she couldn't remember... Why couldn't she remember? Fear made her throat tight. Waves of dizziness were circling round her head and her limbs were too heavy to move, but – something else wasn't right. The smell. It was a disused kind of smell – old cars and petrol and dirty rags. Befuddled as she was, the smell was screaming at her that she was in the wrong place. She forced her eyes open, but – hell no – had she gone blind?

She breathed deeply, forcing back panic. How cold she was; her feet were freezing, and oh hell, she'd peed herself. Hot shame as well as horror flushed through Petra. What was happening to her? Think, stupid... Why couldn't she think clearly?

She strained against the fog in her brain, and chinks of the previous day flashed into her mind. She'd been out in the rain, hadn't she? Yes, she was wearing her leather jacket because of the rain. The fuzziness began to recede and she remembered; she'd been on her way to see the hospital administrator, to complain about Wilma's missing cash.

Petra's stomach heaved, and the pain in her head

increased tenfold. No, no – she was going to be sick. She should shout for Frankie to bring her a bucket to be sick into and a cloth for her head, and to do something about this disgusting smell.

But... no. Frankie was at the hospital, waiting for Wilma to come back from physio. But this wasn't the hospital because hospitals didn't smell of oil. Unless she'd got lost and fallen into the machine room or something. Did hospitals have machine rooms?

Nausea swept through Petra again and she retched; oh God, she couldn't be sick here. She tried in vain to turn on her side but her limbs were weak and uncooperative. Was she paralysed? Blind? A shriek of disbelief rose in her throat, but the only sound she made was a high-pitched whimper as darkness descended once more.

Frankie's home was in a not particularly affluent area near the town centre. Sarah parked in front of the ten-storey block and stared. No hanging baskets with cheerful geraniums were here to interrupt the grey concrete, and a depressing amount of litter and dog poo was scattered around the parking area in front of the entrance.

The lift was working, though smelly, and Sarah followed Frankie out at the third floor, where six flats were strung along a graffiti-covered landing. A little crowd of neighbours had gathered at the far end, and the uniformed officer standing beside one door made it painfully obvious which was Frankie's home.

Sarah introduced herself and Frankie, and the officer disappeared inside, closing the door behind him.

'Why do we have to wait?' said Frankie, her voice high-pitched. 'I live here – why can't we go in?'

'They're only doing their job.' Sarah kept hold of Frankie's arm.

After a moment Harry West came out. 'Morning, ladies. Frankie, I'd like you to have a look round with me and see if you notice anything unusual, because that might help us find your mum. And then you can take your stuff, but we don't want you packing anything that has a big fat clue to your mum's whereabouts sticking to its other side, so PC Mandy will help you. Okay?'

Frankie was escorted inside, and this time the door was left open. Sarah waited on the landing, watching the search. From what she could see the furniture was all either very old or very cheap. The place didn't feel in the least homey, but that might be down to the police and the mess they were making. The contents of a large wall unit in the living room were being lifted out, searched through, and deposited on the coffee table and the floor. It seemed the police were taking Petra's disappearance seriously after all. Or were they looking for the missing money? Troubled, Sarah averted her gaze. The scene before her was like something in a TV crime series – bringing Frankie here maybe hadn't been a good idea.

It wasn't long before the girl reappeared in the hallway, her chin wobbling.

Harry West ushered her out to Sarah. 'We'll come and report progress this afternoon. See you later.'

Frankie had packed two large sports bags, and Sarah gripped one and led the way back to the car. 'You can have a nice shower after lunch,' she said, trying to sound matter-of-fact. 'You'll feel better with a proper change of clothes.'

The child was silent all the way back to Allington Road, and Sarah could find nothing to say that would help her. It must have been horrible, seeing policemen rifling through her home. Everyone said possessions were only things, but things as well as people made up a child's world. So as well as missing her mother, Frankie had been forced to witness the rape of her home. Every bit as bad as burglars. And there was nothing Sarah could do, except hand out more of Mim's hundred-word hugs.

Mim was waiting, and they left for the hospital as soon as Frankie had taken her bags upstairs. Wilma was in occupational therapy, but Nick sent a student nurse down to fetch her back.

'We'll go into Vicky's office,' he said in a low voice. 'All Wilma knows is what we said yesterday, that Petra didn't go to her meeting, and it's anyone's guess if she remembers that now. She's pretty awake this morning so we should grab the chance to talk to her.'

Sarah couldn't remember hearing Wilma speak intelligibly. 'Is her speech okay?'

'Yes. Her right brain was affected so her left side's paralysed. Speech is controlled by the left brain. The problem is she's so weak and sleepy much of the time.'

Wilma was wheeled in and sat peering from one face to the other while Nick explained that Petra was missing. Sarah couldn't tell if she understood or not. And those thoughts she'd had about Nick – if she was right, the man should be given an Oscar for this performance. The caring nurse... On the other hand, nurses did have to 'act', didn't they? They couldn't bring their private lives to work with them. She knew nothing about Nick. Or Vicky. Or the bad-tempered nurse. And the hospital staff would have had the best opportunity to get hold of Wilma's cash.

When the old woman spoke she sounded breathless and weak, but the words were clear enough. 'She was always flighty. Frankie should go to Adam.'

'Oh, Gran, Dad's in Boston,' said Frankie, sounding exasperated. 'Anyway, he hasn't seen me for years. I don't want to be with him.'

'Nonsense,' said Wilma. 'He was here... last week. Why did you bring me back? I was waiting... for tea downstairs.' She closed her mouth in a tight line.

'Okay, Wilma, I'll get someone to take you back down,' said Nick, glancing at Sarah and Mim. He pushed Wilma out of the office.

'I suppose your dad hasn't come back to this country?' said Sarah.

Frankie shrugged. 'I'm sure he's in America. Gran might have been thinking about Bert. He was Mum's boyfriend till Easter. Though he won't have been visiting Gran either.'

Nick came back. 'She's probably confused about your dad,' he said, looking at Frankie. 'It's the effects of the stroke.'

Sarah remembered something. 'Petra said Wilma was still pretty sharp. Was she wrong?'

Nick pulled a face. 'She was still very with-it after her first stroke, but she's had a couple of smaller ones since. I'm afraid we can't rely on what she says.'

He walked them to the lift and shook hands all round,

67

holding on to Sarah's a shade longer than necessary. Sarah put an arm round Frankie as the lift descended. The child's mum had vanished and her grandmother was confused. All the hugs in the world couldn't compensate for that.

They were crossing the entrance hall when someone called Sarah's name.

She turned to see Jack pushing an elderly man in a wheelchair in the direction of the speech therapy department, and he made emphatic gestures to Sarah to wait for him. The day was suddenly one hundred per cent brighter.

'Hello – now who's that?' said Mim, staring after him.

Sarah gave Mim's elbow a little shake. 'We were friends when I lived at Gran's. Why don't you two go for coffee? I'll catch you up.'

Jack reappeared with an empty wheelchair and a huge grin on his face, and skidded to a stop beside her. Sarah felt flattered. When was the last time an attractive man had been so pleased to see her? She felt herself blush with pleasure, and oh, this was a feeling to hold on to, in the middle of all the negative stuff going on around her.

'How's the little girl? I heard on the grapevine her mother's vanished.'

'There's still no sign of her. I'm beginning to be afraid there isn't going to be a happy ending for Frankie.'

'So she's staying with you for the moment?'

'Yes – with my foster mum, officially. I'm an added bonus.'

He laughed, then apologised. 'Sorry. You can't be feeling very humorous right now.'

'It's okay. It's not your problem. And it was kind of you to ask.'

'Oh, I had an ulterior motive. You've saved me a phone call. A bloke in orthopaedics was telling me about a farmhouse a mile or so outside Brockburn where they do fantastic Sunday brunches. You can sit outside – well, in the barn. The forecast's good, so how about it?'

Sarah had to suppress the beam that was trying to escape. It wouldn't do to seem too keen, would it? But Sunday brunch in a farmhouse sounded amazing, and golly, he was attractive. And she liked the way he'd thought to ask after Frankie. 'Sounds good. I can't be a hundred per cent definite, in case anything happens, you know, but –'

He was scribbling on a piece of paper. 'Look. Here's my number. If I don't hear from you, I'll assume you can come and I'll pick you up at half ten on Sunday morning. How's that?'

'Perfect,' said Sarah, putting the scrap of paper into her handbag. 'Let's hope they find Petra soon and everything can get back to normal.'

He waved as he raced off again with his wheelchair. He was obviously one of those people who were never still. Sarah hugged herself. This might just be the start of something significant. Wow. Although – no matter what happened, things wouldn't be 'normal' for a long time. Even if Petra was okay, she had abandoned her daughter and wouldn't get Frankie back straightaway. And if she wasn't okay... Either way, Frankie could be staying at Mim's for a while.

Sarah walked over to the cafeteria, a smile pulling at

her lips. She had a date with a tall, dark, handsome man, and she was going to enjoy herself thoroughly.

Chapter Five

Saturday, 8th July

He sank down on an elegant black kitchen chair and propped his elbows on the new glass and chrome table. At least he didn't have to go to work today; he didn't have to pretend to be a caring, hardworking, normal member of the human race. Which was just as well, for the thoughts going through his mind today were black ones. A woman was tied up in his garage and he didn't know if she was alive or dead. He would have to go there and see what was happening with her – please let her be dead, oh please. He couldn't stand having to kill her.

He dragged himself to the back door, out through the garden and down the lane. The area was deserted; most people would still be in bed at this time on a Saturday. The row of garages was in full sunlight, paint flaking from each of the doors. For a moment he stood with his ear pressed against the warm metal. Was she breathing in there? There was nothing to be heard, no breath rasping, no groans.

A strange mixture of hope and anger moving him

forwards, he pulled the door up and ducked inside, closing it behind him again and – shit, he'd forgotten the torch. But even in the dim electric light he could see Petra's chest rise and fall. Slowly, quietly, rhythmically. She was alive, but she must be unconscious, breathing like that...

Abruptly, he yanked the door up and retreated back into the sunshine. What the heck was he supposed to do with her?

He fled back up the lane and into his kitchen, where he collapsed onto a hard kitchen chair. This was the pits. Deliberately, he banged his forehead on the table, then rubbed the mark away.

He'd been – he was – so proud of his house, especially the kitchen. It was a dream come true. A huge weight was lifted from his shoulders when Dad's rheumatoid arthritis forced his parents into sheltered accommodation, leaving him alone here. They'd never let him have a life of his own. It was as if they were living their lives through him, their only precious child, and it was stifling. Even now they were so needy, always phoning, wanting him to do things with them, to be there, to talk to them about every detail of every day. He'd wanted to move out years ago, but they wouldn't hear of it and he'd never been able to gather the strength to go. But their move and the forced break-up of Mum's perfect family had brought him problems as well as freedom. He had to find money for the mortgage... and the renovations. The old-lady scam was the ideal solution. Or it had been, until Petra poked her stupid nose in, and what the *fuck* was he going to do with her? Two tears dripped off his chin.

If he left her long enough she would die. How long did people survive without food and water? He had a feeling it was longer than you'd think. He still had the sleeping pills – maybe he should try again to give her an overdose. She was helpless on the floor, for God's sake, all he had to do was stuff the remaining pills into her mouth and swill them down. The memory of her choking struggle seeped into his mind. Christ, no. He'd have to touch her... And suppose someone heard them struggling? People could be walking past on their way to the station.

No. He would have to kill her quickly, but without touching her. The contents of his stomach shifted and he raced for the bathroom.

The phone rang while he was drying his face. Dear Lord, it was his mother. It was always his mother first, that was the ritual. A chat with Mum, then a chat with Dad, both of them sucking the life out of him. But he would lift the phone; he always did. Lifting it meant a longer break till the next call.

'Hello, darling, how are you today?'

'Hi, Mum. Fine, thanks. I'm on my way out, though – I'm doing a course in Manchester.' A necessary lie.

'That's a pity, dear. I wanted you to come for lunch and fix the shower and help Daddy with his bank paperwork, you know how he worries. Come for dinner then. I'll expect you at six.'

He cast his eyes heavenwards. Fixing the shower was up to the sheltered housing people, and as for the accounts – his father was better with money than the Chancellor of the Exchequer. It was nothing more than an excuse to get him round there.

'Sorry, Mum, the course lasts all weekend. I'll give you a call and come by next week sometime.'

'Oh no, darling, you must come sooner – after your course tomorrow. You didn't come last weekend and Daddy was so hurt, so you really must come now. We can't do without our boy all this time. Tomorrow at six, darling. I'll do a nice roast.'

Rage and exasperation choking him, he held the phone away from his face and took a couple of steadying breaths. He couldn't stand this. Why did he let her do it? He was a grown man, supporting himself and choosing what he did in his own free time. Or not choosing.

'Right, Mum. I have to go or I'll be late. See you tomorrow.'

'Tell you what, would you like me to come round today and do a nice clean for you?'

'No! No. I'm still redecorating. No use cleaning until it's finished.'

'All right, dear. I –'

He slammed the handset down on the base station and laughed through tears of outrage and frustration. She might come round, but she wouldn't get in. He'd had the locks changed the day they left.

Back in the kitchen, he put the kettle on. A cup of tea would settle his stomach.

He should never have taken Petra. But if she'd gone to the authorities, the police would have been involved, and if a smart young DI started nosing around it would be all up with his new life. He couldn't risk that. And he couldn't risk Petra attracting attention in the lock-up, either. There was a spade in the garden shed... Thanks,

Mum. He could harness the aggression she'd inspired in him.

Thick regret filled his head as he went to put on old clothes in case there was a mess. All he'd ever wanted was a home of his own and freedom, but he was still trapped.

Her head hurt, but the buzzing was slackening off. Petra came to with the feeling she'd been out for some time. Her feet had gone numb, and the stench of stale urine mingled with the petrol smell burning in her nose. God help her. Nothing could be worse than this. She was ill or hurt, but she wasn't in hospital, and everything was dark and she couldn't move.

But no, that wasn't right – she *was* getting better. The realisation made her pant with relief. She could move her head without pain stabbing through her eyes, and her arms, yes, she could move them too and – no! There was something binding her wrists together, and – no, no – her feet were tied as well. And some disgusting kind of cloth was covering her head, in her mouth and all... that was where the petrol smell was coming from. She raised her bound hands and tugged at the cloth; it was a sack, Christ, her head was in a sack, and it was somehow fastened round the back where she couldn't reach. Someone had done this to her. God Almighty, no.

She had to get help. She had to shout or bang – but she didn't have the strength. No-one would hear these pathetic little bumps her feet were making.

Panting into the gag, she lay still. Think, think – if she

remembered how she got here it might help her escape. The hospital. She'd been going to see the administrator... in the rain. She was soaked through and fighting with her umbrella, going up the main roadway. And then... the car. He'd called out and she'd been so pleased to see him... but the memory stopped there. He must have knocked her out and brought her here. It was the only explanation.

Why had he done this? Was he going to keep her here and rape her? No, no – she had to get away, back to Frankie. What was her girl doing without her? What day was it?

Pain burned into her wrists as she pulled them against the bonds. Hopeless, hopeless. What more, what else could she do? If she rolled over she might find something to bang with. Hot, shocking pain crashed through her head as she forced herself onto her side, stretching her arms out, feeling for something to grab hold of. But – oh God, someone was coming. She could hear footsteps approaching from a distance. Petra froze, her breath coming in shaky pants. Was it him? A door screeched open – it sounded like a garage door, the metal kind you swing up towards the roof. A faint sensation of light came through the covering on Petra's head and then vanished as the door banged shut. Motionless, she listened to the footsteps crossing a concrete floor, her heartbeat loud in her ears and her stomach cramping. He was breathing heavily, almost panting. What was he going to do to her? Little moaning noises were coming from her throat; she couldn't suppress them. The sour taste of sick burned in her mouth and she could feel her bowels loosen in fear. Was she going to be raped?

The footsteps shuffled around some distance away, and something metallic scraped on the floor before silence fell again. Her own whimpering breath was the only sound now.

Brisk steps came towards her. A blinding flash split her head and the world stopped.

He would have to dump the body. Lift it up and put it into the car and drive it somewhere and touch it again... The mental picture made him retch anew. Petra was *dead*. There was no way back from that. All he could do was cover up his crime, and thank God there was nothing to tie him to Petra. Except old Wilma, and she was in a bad way.

He opened a can of coke to settle his stomach and sat in the kitchen sipping, feeling the cool liquid bubble down his throat. The canal. He could drop her into the part by the old factories. He'd have to drive through a busy area to get there, but the canal bank itself was ideal; the buildings were derelict and no-one ever went there now. Southside supermarket was nearby, so he'd go there first to give himself an alibi for being in the area at that time, in case anyone saw him drive by. They had a '2 for 1' evening on wine every Saturday so it was a good excuse to go.

The day stretched drearily into evening dimness, but thankfully his mother didn't appear at the door. That would have pushed him beyond breaking point. At last it was time to go. Upstairs, he pulled on the jeans and pullover he'd worn to kill her. Old clothes and dark colours to dispose of Petra, because he might get bloodstained this time. He could still feel the way her skull had smashed below the spade.

He shuddered, one hand on his stomach. The sack over her head had absorbed most of the mess, and he'd flung another over that to hide the spreading stain, but thinking about it was making him feel sick again.

The supermarket was packed. Impatience seethed inside him as the queue inched towards the checkout. All he wanted now was to dispose of Petra safely, and forget her.

The crowd of teenagers in front moved forward and it was his turn to scan his purchases; a few minutes more and he'd be out of here. How glad he would be to get to bed tonight. It felt like a million years since he'd got up this morning.

Shopping packed into plastic bags, he scurried towards the furthest corner of the car park. It was gloomy here under the bridge that led to the upper level car park, the perfect place to leave a car if you didn't want people to notice what – or who – you had in it. He placed his bags on the front passenger seat and turned to stare at the bundle in the back. The body was covered by a blanket, but he knew what was underneath. From the shoulders down she looked like any other woman. But covering her head was the hideous, stained sacking. And beneath the sack... no, no, he couldn't think about that. He was getting rid of her. His new life was beginning and it was going to be a good life. He swallowed the bile in his throat and turned the key in the ignition, heart pounding as he drove towards the canal. He'd chosen a good time to do this; most people were either in the pub, or at home in peace and comfort. Soon he would be too.

The Brockburn-Witherton canal wound round the southern part of town before meandering on through woodland and green countryside towards the coast. It was a favourite spot with courting couples in summer, but the part he was heading for was in the industrial area, not such a scenic place for a snog, and at this time of night there was unlikely to be another soul in sight. Please, please, don't let there be another soul in sight. Enough had gone wrong already.

Approaching the spot he had in mind, he saw he'd been right. The only other living creatures at the back of the old carpet factory were rats, scattering in the twin beams from his headlights. Heart thudding behind his ribs, he pulled up by an old crane at the waterside and switched off the engine. Now for it.

The ground squelched underfoot and he inhaled sharply. He'd be leaving footprints and tyre tracks behind here. But more rain was forecast for the night; that would get rid of any tell-tale signs. He opened the back door and was almost overcome by nausea. Putting her into the car had made him vomit the bacon sandwich he'd forced himself to eat that afternoon onto the garage floor. He couldn't touch her again. But he had to. Deep breaths...

He grasped the edge of the blanket covering the body and yanked it away, averting his eyes while he struggled to control his gut. Okay. Now to weigh her down. He'd brought a couple of bricks with him; there'd been a few left over from last year when Dad repaired the garden wall.

Shuddering, he pulled at the zipper on Petra's jacket and shoved the bricks inside, then zipped it up again as far as he could and spat sour saliva on the ground beside the car. Sobbing under his breath, he heaved her out of the car, her arms with the bound wrists sticking out awkwardly in front of her. He stood for a moment getting the weight, her body clutched to his chest and her head rolling horribly against his shoulder. His legs shook. That terrible face was next to his neck, no, no, how disgusting. Tears ran down his cheeks. This should never have happened, stupid, *stupid* woman. It wasn't his fault – he wasn't a killer. But he had to finish the job or he'd never be safe again. It took all the strength he possessed to stagger the few steps to the edge, where he dropped Petra into the murky waters of the canal, watching as she sank, down, down, down and gone.

It was over.

The rain began again when he was reversing away from the canal, and he flipped on the windscreen wipers. Forget the bad stuff. Forget Petra and her flat, hidden face. Concentrate on better things.

Sarah.

Chapter Six

Sunday, 9th July

Sarah smoothed the iron over her grey trousers. It was difficult to know what to wear to Sunday brunch at a farmhouse; she had opted for 'smart but casual' so hopefully everyone else wasn't going to be in shorts. Steam from the iron rose to her face and she leaned back. She'd already done her make-up; she didn't want it sliding off before she left the house.

Okay... that should do. Sarah held her trousers up and glared at them. She still wasn't sure if she was doing the right thing, leaving Mim alone with Frankie for so long.

'You look like the cat who's lost the cream,' said Mim's voice behind her.

Sarah unplugged the iron. 'I don't suppose it's any use me suggesting that Jack and I postpone this date until things are a bit more settled with Frankie?'

'Sarah, we'll be fine. Remember how many kids I've fostered over the years. And most of them were more of a handful than Frankie.'

Sarah frowned. 'I know, but you've never done it with a bashed knee, have you?'

'Are you expecting Frankie to run away? Because I'm not. Where is she, anyway?'

'Still getting dressed. She had a bad night but she kept it to herself.'

Sarah turned towards the door, realising Mim meant what she said. And of course it would be great to allow Jack to spoil her for an hour or two. She'd come home to Brockburn expecting to go on a fun trip with Mim, confide her frustration about breaking up with Andreas, and generally get her life together before taking the Geneva job in October – because that was what she wanted, wasn't it? Now she was living with an injured foster parent and a hurting child.

The sound of tyres on gravel interrupted her thoughts, and Sarah made a face. 'Help, here's Jack already. Entertain him for me, would you?'

She fled upstairs to dress as the doorbell shrilled behind her.

Lilian Jennings pulled on an old blue windcheater and pushed her feet into mud-splattered wellingtons. The ground would be soft and wet after all the rain they'd had these past few days. She untangled the two dog leads hanging by the front door, then grabbed a couple of poo bags from the shelf, grinning as a hopeful face appeared in the kitchen doorway.

'Hello, Boris! Come on, Tequila!'

Two yellow-gold bundles of power raced along the front hall, panting to get outside. Lilian clicked on the leads. 'Come on. And there's no use trying to make me feel guilty about not going walkies earlier. Everyone deserves a lie-in on Sundays.'

She zipped her phone into her pocket and left the house, the dogs pulling her down the path as soon as she'd locked the door. At the gate they both turned left. Okay, so this was to be a canal walk and back through the woods. A right turn at the gate led them to open countryside and a good run. It was warm today, the warmest day of the year so far, so the coolness of the woods was the best option in spite of the mud.

As usual, after charging along like wild things for the first hundred yards, the dogs settled down and trotted at her heels, stopping frequently to investigate some interesting bush or lamp post. Lilian waited patiently while they sniffed around. She had all the time in the world today.

They arrived at the canal bank and Lilian let Boris off the lead. At his age he could be trusted not to take a running jump into the cold and murky waters of the Brockburn-Witherton canal. The dogs sniffed their way along the canal path, Lilian following. Normally they would meet other dog walkers here, but today she was later than usual and the place was deserted.

Lilian strolled along, Boris five yards behind her, Tequila straining ahead as far as the long lead allowed. Lilian sighed appreciatively. How lucky she was to be out in the fresh air – woods on the left, the canal and fields on the right, and today there wasn't even the buzz of traffic from the bypass. Mind you, the canal was a bit pongy here. It must be the high temperature. The water wasn't sluggish enough to smell on a cool day.

All at once Tequila stopped, ears pricked, and gave a short bark before hurling herself towards the canal bank and into the water. Caught off balance, Lilian dropped the lead, yelling, 'Tequila! Come here!' But Tequila took no notice, and to Lilian's surprise and dismay old Boris shot past her and took a flying leap into the water too. Seconds later, both dogs were splashing around the shallow waters of a narrow channel at the side of the main canal.

'Boris! Tequila! Come back here!' shouted Lilian, picking up the lead and pulling as hard as she could. It was no use. Tequila was stronger. Lilian set her teeth and jumped down to the edge of the water.

What was that? Something large and ungainly was floating just below the surface, close to the bank. Lilian took a few steps forward, then stopped, horror swamping through her. Cold sweat broke out on her brow. A broken body was bobbing in the swirling water – a woman. Some kind of bag was hanging off the head... reddish hair was streaming into the water and the skin was a funny yellow-grey colour and the face – the face was... flat.

Lilian retched. Saliva drenched her mouth and she spat, several times, into the weeds at the water's edge. Dear Lord. This woman had been killed – and she and the dogs were all alone here.

'He – elp!' she shouted, twice, and listened as the woods swallowed her call. No answer came. Lilian swallowed painfully. No help would be in time for this poor creature in the water. There was no need to rush for ambulances or phone for doctors. The most important thing was to get the dogs away from the body and call the police.

'Boris! Heel!' She spoke quietly, but Boris realised she meant business and waded towards her. She seized his collar and hauled him up the bank, then reattached his lead and tied him to a tree. Now for Tequila. She grasped the dog's collar and shook hard, shouting her name and yanking her towards Boris. Tequila was so surprised she allowed Lilian to pull her to Boris's tree and tie her on.

Lilian's teeth were chattering as she scrabbled dog snacks from the pocket of her windcheater and dropped them on the ground beside the two dogs. A quick look behind her confirmed this wasn't a nightmare. There was a body in the canal, and it hadn't fallen in and drowned.

With shaking fingers Lilian pulled out her mobile. It was the first time in her life she'd ever done this. She held the phone in her right hand and punched out 999.

'This is brilliant! I'd no idea they did brunches here. Look at the cats!'

Sarah banged the car door shut, gazing round in delight. The farmhouse was only a ten-minute drive from Brockburn, but it was right out in the countryside, surrounded by fields of grain. A little stream crossed a corner of the yard, tumbling downhill to join the River Brock. Grey sandstone farm buildings contrasted with the terracotta window boxes overflowing with pink geraniums, and cats of all colours were lazing around in the sunshine. Sarah counted seven before several chased after a piece of paper blowing across the yard, and she gave up, laughing.

Jack took her elbow as they left the car park. 'Thought you'd like it.'

He led her towards a large wooden building behind the farmhouse. One wall was open to the orchard, where trees with still-tiny apples and pears gave shade to the tables beneath them.

A rosy-cheeked woman showed them to their table, halfway up the barn. 'The cold buffet's self-service, and if you're having anything cooked we'll bring it over,' she explained, indicating three laden trestle tables, one of which had gas hobs at one end.

'I hope you're hungry,' said Jack.

Sarah walked along the cold table. 'I am, but way too much of this looks delicious. I'm going to have tiny portions of lots of things.'

She poured them both orange juice and coffee, and went back to their table with a small bowl of muesli, having ordered scrambled egg and bacon. Jack joined her, a selection of cheese and cold meat on his plate.

Sarah's gaze wandered round the barn as she started to eat. All the tables were occupied, and chatter and laughter filled the air. Some people had dressed up, while others were wearing jeans and t-shirts. Everyone looked relaxed and happy.

She turned back to Jack. 'This would be a fun thing to do for a birthday, wouldn't it – something a bit different.'

'Glad you like it,' said Jack, balancing a gherkin on a forkful of ham. 'What do you usually do on your birthday?'

'Mim and I always used to go out for lunch, but I haven't been here the past couple of birthdays. My last job was in Zürich, and I have the chance of another in

Geneva this autumn.'

'Doing...?'

'Teaching. I was at the International School in Zürich. Kids from all over the place, and great travel opportunities, too.'

'Tell me more,' he said, leaning forwards.

Sarah didn't miss the interest in his eyes, and it wasn't for Zürich, either. Flattered, she began to talk. Jack asked a lot of questions, and she toured happily round Europe until she'd finished her muesli.

Jack went for more coffee, and Sarah pulled out her mobile. No calls. Should she text Mim and check that all was well? But Mim would only remind her that she was the foster parent, not Sarah. Mrs Jameson had completed the paperwork on Friday, and Frankie was back at Mim's for an unspecified time. It was apparently correct that the child's father lived in the States, though Mrs Jameson hadn't located him yet.

Sarah bit her lip. It was all very well saying Mim was the foster parent, but Sarah was the one Frankie turned to with questions about the police, and the one supplying comfort in the night, too. She sipped her juice, ignoring the dragging sensation of not having had enough sleep. Frankie'd had a restless night, but every time Sarah went through the little girl pretended to be asleep. It was horrible. Frankie was much too young to be worried sick all by herself.

Stop fretting, Sarah told herself. Mim's there; she and Frankie'll manage without you for an hour or two. This is your treat, enjoy it.

The barn was packed, brunchers of all ages milling

round, choosing food and chatting to friends and families. Jack came back with the coffee, closely followed by the woman with Sarah's eggs.

Sarah lifted her fork. 'What do you do, Jack? I think you said you were between jobs too?'

'Yes. I did a degree in electronics, and I've worked all over the place, mostly in the north-west.'

'Sounds like you change jobs every five minutes,' said Sarah, laughing.

'Oh – no – well, not very often,' he said, stumbling over the words and scrunching his napkin under one hand. His eyes slid away from hers and he wiped his face with the napkin.

For a moment Sarah was lost for words. It seemed an odd reaction to a humorous remark. Had he been sacked at some point, perhaps? Time to change the subject. But Jack got there first.

'Have you been to that revolving restaurant in Switzerland where they filmed one of the James Bond films?'

She had, and told him about it while she ate her eggs. Like her, he was a James Bond fan, and they had a lively conversation about who'd made the best 007.

'Definitely Roger Moore – he brought a bit of humour with him,' said Jack. 'The way he raises an eyebrow is classic.'

'Daniel Craig made Bond look like a real person,' said Sarah. 'But maybe that's more of a girl thing, huh?'

Jack was laughing now, the brief awkward moment seemingly forgotten.

Mim's back door slammed, and Caitlyn frowned. She'd watched earlier as Sarah and her handsome date drove off, so Mim was home alone with Frankie now. If the girl went off in a strop Mim wouldn't be able to chase her. Time to be a good neighbour and pay them a visit. Caitlyn slid her feet into flip flops.

Mim's front door was unlocked, and Caitlyn rang the bell and stuck her head in. 'Anyone home?'

Mim's voice answered from the kitchen, where she was arranging roses in a vase. She waved Caitlyn to the table. 'Aren't these lovely? They're from Jack, an old friend of Sarah's. He's taken her for a farmyard brunch.'

Caitlyn watched as Mim finished the roses and put the cut-off stems into the bin. 'Sounds fab.' She gazed outside where Frankie was throwing ping-pong balls for Thomas. 'He won't be Fat Cat much longer if she has anything to do with it.'

Mim snorted. 'Poor old Tom-puss. But I'm glad she has the distraction. Coffee?'

'Please. But let me make it.'

Mim sat down and stared out at Frankie. The older woman's eyes were bleak, and Caitlyn could see why. Frankie's face was closed-in even when she was playing with the cat. It was plain the girl was miserable.

'I've never had a child of this age who's had to worry if her mother has deliberately abandoned her,' said Mim. 'Oh, we've had difficult cases – remember that little family whose parents were jailed in Morocco? And we've had children anxious because their mother was in hospital – but this is a different kind of anguish...' Her voice trailed off.

Caitlyn put two mugs of coffee on the table and sat down. 'Sounds to me as if something's happened to her mother.'

Mim heaved a sigh. 'It's dreadful. The best the poor child can hope for is that Petra has cold-bloodedly left her to fend for herself. We've tried to be upbeat without giving her false hope, but all we can do is tell her that she isn't alone, and try to take her mind off what's going on. I'll get her to help me with my stair exercises in a moment, but really – it isn't much of a distraction, is it?'

Caitlyn sipped her coffee. She could help Mim here, even if there was little comfort in it for Frankie.

The back door opened and Frankie came in, glancing at Caitlyn with the same non-expression.

'The very person,' said Caitlyn, smiling at the child, who gave her a blank look. 'Mim was saying she hasn't done enough stair practice. You and I can help her.'

'Huh?' Frankie didn't look convinced.

'I want to try without my crutches,' said Mim quickly. 'If you and Caitlyn are in front and behind, you can catch me if I take a sudden nosedive. If you don't mind, lovey.'

Frankie's face was apprehensive as Mim solemnly ascended and descended the stairs, and Caitlyn almost laughed. She cheered when they were back at the bottom, and this time Frankie smiled too. Caitlyn and Mim exchanged glances.

'Thank you so much, Frankie,' said Mim. 'I hope I can get rid of the crutches officially soon. We'll see what they say at physio tomorrow.'

Frankie nodded dumbly, and Caitlyn saw tears gather

in the girl's eyes at the mention of the hospital.

Mim evidently saw them too. 'Would you like to come with me tomorrow? You could watch me do my exercises, then we could visit your gran before lunch.'

Frankie shrugged, and Caitlyn saw Mim's shoulders droop. Another chance to be neighbourly. 'If you ever need a lift, Mim, I can take you.'

Mim gave her a 'thank you' look. 'Excellent. And talking about lunch, let's see what there is in the fridge. You'll stay, won't you, Caitlyn?'

During the meal they chatted about Mim's plans for the house. Frankie was silent throughout, and Caitlyn could see Mim was glad to have someone to keep the conversation going.

When they'd finished their salad Mim touched the child's head. 'I know it's hard, but you're not alone in all this, Frankie love. Sarah and I'll both help as much as we can. And soon you'll see Rita and her family too, remember them? No matter how it feels, you're not alone.'

Frankie didn't answer. After a moment she stood up and began to stack the dishwasher.

'Mim – sofa – now. I'll help Frankie clear up,' said Caitlyn.

The exhausted look was back on the older woman's face. Mim nodded, and crutched her way towards the living room, the phone in the hallway ringing while she was approaching it. Caitlyn watched as Mim lifted the receiver, her right crutch hanging on her elbow.

'Hello?' The appalled expression that came over her neighbour's face told Caitlyn everything.

She closed the kitchen door and lifted the salt and pepper from the table. 'Where do these go, Frankie?'

'In there.' The girl's voice was tranquil; it didn't seem to have entered her head that the phone call might be about her mother. Caitlyn swallowed. Of course lots of people would be calling to ask how Mim was. Frankie would be used to people ringing up.

A few minutes later Caitlyn heard Mim replace the handset, and went to join her in the living room, dismayed when Frankie followed on.

Mim was on the sofa, her face pale. 'Frankie, could you fetch me the packet of paracetamol from the bathroom cabinet, please?'

The child ran upstairs, and Mim gazed up at Caitlyn, her voice a mere whisper. 'They've found a body in the canal, and it matches Petra's description. Someone from the police will be round in an hour to tell us more.'

Caitlyn's hands flew to her face. So it had happened. The worst possible outcome; the nightmare ending. 'Was she – murdered? It can't be suicide, surely?'

'He talked about a head injury. Oh, Caitlyn.'

Caitlyn bent down, her hand on Mim's shoulder. 'What do you want me to do?'

Mim's hands were shaking, and she clasped them together. 'I'll have to tell Frankie something. But I need Sarah here. Could you phone her for me?'

Caitlyn pulled out her phone while Mim leaned back into the sofa, looking ten years older. What a horrible thing to have to do, tell a child her mother was dead. What had happened – who had done this to Petra?

Frankie walked back into the room, an apprehensive,

silent question forming in her eyes as she glanced from Caitlyn to Mim. Caitlyn put a hand on her shoulder. The child wasn't stupid; she could see something was badly wrong. Explanations couldn't wait until Sarah was here.

'Oh, Frankie,' said Mim, tears dripping off her chin. 'It was the police on the phone, lovey. They –'

Frankie's face went chalk white. 'She's dead, isn't she?' It was little more than a whisper.

Mim held out her arms, but Frankie flung herself into the opposite corner of the sofa and buried her head in a cushion. Loud sobs shook her body. Mim inched along until she was sitting beside the girl. Caitlyn bit her lip. There was nothing she could say or do to help, so she crept back to the kitchen to ruin Sarah's date.

Sarah finished her croissant and honey and sat back, patting her tummy. 'I'm full! I should jog home after all this. Where do you live, Jack?'

'Ceres Road. It's near the bypass –'

'Oh, sorry.' Sarah's mobile was buzzing and she fished it out.

Caitlyn's number was on the screen and Sarah drew her breath in. Was everything okay at home? She accepted the call with shaking fingers. 'Caitlyn?'

'Sarah, it's bad news, I'm afraid. They've found a body in the canal and it looks like it's Petra. Mim asked me to call you – you're needed here. Do you want me to come and get you?'

'Hell – hang on a second, Caitlyn.'

Jack was staring at her, his eyes wide. Forcing back

tears, Sarah whispered what was going on.

His face paled, and he clutched her hand over the table. 'Oh no, how dreadful. I – I'll pay and we'll get straight off.'

He strode across the barn and murmured in the woman's ear, handing over a banknote as he did so. Sarah ended the call, dropped the phone into her bag and weaved her way to the door. What a horrible end to their brunch, and oh, was Mim coping? Thank heavens Caitlyn was there.

Jack drove swiftly towards Brockburn, Sarah fidgeting in the passenger seat.

'This is awful. Poor Frankie.'

'I know. She'll need all the help you can give her.' His voice was tense, and she glanced across. This had upset him too.

'Hell yes. What can have happened to – Petra?' Was there any hope it wasn't Petra?

Jack slowed down for the turn into Allington Road and pulled up outside Mim's gate. 'Sarah, you know where I am. Promise you'll ask if you need anything.'

'I will. Thanks, Jack.'

Sarah ran up the path and burst into the hallway. The house was in complete silence.

'Mim? Frankie?'

They were in the living room. Frankie was wedged into the corner of the sofa, her face pale and tearstained, a black velvet cushion clutched to her chest. Mim was beside the girl, one hand on Frankie's shoulder and the other clenched in a tight fist on her lap.

Caitlyn came over from the window, a helpless

expression on her face. 'I'll leave you now, Sarah, but let me know if I can do anything.'

Sarah's heart sank as her eyes met Mim's. Offering Frankie any kind of comfort under these circumstances would be futile – impossible to imagine what was going on in the child's head. What could it feel like – *not knowing* if it was her mother's body in the canal? But it must be.

Sarah crouched beside the sofa – how many times had she sat huddled in the corner where it was soft and warm, grieving for her gran? It was a different sofa in those days, and a different situation. The death of an old lady was something even a child could understand, something almost logical, in spite of the pain it caused. Petra's death was unexpected and unfair, and Frankie would feel as if the bottom had been ripped out of her world. And it was clear she wasn't looking for hugs and reassurance; her entire posture was one of disbelief and aggrievedness.

'Frankie, love, I'm so, so sorry,' whispered Sarah, touching the child's hand. 'We'll help you all we can.'

Frankie snatched her hand away and turned a white face to Sarah. Her eyes were wild. 'How can you *help*?' she choked, her voice shaking with anger. 'No-one can help because she's dead, she's fucking *dead* and she's not going to come back, is she, so how can anyone *help*?'

Sarah winced. This was how she'd felt too, half a lifetime ago, but her upbringing hadn't allowed her to voice her anger so bluntly.

'I know. I do know,' she said helplessly. She turned to Mim. 'The police?'

'They'll be here soon. They'll be able to tell us more,'

said Mim, rubbing Frankie's shoulder. 'A body was found in the canal, that's all I know.'

Frankie gave a little gulp. The anger was gone for the moment and her voice was puzzled and childish. 'What was she doing in the canal? And she can swim. Why didn't she swim? Maybe it isn't Mum?'

'I don't know,' said Mim. 'The police'll be here soon. Frankie, I'm going to take you upstairs and then I'll stay with you while you have a little lie down until they arrive. You've had a shock, you need to rest. Come on, lovey.'

That was neatly done, thought Sarah, as Frankie preceded Mim out of the room. The police might well want to talk without Frankie's presence first, and now they could. She flopped into an armchair and listened to Mim's voice talking comfortingly as she crutched her way upstairs. Her foster mother sure had power when things got tough.

A car drew up outside, and Harry West, an older man, and a young woman carrying a bulky briefcase got out. Sarah hurried to open the door before they rang the bell.

'This is Doctor Maxwell, she's a police surgeon and she's here in case Frankie needs anything,' said Harry West. 'And this is DI Summers from CID.'

His face was grim, and Sarah wondered fleetingly how on earth the police learned to cope with situations like this. How could anyone *learn* how to talk to a child whose mother was found dead?

'Frankie's upstairs with Mim.' Sarah motioned them all to sit down, feeling her heart beat faster. What was she going to hear?

'The body was found at midday by a woman walking her dogs by the canal,' said DI Summers in a low voice. 'From the clothes she was wearing, and the physical description, we're convinced it was Petra Walker. We'll know more about the time of death after the post-mortem.' He dropped his voice even further. 'Her face had been badly beaten, whether that was the cause of death or not we don't know yet.'

Sarah's gut started to churn. What had Petra done to deserve that? And who on earth could have done this to her – and *why*? She struggled to keep her voice steady.

'Had she been –' She choked, unable to bring herself to say the word 'raped'. It was there in her head; she could picture the letters, but the word stuck in her throat.

'She was fully clothed, but again, we won't know until later,' said Harry West. 'We need someone to officially identify the body. Could you do that?'

Sarah felt as if he had doused her with cold water, the shock was so great. '*Me?* Isn't there anyone else? I wasn't really a friend.'

'The neighbours aren't being cooperative,' said Harry West. 'She wasn't popular in the flats. And we haven't found any family nearby except of course Frankie and the grandmother. We can do DNA testing, but that takes time and it would be better for Frankie to have things official sooner.'

'I'll do it,' said Sarah miserably.

Brilliant. What a horrible thing to have to do. And there wasn't anyone she could ask to go with her, either. Mim would have to stay with Frankie, and Rita in her pregnant state was out of the question. Caitlyn? For a moment Sarah wavered, then grasped her courage with both hands. If there was no shoulder to cry on, she wouldn't cry. Best just get it over with quickly.

The doctor leaned forward, speaking rapidly. 'We have to decide how much Frankie should be told today. The fact that her mother is dead, and we can say from a head injury, is perhaps enough for the moment.'

'She knows about the canal,' Sarah told her.

'Then I suggest we leave it at that for today. I'd like to–'

Mim's head appeared round the door. 'We're back down. Frankie wants to see you,' she said, looking at Harry West.

Sarah could only admire the way DI Summers told Frankie about her mother's body being discovered. Although she wasn't given much information, everything he said was true. Frankie asked about the cause of death, and the doctor explained that Petra had suffered a head injury, and wouldn't have been aware of what was happening.

The girl was staring at the doctor, her eyes wide. 'But what was she *doing* beside the canal?' she whispered, tears starting again. 'That's what I don't understand. She never goes there.'

DI Summers stood up. 'Clever girl. That's what we have to find out. Where *did* Petra go after she left the rehabilitation unit? Someone, somewhere, must know, so we have to find that someone. We'll get back to working on that now. The doctor'll stay with you and Frankie for a bit, Mrs Dunbar, and Sergeant West will keep you up to date with the investigation. Ms Martin, if you'll come with us we can...'

He touched Frankie's shoulder briefly, shook hands with Mim, and left, Harry West behind him.

Sarah exchanged a look with Mim, and saw that her foster mother had realised where she was going. Mim's face was paler than when she was in hospital, and Sarah hugged both her and Frankie.

'Won't be long,' she whispered.

The mortuary was in the oldest part of the hospital, up at the back and not far from the rehab wards. Harry West drove into the covered staff car park and pulled up beside a shiny black Jaguar.

'One of the perks of being a consultant, I guess,' he said, nodding towards the other car.

Sarah attempted a smile. He was trying to bolster her up, but her legs felt like jelly as she followed him into the lift, where going down and not up as she was expecting did nothing for the feel-good factor. The mortuary was in the cellar. Yikes.

'This won't take long,' said Harry, holding a grey metal door open for her.

The smell was everything she'd ever read about and Sarah clamped one hand over her nose and mouth. How did people work in an atmosphere like this? Thick and cloying and a mixture of disinfectant and something indescribable, it caught in the back of her throat and made her cough. Eyes watering, she followed Harry West, who seemed completely at home in the department. He led her along a badly-lit corridor and into a dingy little waiting room. Her stomach was churning like mad – dear heavens, supposing she was sick?

Breathing carefully through her mouth, Sarah perched on the edge of a plastic chair. Everything was grey here. Were the bodies... Her insides lurched anew, and she was concentrating on keeping her stomach under control when the mortuary attendant, an Asian woman a few years older than Sarah, came in and smiled sympathetically.

'Hi, Sarah, I'm Reena. The body is in the viewing room next door. You'll see it through a glass window.'

Sarah stood up, and Reena took her arm. The human contact was comforting.

'The face will stay covered. Don't think about that. Look at the hair, the hands. See if you notice a definite sign that this is Petra Walker. When you've seen enough, say if you recognise her or not.'

The room they went into was small, white tiles on the walls giving way to institutional green on the ceiling. Sarah's knees began to shake. What a hellish colour to paint a mortuary. A window on the long wall opposite the door was curtained. That was where –

Harry West gripped her free elbow. 'One good look will be enough.'

Sarah nodded to Reena, who slid the curtain to the side before returning to Sarah's side.

Sarah's head swam for a second before she saw the body of a woman, lying on a trolley and covered by a green drape from the chest down. One arm and hand lay free beside the torso. White gauze was covering the face, and Sarah's throat closed. Flat... the head of this poor woman had been battered almost flat. The killer must have used an incredible amount of force. The thought was appalling. She retched, and Reena gripped her arm so hard that it hurt.

'Do you know who this is, Sarah?'

Sarah nodded. She wrenched her arms free and raised clasped hands to her mouth, feeling her fingers shudder against her lips. Recognition had been instantaneous in spite of the distraction of the flat head. The earrings. She'd noticed them in the cafeteria on her first day back, four pathetic little studs, all different colours, the bottom one looking like a diamond. And of course the hair, the dyed red hair that clashed so horribly with the top pink stud.

'It's Petra,' she said in a low voice, surprised at how steady she sounded.

'Well done. Come and have a cup of tea, then I'll take you home,' said Harry West.

Later that evening the phone rang, and Sarah hurried to answer it, glad to hear the buzz of voices in Frankie's room, where Mim and the little girl were. What a good thing Frankie had come back to her old foster home. It would have been ten times worse for her if she'd been with strangers today.

'Sarah, hi. How are things – how are *you?*'

It was Jack. Sarah took the phone back to the sofa and snuggled into the corner cushion. 'Oh, Jack. I'm – I'll be okay. I had to identify the body and it was horrible.'

She heard his breath catch, and his voice when he

spoke was unsteady.

'Oh no. That's terrible. So it *was* Petra. You take things easy, Sarah. Have an early night.'

Sarah put the phone down feeling comforted. Jack's call showed she was important to him – and look how upset he'd been in the restaurant, when she'd told him what was going on. It was good to know she had a supportive friend nearby.

An hour later she was in bed, the events of the day churning round her brain. Just this morning she'd been enjoying scrambled eggs at Rushglen Farm. It seemed like half a lifetime ago. What a terrible day it had been for Frankie, but at least the girl was asleep now, helped by the doctor's pills.

Sarah shivered. Every time she closed her eyes, she saw those earrings, and Petra's battered, hidden, flat face. Sleep was a long way off. Perhaps she should take one of Frankie's pills. She began to sit up, then collapsed into the mattress again. Hell, no – what if she had a nightmare about Petra's no-face and couldn't wake up because she'd taken a pill? Better to stay awake. That way, at least she was in control.

Chapter Seven

Monday, 10th July

It was on the radio. 'The body of a woman identified as the missing Petra Walker has been found in the...' He switched it off, his stomach shifting. It was happening too soon. The body hadn't been in the water long enough – less than twenty-four hours. Would any trace of him still be lingering on Petra? But the canal would have got rid of any stray hairs he might have shed on her, and surely there wouldn't be fingerprints... He was still safe, and in a few weeks all this complicated stuff would be behind them and he could concentrate on getting to know Sarah. What God-awful timing it all was.

So what should he do now? He was free this morning, but he couldn't sit at home – he had to be active, because doing something would take his mind off the body. Petra's bloody face, haunting him every time he allowed his mind to relax. Ward Five would be the best place to gather information – so he would go and get the gossip. He had to keep up with what was going on behind the scenes as well as what the media was reporting.

The rehab unit was busy with therapists and patients going about their normal weekday routine, and a few relatives taking advantage of the open visiting hours. Ignoring the lifts, he ran upstairs.

Ward Five was buzzing, but that was maybe a good thing. He wandered along to the nursing station, which was deserted, then looked into the kitchen, where a first-year nurse was drying her eyes on a tea towel. He started to reverse out, but she gave him a shaky smile, batting her eyelashes even in the midst of her tears.

'Come for a cuppa? I'm just having a moment – Vicky bawled me out about old Wilma's money, and yes, I know I deserved it.' She clicked the kettle on.

He made an inquiring noise in this throat and she went on.

'I saw it in her locker when I was helping her look for her reading specs, back when she was well enough to know if she had the right specs on. She warned me not to say anything, and when I looked later it was gone. Gawd knows what happened to it. I didn't tell anyone at first but today I thought I'd better, with Mrs Walker's body being found, you know... Vicky says we'll have to call the police, and it won't look good for the hospital.' She mopped her eyes again.

He thought swiftly. 'She might be better just to wait until the police come back here. They're bound to do interviews soon.' It was clutching at straws, but any delay would help him.

A shout came from the corridor. 'Nurse Bruce!'

The girl left, and he walked back up the ward and out to the stairwell. Did he need to do anything about this?

Not yet, he decided. The less complicated he kept his involvement here, the better. But he'd keep a close eye on student nurse Bruce. He should go home again and have a good think.

He drove back slowly, thinking about the body. It was horrible he'd been forced to kill her. All he wanted was a nice home – it was only what he deserved and in a fairer world he'd have had it long ago. Huh. He'd never had justice, never had what all the other kids had. And now... if only he could *forget* Petra and her battered, bloody head under the sacking. What did it look like now, that head?

Home again, he stretched out on his sofa, looking up at his brilliant white ceiling, and in spite of the horror a sense of peace soaked into his soul. The darkness of Mum and Dad had vanished from the ground floor. Memories of miserable weekends spent in his parents' company when his mates were all out enjoying themselves flashed through his head. They'd always been there, pushing him, suffocating him, making him their puppet to dance as they pulled the stings. Even when he was a grown man they'd never let go. He thumped his hand on the sofa so hard his fingers tingled. Life here had been hell. God bless Dad's arthritis; it had freed him. And his renovations were freeing the house – such a difference to three weeks ago. Petra had been an accident; he hadn't meant her to die.

Drowsiness washed over him and he closed his eyes. He would dream of lovely Sarah. How perfect...

Sarah drummed her fingers on the kitchen table. She'd

been trying to organise her online banking account for over an hour now, and getting nowhere fast. It was a welcome distraction when her mobile buzzed beside her, and she grabbed it, pushing the laptop away. Was this Jack? No, help – it was the hospital. Vicky the ward sister had called that morning with the news that Wilma'd had another small stroke, and the consultant would be coming to examine her shortly.

Sarah leaned across and swung the kitchen door shut. Frankie was in the living room, and it might be better if she couldn't listen in here. 'Hello?'

'Sarah, it's Nick. The consultant's been, and he's organised for Wilma to be transferred back to a medical ward. Rehab isn't the right place for someone with a condition as acute as hers is now.'

'Okay,' said Sarah. It occurred to her that Wilma had no-one left in her corner. Petra would certainly have wanted to know all the reasons and ramifications, but there was only so much they could cope with here. She compromised guiltily. 'We might want to talk to a doctor about her sometime, to give us an idea what's happening. For Frankie's sake.'

'Good idea. Give them a day or two to get her settled into the new ward, and then organise something there. It's Tyne, that's Ward Three in the medical block.'

'Right. When's she going?'

'Any moment. So you won't be back here visiting her. Um – how about that coffee we talked about?'

Sarah closed her eyes. What was going on here? Just a coffee invitation, or something more sinister? By staying in contact with her, he'd also be in contact with the investigation, and if he had anything to do with the missing money that's what he'd want. But *surely* he hadn't... She would have to think of a way to find out his motives. 'I'm sort of seeing someone,' she said. 'But maybe we can pop up sometime and say thanks and goodbye to you all. I'll bring some chocs for the nurses.'

His sigh echoed all the way down the phone. 'Ah, well. Fair enough. All the best, Sarah.'

The connection broke. Sarah turned back to the laptop, but her concentration was gone and she leaned her elbows on the table, massaging her head with both hands. She would worry about Nick later. What this mess on her laptop needed was a trip to the bank. Why was it so complicated? All she wanted was to transfer the bulk of her money from her Swiss account back to her English bank. The way things were developing it didn't look as if she'd be going to work in Geneva, so she needed her main account to be in this country. A job was something else she'd need, of course, but she could worry about that another time too. She glanced at the clock on the microwave. Three o'clock, and as the bank might not appreciate her waltzing in ten minutes before closing time with something this complicated, she should get a move on. Was Mim awake yet?

A peek into her foster mother's room revealed Mim still fast asleep, and Sarah closed the door softly. Mim had been dead tired after her physio session that morning. Frankie had refused to go anywhere near the hospital, so Caitlyn had taken Mim while Sarah did her best to distract the child.

Sarah hesitated in the hallway – no way was she going

to wake Mim. Could she leave Frankie to her own devices for half an hour?

The girl was huddled on the sofa, watching cartoons. She'd had a long cry that morning when Vicky phoned with the news of Wilma's stroke, but now the Simpsons were bringing a smile to her sombre little face. Pity tugged at Sarah's heart. Poor scrap. It seemed likely that Wilma and Petra would soon be in the same place. Another death in her family would be a lot for the child to cope with, and one day soon she'd have to be told that her mother had been murdered. And heaven forbid, but it was possible that Frankie knew the person who killed Petra. Sarah remembered the vicious expression on the little girl's face on hearing about Petra's death. Thank goodness social services were setting up counselling for Frankie; she was going to need help to get through this.

She leaned over the back of the sofa. 'Frankie? I have to go to the bank, will you be okay for half an hour or so? Mim'll be awake soon.'

Frankie switched the TV off, the smile gone. 'Can I come with you?'

Sarah thought for a moment. She didn't want Frankie listening in on a conversation about her bank accounts, but the child was grieving for her mother, and Sarah of all people... She scribbled a note on the telephone pad. 'Okay. I'll leave this for Mim in case she wakes up before we're back. Let's go.'

The bank was at the far end of the High Street, and Sarah parked in front of the dry cleaner's. She put an arm round the girl's shoulders as they walked to the bank. Hopefully there'd be a kids' waiting area inside – but

Frankie might consider herself too old for jigsaws and Lego.

As Sarah feared, the children's area was populated by four- and five-year-olds, but there was a small waiting section with magazines, and Frankie agreed to being parked there while Sarah approached the advice booth. She started to tell the clerk about her problem, and was about to access her Swiss account details on her iPad for him when a woman's voice called out.

'Steady, love – is it asthma? Who's with this girl?'

Sarah swung round to see Frankie bolt upright in her chair, clutching her chest and panting, her face shiny with sweat. A couple of people rushed to help, one of them a red-haired young woman wearing tight black trousers and a denim jacket. The superficial resemblance to Petra made Sarah wince, and she ran over to take Frankie's hands. This was her fault; she should never have brought the child here.

'She's having a panic attack,' said a tall man further down the queue. 'Get her to breathe into a paper bag.'

The bank clerk, whose name badge identified him as Ralph Bailey, came round the front to help.

'Is there anywhere we can take her?' said Sarah urgently. This was too cruel; the red-haired woman was bending over Frankie.

Ralph Bailey opened a door in the side wall, and Sarah saw it was a conference room, with a large wooden table and about ten chairs.

She supported Frankie away from the crowd and helped her sit down. 'Cup your hands over your mouth and breathe as normally as you can,' she said firmly. This was horrible – why hadn't she taken two seconds to think before rushing out to do business that could quite well have waited till the morning? She turned to Ralph Bailey. 'Could you find a bag for her to breathe into?'

He opened a cupboard door and produced a paper bag.

Sarah helped Frankie hold it against her face. 'Nice normal breaths, sweetie.' She breathed along with Frankie for a moment, and the distress in the child's eyes lessened. 'Any better?'

Frankie nodded and pushed the bag away. 'I thought that woman was my mum.' She burst into choking sobs.

'Shall I call an ambulance?' Ralph Bailey was hovering behind Frankie.

Sarah rose and pulled him to one side. 'No. Her mother was – found dead yesterday. I just want to get her home now,' she said in a hushed voice, conscious of the man's shocked expression. And he was right. Who needed a wicked stepmother when they had a foster sister like her?

Sarah went back and hugged the child. 'I'm so sorry, Frankie. We'll go home straightaway.' She glanced over Frankie's head at the bank clerk. 'I'll come another time and get my accounts organised.'

Frankie heaved a sigh and leaned back in the chair. Sarah was glad to see more colour come into her face. The girl was staring at Ralph Bailey. 'I saw you at the hospital when I was visiting my gran.'

Ralph Bailey stared back at her and Sarah noticed that he was paler than Frankie now.

'Oh – um – I expect I was doing a shift at the hospital

branch. I'm there a couple of times a week.'

'My gran lost some money from the bank.'

Frankie's face crumpled and Sarah cuddled her, noticing that little beads of sweat had broken out on Ralph's forehead. Why was he so ill at ease?

'Do you know Wilma Murray in rehab Ward Five?' she asked.

His gaze shifted around the room. 'Mrs Murray is one of our customers. I've met her on bank business. How – how is she?' His hands were shaking.

Sarah frowned. Something was wrong here, but this wasn't the time to ask questions. She would find out about Ralph Bailey later. 'She's stable. Frankie, if you're able to walk to the car we'll head back home.'

Frankie stood up, thrusting the bag into her pocket.

Ralph Bailey accompanied them to the door and handed Sarah a business card. 'Email me about your problem, and I'll get onto it for you.'

Sarah ushered Frankie back to the car. 'Mim'll tell me all about it for taking you out like that.'

'I'm okay,' said Frankie drearily. 'Don't tell Mim.'

Sarah started the engine. 'I can't do that.'

'Then wait till I'm not around. I don't want a fuss.'

Sarah nodded, relieved in spite of the guilt. Frankie was beginning to decide how she wanted to be treated, and that was good. People with some sort of control over their lives were less likely to fall into depression. The girl with her now was very different to the child Sarah remembered three years ago.

A dark blue Ford Escort was sitting in the driveway when they arrived home. Sarah pulled up beside it. 'Mrs

Jameson's here. Let's go and see what she has to say.'

Mim was sitting in the living room, looking much the better for her long sleep. 'Sorry, Sarah, I didn't mean to fall asleep for a hundred years,' she said, holding out a hand to Frankie. 'Okay, sweetheart?'

'Uh-huh,' said Frankie, flopping into the corner of the sofa beside Mim and looking over at Mrs Jameson.

'I was telling Mim we've got some information about your family, Frankie,' said the social worker, leaning towards the girl. 'As you said, your father's in Boston, but he's not able to help us at the moment, I'm afraid. But there's also your mother's mother, your grandmother. Her name is Alison Kerr, and she –'

'She had Mum when she was eighteen and dumped her with Wilma. Then she left,' said Frankie, her voice bored. 'She probably doesn't even know I exist.'

'She does, you know,' said Mrs Jameson mildly. 'She lives in Australia now. There's a big family out there, you've got aunts and uncles and cousins as well as your grandmother and step-grandfather. We'll be in touch with them, but don't worry, no-one's going to rush you off to Australia.'

Mim took Frankie's hand in both her own. 'You can stay here as long as you want, Frankie, be a long-term foster child, like Sarah was. But you should have some kind of contact with your Australian family. You might want to go and see them one day.'

Frankie sniffed desolately. 'I don't care.'

Mrs Jameson stood up. 'Have a think about it. We're setting up bereavement counselling for you too. You'll be able to talk to someone who helps people sort out how they feel after a death in the family.'

'I don't want to.' Frankie stared at the floor, kicking the leg of the coffee table.

'We'll talk about it in a day or two,' said Mrs Jameson. 'But I'll contact your grandmother tomorrow and we'll take it from there. Oh, have you heard Wilma's been moved to a medical ward?'

'They phoned this morning. Apparently she's –' Sarah hesitated, not wanting to use the word 'unconscious' in front of Frankie. '– a bit woozy today, so we thought we'd go and see her tomorrow when she might be feeling better.'

She saw Mrs Jameson to the door, and returned to find Frankie in front of cartoons once again, and Mim in the kitchen shaking paprika over chicken legs.

'We'll leave her for a bit. She has a lot to think about,' said Mim, jerking her head towards the living room. 'Her father's in prison, by the way, but we're keeping that to ourselves for the moment. Well, Sarah love, this holiday's not turning out quite how we planned it, is it?'

Sarah grinned wryly. 'You can say that again.' She pulled out a stool and perched at the worktop beside Mim. Now seemed as good a time as any to tell her about Frankie's panic attack. Mim wasn't going to be pleased. She took a deep breath and began.

After dinner Sarah went up to her room to email the details of her banking request to Ralph Bailey. The problem was explained in a few sentences and she pressed 'send' with a sigh of relief. He could sort things out first thing tomorrow, though she'd have to go to the bank again to make the final arrangements for the transfer. But next time, she'd go alone. Her mobile rang while she was still at the laptop, and Sarah picked it up. It wasn't a number she recognised. 'Hello?'

'Hello, Ms Martin, it's Ralph Bailey at the bank. Thank you for sending your details.'

Sarah blinked. 'Goodness – are banks open so late here now?'

'Um... no, only on Thursdays. I saw your email, though. I'll get onto your problem in the morning. Um – I was wondering about poor Mrs Murray. How is she?'

Sarah searched for words. This seemed a very odd conversation to be having with her financial advisor. 'She's been moved to a medical ward. I'm not sure what to tell you – why are you asking?'

'I – you may know she called the bank from the hospital, about two weeks ago. She wanted to withdraw money for a surprise of some kind for her granddaughter. It was a lot of money, from her savings account, and I told her about the hospital branch...'

His voice trailed away and Sarah felt like shaking him. She made an encouraging sound without speaking.

'Ah, so we organised that, and I was at the hospital branch the following day so I took her the cash and she signed for it and everything was fine, but, ah, she wouldn't hear of putting the money in the ward safe. She insisted on having it in her bedside locker... I've been a bit worried about it.'

Sarah could hardly believe her ears. It couldn't be bank policy to leave large sums of money with frail elderly patients, could it? 'Didn't you tell anyone?'

'Well, no... but later I wondered if I should have. And when you said about her granddaughter dying...'

Sarah didn't know what to say. She didn't want to fall out with the bank advisor, even if he was a complete prat. He should have insisted on leaving the money in a safe place, and now he was afraid Petra's death would mean his lapse would be discovered... which was absolutely right because she would tell the police about it herself the minute he got off the phone. The money was almost certainly connected to Petra's disappearance. Was Ralph mixed in there somewhere too? But if he was, they would hardly be having this conversation... unless he thought that by telling her, he would make it seem as if he had no connection to what happened to Petra. How complicated. Definitely something for the police.

Sarah decided to end the conversation. 'As far as I know Wilma Murray was quite with-it up until very recently,' she said briskly. 'But in view of what's happened I'll have to tell the police about this.'

She rang off, Ralph Bailey's wails of dismay in her ear. What an idiot the man was. He was afraid he'd lose his job, and it would be no more than he deserved. And now she'd better call Harry West.

'We'll be round as soon as possible,' he said. 'We need to speak to Frankie about this surprise for Petra.'

Fifteen minutes later a car arrived with both Harry West and DI Summers. Frankie's eyes widened when she heard about the money. 'Gran was going to spend all her savings on a surprise for Mum? She hardly ever bought anything expensive! Although...'

115

DI Summers leaned forward. 'What? Anything you can tell us about this might be very important, Frankie.'

Frankie shrugged. 'Gran said once that money in the bank was no use and you couldn't take it with you when you died. But she didn't say anything about a surprise.'

'And was she at home or in the hospital when she said that?'

Frankie sat straighter. 'In the hospital. I remember now, it was a day or two after she went into Ward Five. We thought she was getting better.' She slumped back into the sofa, and Sarah took her hand. Up and down, that was how Frankie's life was going. And there were more downs than ups.

DI Summers almost smiled. 'Excellent. So what we have to do is work out what kind of surprise this might have been, and who could have been involved in planning it.'

It sounded as if it should have been easy, but over an hour later they were no further forward and Frankie was wilting. She had dredged up details of Petra's friends and the things they used to do together, and remembered places Petra had wanted to visit, but the biggest surprise the girl remembered Wilma planning for Petra was knickerbocker glories at Blackpool, and she had no idea who might have been helping Wilma plan an expensive surprise.

'She must have had something concrete in mind or she wouldn't have had the money brought to Ward Five,' said Harry West eventually.

The DI nodded. 'One of the nurses saw the money in an envelope, but Wilma told her it was only for a few hours

– and a few hours later the money had in fact vanished. Maybe Wilma'll be able to tell us more, sometime.'

He didn't sound hopeful, and Sarah flinched.

Harry West and DI Summers left, and Sarah, Frankie and Mim sat looking at each other.

'Hot chocolate,' said Mim. 'Come on, Frankie, we can make it while Sarah puts the cat out.'

Frankie brushed past. 'I'll go out with Thomas.'

Sarah stood at the stove, stirring the chocolate and staring out to the darkness of the garden. Frankie was probably crying out there. Who could blame her?

Chapter Eight

Tuesday, 11th July

Sarah pulled into a space as close to the supermarket entrance as she could get and slumped for a moment, blinking gritty eyes. It had been another long night with Frankie – this must be how mothers of babies felt. But as sitting in the car would get her nowhere, she'd better start the round of the aisles. She dragged herself to the entrance, wrested a trolley from the trolley-park and pushed it towards the dairy produce section.

She was wandering round choosing an assortment of foodstuffs when she spied Caitlyn coming towards her, a basket slung over one elbow and a list clutched in her hand. Sarah tossed a packet of pasta into the trolley and set off to meet her.

'Sarah! Hi – you look terrible! What's up?' Caitlyn's pleased expression changed to a frown, and tears rushed into Sarah's eyes. It was good to have someone concerned about her.

She tried to smile. 'Well, you know how to make a girl feel good. I'm not sleeping much, that's all. Poor Frankie

– she has sleeping pills but we still have three a.m. crying jags nearly every night. And the bank's really bugging me.'

'You're doing too much,' said Caitlyn firmly. 'Come on. Auntie Caitlyn is taking you for a coffee at the De Luxe coffee bar at the back of this very establishment. Bring your trolley.'

Sarah didn't need to be asked twice. A few minutes later they were sitting on stools at a high bistro table, cappuccinos and warm croissants in front of them.

'Tell me all about it,' said Caitlyn.

Sarah launched into an account of Ralph Bailey's phone call and the visit from the police. 'They didn't leave until after ten, and then we were up half the night. My energy levels are kind of depleted today,' she finished.

Caitlyn stirred her coffee and licked the spoon. 'Poor all of you. But that's a weird story, Sarah.'

Sarah sipped her coffee, feeling her stamina return. God bless caffeine. 'Wilma must have had someone helping her with the surprise. She wasn't in a position to go to the jeweller's or whatever. It's so strange, her withdrawing all that money – it was two thousand pounds – while she was in hospital. At that point she was expecting to get home soon.'

'And she was fully responsible at the time?'

'Apparently she was mentally fine when she ordered it so there was no irregularity there, and she certainly signed for it. The off part is the bank clerk left it with her in the ward, but that might have been genuine stupidity.'

'Or not.'

Sarah stared. Or not. An old lady, and an envelope

full of cash, which then disappears off the face of the earth... 'Either someone took the money without Wilma knowing, or else she gave it to someone. The ward staff were there. Ralph Bailey was there. I wonder who visited her that day? It'd be difficult to find out – it's very open and easy in the rehab unit.'

'The money must have something to do with Petra's murder, too.'

Sarah massaged her temples. 'I wish my brain wasn't so woozy. And there's something wrong with all that – let's put it in the order it happened. Wilma ordered the cash, at the hospital. It was to be a surprise of some kind for Petra, so presumably Wilma was planning to give it to someone to pay for something, but we don't know who or what. But – yes, that's it – we can assume the correct person ended up with the money because Wilma was still compos mentis at that point. She'd have been quick enough to yell if the cash had been stolen.'

Caitlyn looked impressed. 'Golly, you're good at this. You should have been a journalist. So what went wrong with the money plan?'

Sarah leaned over the table and spoke in a low voice. 'Wilma had another stroke a day or two later, and four or five days after that, Petra disappeared. And we don't know if she'd seen something, or found out where the money went. That's the mystery – what did Petra know? And I'm not sure how hard the police are trying to find that out.'

'I suppose Wilma didn't just give the money to Petra? Or maybe Petra took it, and made up the missing money story to cover her tracks. That way she'd end up with two grand plus another two compensation.'

Sarah thought for a moment. It was possible, but... 'I don't think she had it. Petra, I mean.'

'Why not?'

'The way she spoke about it. Problems paying Wilma's bills, and so on. She seemed genuinely worried and puzzled about it all.'

'And when she disappeared she was on her way to talk to the hospital administrator.'

Sarah stared at Caitlyn. They had reached a dead end. 'Visitors,' she said. 'I could try to find out if she had any visitors around then who were new, or unusual, one-off, whatever. I'll ask at the ward next time we're visiting Wilma. No, heck – she's in a different ward now. But I could ask in therapy, and Frankie might know something.'

'I could help. I've been in the hospital a few times for this article, and some of my contacts might know something useful. I'm driving Mim to physio again tomorrow so I'll see what I can find out at the rehab unit, and you can do the same on Friday. We can ask in the cafeteria, nurses, therapists, anyone.'

'I'll ask Jack as well. You know, the guy I was having lunch with on Sunday? He's working as a hospital porter this summer, and he's often transported Wilma about the place.'

'Good idea. And we should try to find out who was at the old ward the day the money arrived. And – the bank person –'

'Ralph Bailey. I can't believe he'd jeopardise his career by swiping customers' cash... but I suppose we only have his word for it that Wilma signed voluntarily. And he was working in the hospital branch that day. He could have gone back for it later.'

'You should definitely have been a journalist. Let's meet tomorrow after I've asked around – coffee at my place about four? – and do some more brainstorming.'

'Good idea. It's amazing how much you come up with when there's two of you, isn't it?'

Happier, Sarah left Caitlyn to finish her shopping. Maybe they would find out something that would help track down Petra's killer. It couldn't hurt to try, anyway. Petra's killer... he must be the same person who took the money. Sarah's steps slowed down on the way to the checkout. Supposing Nick was 'the correct person' who ended up with the money – or another member of the ward staff, or Ralph Bailey – that would mean the killer was very close. How unreal it seemed...

The landline rang while she was transferring the shopping from car to kitchen, and Sarah dropped her bags to answer it. It was Jack.

'Sarah – that was quick!'

'I'm just this second home from the supermarket. I was right beside the phone when it rang.'

'I won't keep you, then. How're things?'

'Up and down, as you can imagine. You'll have heard Wilma's been transferred to the medical block?'

'Yes, poor old soul. How is she?'

'So-so, I think. We're going up today. Jack, did Wilma ever mention any of her visitors while you were taking her to therapy?'

There was a short pause before he spoke, and Sarah smiled to herself. He was taking the time to think about it.

'No, but I saw a couple of old people with her a week or two ago. Women. And a bloke from the bank, too, a young chap. I've seen him in the ward a few times. That's all, though.'

'Thanks, that's helpful. Is this a day off for you?'

'That's right. I was wondering if you'd like to come out for a meal this week – how about Thursday evening? There's a new Italian on the High Street and it's supposed to be fantastic.'

'Sounds great. I'm a real pasta freak. But listen, this time it's my treat.'

'Well – okay. Thanks. I'll pick you up at seven on Thursday, shall I?'

Sarah put the phone down and hugged herself. At last, at last, something was going right.

He put the kettle on for tea and stood flicking through the morning paper. This was one of the perks of weekend and evening work – days off during the week. He liked it. The problem was, it gave him time to think, and he didn't need that this morning. The picture of Petra and the smashed face he'd never seen wheeled round his mind for the nth time that morning, and sweat broke out on his forehead. Shit. All he'd wanted was some extra cash to provide him with the happiness he'd never been allowed, and now the fear that everything was going to catch up with him was – dire. He closed his eyes in despair. This wasn't his fault. He had to put it out of his mind; think about the job in hand.

This morning he was planning a trip to the DIY store to

look at bathroom fittings. A lemon yellow suite would be bright and fresh, unlike the dreadful avocado affair that was upstairs at the moment. He would choose new paint for the bedrooms too. There was 1950s wallpaper to come off, and he wouldn't be a bit sorry to say goodbye to that. Faded roses in twee wicker baskets all over the bloody place. He would have the walls painted white, a Grecian look. Simple and elegant. Colour would come from the soft furnishings. It was going to be so great.

And so expensive. Never mind, he still had a large chunk of old Wilma's cash left. That was another advantage of working in a hospital – he met so many susceptible old women.

He grimaced. Stupid Petra... lying there with a sack over her head... and the throaty little sound she'd made when he hit her with the shovel... and the way the blood had seeped through afterwards...

No, no... Don't *think* about it... The kettle's shrill whistle was a welcome distraction, and he poured water over his teabag, sweat drying on his brow. It was over, and next time he'd be more careful choosing his victim. He could earn enough for a nice attic conversion. Then he'd need someone in to landscape the garden, and then – then his home would be finished. He could be his own person at last.

He was hunting round for the car key when familiar voices outside interrupted him. Mrs Grant across the road and – his mother. He punched the wall so hard his fist stung. With the car beside the house he couldn't pretend to be out, and anyway, if he did that Mum would only get her keys out and discover they didn't fit the lock anymore. He fixed a happy smile on his face and opened the front door.

'Hello, darling! I dropped your dad at the barber's and I thought I'd come for a nice cuppa before collecting him again. We can all go for lunch somewhere since you're off today. Oh – you've taken the carpets up. I don't know, dear – a nice carpet will be so much softer to walk on than bare wood. I'll help you choose one. What else have you done... oh, my...'

'Modernisations, Mum. It's not finished yet. Now, a quick cuppa's fine but I'm going on another course this afternoon so I'm afraid I won't manage lunch.'

He bundled her into the living room and almost shoved her down on the sofa, glorying at the surprise on her face. This was good. Dealing with Petra had helped him find some assertiveness. At last.

She stood up again. 'Darling, your manners! We'll have to do something about that. I'll have a quick peek into the kitchen, you said you were decorating it too... oh my goodness. That table will be dreadful to keep clean, dear. You should have asked me first. Never mind, I'll help you plan the upstairs. You don't want to spend too much money and often a good clean's just as good as...'

She fussed around behind him and he seethed inwardly. It was unbearable. Here she was, interfering and taking over his life like she always did.

His stomach gave a sickening lurch as he realised he would never get away from her. Not while they were living in the same town.

Glynis Brady peered at her bank statement and frowned. Stuart hadn't paid the money back yet. How very odd.

She bent to lift the paperknife which she'd dropped when she opened the statement, appreciating even in the midst of the worry that she was able to bend to the floor without that excruciating pain in her left hip. You'd never think the operation was only eight weeks ago – here she was, dancing about like a young thing already – well, not quite, but very nearly. After all those years of incapacity it was wonderful.

But the money... Stuart had said it was for 'a few days'. She remembered it perfectly. He'd phoned a couple of days before she left the hospital to go to York, to ask if he could borrow the money to book a holiday as a surprise for Ellen – he was worried she'd notice if he used one of their accounts. It was one of those last minute things, he said, so he had to pay cash. And there was no reason not to lend her own son-in-law some money, though she'd thought at the time it was a lot to spend on a holiday. But she organised the money and he sent his clerk to collect it... Not very polite under the circumstances, but that was none of her business. He was going to repay everything as soon as he'd told Ellen. Glynis rubbed her forehead. Three thousand pounds was a lot of money, and it should have been back in her account long ago.

And – now she thought about it – Ellen hadn't said anything about the holiday, either. Glynis bit her lip. Of course she hadn't seen them recently and Ellen wasn't one for phoning... What was going on?

She perched on a dining chair, the bank statement flattering in her hand and a nasty churning feeling in her stomach. Something was wrong... Her savings... Think, think. When *was* the last time she'd spoken to Ellen and Stuart? In York, that was it – she'd spent two weeks in the convalescent place, because with George gone there was no-one to help out at home anymore. And Stuart and Ellen had only visited once because Ellen came down with that bug that turned out to be chicken pox. Of course. That would be it. They must have postponed the holiday because Ellen wasn't well. But that was no reason for Stuart not to pay her back. And she hadn't seen them since. Oh dear. She was getting worried now.

She would phone Stuart right this minute. If nothing else, all these senior citizens' classes she'd been going to since George died had given her more self-confidence dealing with people. She would call and ask Stuart politely but firmly when she was going to get her money back. He must have forgotten about it. There was nothing to worry about; she was being silly...

A nice cup of tea settled her nerves, and she sat down at the old-fashioned phone table in the living room. At this time in the morning Stuart would be at work, but she had the number written in her little book. It was a pity she didn't have his mobile number too – she could have texted him, what a shock he'd get! She was the best in the OAP mobile phone class at the community centre. And when her hip was a little better she was going to take up Nordic Walking as well.

She punched out the number and listened as it connected. Deep breaths, and remember to sound firm. Pleasant, but firm.

Her son-in-law's voice was distant over the phone and

Glynis had to make an effort not to stammer.

'Hello, Stuart dear, it's Glynis. How are you?...Excellent, thank you. Stuart, I was wondering when you were going to pay my money back – there's something I'm planning to buy soon.'

There! That was tactful; no-one could take exception to that.

Stuart was speaking, and what he said caused her to grip the phone tightly. Even in her own ears her voice sounded old and tremulous when she answered.

'But you did, dear, a lot of money... When I was in hospital... No, you phoned and asked if I could lend you three thousand pounds in cash to take Ellen on holiday... Yes, of course I did, I called the bank and they brought me the money that very same day... No, your clerk collected it – you had an important meeting... Oh no – no. Oh dear Lord.'

Glynis Brady dropped the phone and stumbled to her knees on the floor.

Sarah put the last of the frozen food into the freezer and closed the door. That conversation with Caitlyn had been an eye-opener. She hadn't thought the situation through like that before – logically. The missing money and Petra's death – had Petra found out who the thief was? She must have.

And how interesting it was to hear that Ralph Bailey was a regular visitor to Ward Five. Was there really so much bank business going on in a neuro rehab ward?

Frankie came in as Sarah was piling yoghurts into

the fridge. The child's eyes were red-rimmed – did she remember last night's bad dream? She hadn't been properly awake, though she'd thrashed around for over an hour.

Sarah shifted her bags from the table. 'Hello, Frankie love. You had a long sleep today. Want some breakfast?'

Frankie collected the cornflakes and a bowl and sat down with them. 'Sarah – what's happening about my mum's funeral?'

Sarah winced. The F word. The situation with Frankie and Petra was raking up her own bad memories and it wasn't fun. The day of Gran's funeral had been almost as bad as the day she'd died. The only thing that made it bearable was Mim, sticking to little Sarah like a limpet.

She clicked the kettle on and made herself sound calm and reassuring. 'I think that's something Mrs Jameson could help us with. The police'll have to – um, they have to say when, too.'

Frankie sat picking at her nails. 'When people die there's a funeral. I want my mum to have things done properly.'

Sarah rubbed the girl's back. Poor scrap. Frankie's world wasn't a happy place. But a funeral would have to wait until after an inquest, and that could take time.

'It might be a week or two before we can have a service, Frankie.'

Frankie burst into tears and Mim came through from the living room, walking carefully with one crutch. Sarah explained and Mim nodded.

'It's true we can't have the funeral until the police, um, say we can, Frankie, but there's nothing to stop us having a memorial service for your mum. Then we can have a quiet family funeral later. Would you like me to organise a memorial?'

Frankie wiped her eyes on her sleeve. 'Can we have flowers and everything?'

'Of course. I'll get onto Mrs J now, and then call the vicar.'

Sarah nodded at Mim as she turned back to the hallway. A memorial was an excellent idea – it would give Frankie the beginnings of closure, and the chance to move forward into her new life.

The little girl obviously had the same thing in mind. 'Sarah, where will I be going to school after the holidays?'

Sarah pushed yet more painful memories away. Twice she'd had to change schools because someone had died. Mind you, a fresh start was maybe a good thing in Frankie's situation, and she'd get that. The authorities had excused her for the last couple of weeks of term, sparing her the trauma of going into her old class and facing the eyes of the other kids.

Sarah took three mugs from the cupboard and turned back to Frankie. 'I expect you'll go to Brockburn High. Mrs J'll have all that organised as well.'

Mim appeared back in the doorway. 'Mrs J thinks a memorial is an excellent idea, Frankie. And the sooner the better, so I made an appointment with the vicar before lunch. Is that coffee?'

Sarah pulled out a chair and waved Mim onto it. 'Coffee approaching at speed, and well done you. Let's fix up when we're going to visit Wilma. Does the new ward have open visiting too?'

'No, it's afternoons from three till four, and evenings from seven till eight,' said Mim.

'Let's go this afternoon,' said Sarah. 'Wilma's more likely to be awake then.' She remembered her talk with Caitlyn. 'Who else has visited Wilma, do you know? I was wondering if they might know something that would help find out about the money.'

Mim stirred her coffee. 'I saw her in the TV room a couple of times with an elderly lady. Electric blue hair.'

'That would be Mrs Chisholm next door to Gran,' said Frankie. 'She visits sometimes, and so does Mrs Baker across the road. That's all, I think.'

Sarah scribbled the names on the shopping pad. Two elderly ladies didn't sound like candidates for kidnapping and murdering Petra, but they might know of other visitors she could ask. And she would go to the bank – without Frankie this time – and see Ralph Bailey. He hadn't seemed like a swindler, but a real swindler wouldn't. And a chat with someone in Wilma's old ward would be good. Vicky, the ward sister, might be best, just to be sure she was given correct information. If they found out something new it might make the police more active with their investigation.

Sarah stood up and put her mug into the dishwasher. 'I'm going to the bank this morning, ladies. Can you two amuse yourselves till lunchtime?'

'We certainly can,' said Mim. 'We have our meeting with the vicar. He's coming at eleven. Oh, and Harry West phoned while you were out, Sarah. He'll be here around five.'

Good, thought Sarah. Maybe she'd be able to judge

better how the police investigation was going. They had to get this cleared up, for Frankie.

She drove the short distance to the High Street, parked as near to the bank as she could get and reached for her mobile. Here in the car she'd have peace and quiet to call Wilma's elderly neighbours.

The online phone book soon had her in possession of the relevant numbers. Now, if only the ladies were at home.

There was no answer at Mrs Baker's number, but Mrs Chisholm's phone was lifted on the third ring. Sarah explained who she was, and asked which of Wilma's friends were in the habit of visiting her, 'so that she could tell them about Wilma's new ward'.

'Oh, that's kind, lovey, and you're right of course, it's a real trek up to that rehab unit, and the medical wards are so much nearer the main gate, aren't they? Let me see, there's Ma Baker across the road –' Sarah gave a little snort of laughter. 'Yes, that's what we all call her and it was our Wilma that started it, you know, quite a comedienne she is, lovey – and me, and Mr Paul the church minister but you don't need to tell him because he gets a list every week from the hospital and Wilma's new ward'll be on it, and there's Mrs Travers from the Woman's Guild, and that's about it as far as I know, lovey, apart from poor dear Petra and that little Frankie, bless her heart.'

Sarah wrote the names down, thanked Mrs Chisholm, and rang off. Heavens, what a live wire the old lady was. But her information hadn't exactly turned up dozens of prospective criminals. Surely Mr Paul and Mrs Travers could be scored off the list of suspects. But she would call them anyway; they might know of other visitors that Mrs Chisholm wasn't aware of.

It took nearly half an hour, but eventually Sarah had spoken to each of the people mentioned as Wilma's visitors. Mrs Travers came across as very clued-up, and assured Sarah that Wilma was unlikely to have had any other visitors. Sarah was inclined to believe her. She came to the conclusion that none of these people would be any help in finding out about the missing money. Another dead end. All the more reason to go and see what Ralph Bailey had to say for himself.

Ralph was busy with another customer, and Sarah sat in the waiting area, where two children were arguing in loud whispers over a jigsaw. She whiled away the time by making a list of the events running up to Petra's death, but nothing new came to mind. They were missing something – but what?

'Ms Martin? You can come over now.' Ralph Bailey was standing beside her chair, and Sarah jumped in fright. What was the man doing, creeping about like that?

She followed him into one of the advice booths and listened as he explained what he had set up with her accounts. The problem had been neatly sorted out, and Sarah signed release papers for her Zürich bank with the feeling that Ralph knew what he was doing job-wise, at least. Which might make it all the more likely that he had something to do with Wilma's lost money.

'I'm taking Frankie to see her great-gran this afternoon,' she said conversationally, sliding the last paper back towards Ralph.

His fingers twitched as he took it. 'Oh? I hope she's improving?'

'I'm afraid not. When was it you last saw her?' She noticed that once again, pearls of sweat were shining on his forehead.

'A – a couple of weeks ago, when I took her the money. It would be the Wednesday. It's my usual day at the hospital branch, and then I work late here most Thursdays and have time off another day.'

Sarah narrowed her eyes. That was more info than she'd asked for. Was he trying to be super-cooperative in the light of his mistake, or was he trying to distract her from Wilma? Or was he just nervous? And if so, why?

'Did you notice much change in her condition, compared to the time before that?' Sarah leaned over the table. She was getting good at this – putting questions in such a way as to get the information she wanted.

Ralph shuffled in his chair, twiddling the pen he was holding. 'I only saw her that one time. She was very bright, I must say. I – I'm sorry I bothered you on the phone like that.'

He put the pen down then immediately lifted it again, turning it over in his fingers. Sarah could almost smell his nervousness. She should keep him talking; he might give something away.

'That's all right. I called the police to make sure they knew about it and they were very interested, so it was good you did tell me.'

Disconsolate brown eyes met hers before sliding away. 'I know. They were here this morning. The police. None of this is my fault, you know.'

He sounded like a peeved child and Sarah was hard put not to laugh. She could well imagine Harry West cutting through Ralph's dithering and extracting the right information. Which was – what?

'Oh dear. Were you able to help them?' She put all the sympathy she could muster into her voice, wondering if she was overdoing it. But Ralph was lapping it up. Leaning over the table, he told her about the interview.

The questions had been easy enough at first. He hadn't known if other people were involved in the surprise for Petra; Wilma had mentioned no-one else during his visit. The police were scathing about him leaving the money on the ward, and the fact that she'd signed for the cash had been given a grilling too.

'They said I should have made her put it in the safe. But when I asked her about that she said no, she wanted it in her locker.' He wiped his forehead, smiling at her, obviously thinking that she was on his side. The short dark hair on the side of his head was damp with sweat.

'Mm,' said Sarah. It didn't seem likely that Ralph was their murderer. No matter what had happened to the money, she couldn't imagine this nervous man attacking Petra so violently. 'Did they ask anything else?'

As soon as the words were out Sarah bit her lip. That was a bit direct; this was none of her business.

But Ralph seemed eager to talk. 'They asked about other people. I said the room was empty, but people were going up and down the corridor. That sergeant wasn't happy that anyone could have passed by and seen Wilma with the money. I had to show them the document she signed, and a signature from before her illness, too.'

'Well, now they have all the facts they'll be able to investigate more fully,' said Sarah, glancing at the clock on the wall. Time she wasn't here. 'I hope for Frankie's sake it gets cleared up sooner rather than later.'

She stood up, and he rushed to open the booth for her.

'Thank you very much for fixing my accounts.' She made her smile as sweet as she could and offered her hand. The hand shaking hers was limp and sweaty, and Sarah walked out of the bank wondering if she had heard the whole truth from Mr Ralph Bailey. Did his nervousness mean he was hiding something? It was impossible to tell.

Frankie was leafing through a magazine in the living room, her feet on the coffee table. Sarah gave her a smile and went on through to the kitchen. If Petra hadn't been in the hospital cafeteria last Tuesday, or if Mim hadn't gone to watch the tennis that last afternoon, Frankie would have been placed in a different foster family. It was an odd thought.

Mim appeared from the study, using one crutch and with two empty mugs balanced on a plate in her other hand.

Sarah rescued them. 'Did you get fixed with the vicar? And for heaven's sake tell me when you have stuff to carry about,' she said, regretting the last sentence the moment it was out.

Mim gave her an old-fashioned look. 'The memorial will be on Friday. We had a good chat, didn't we, lovey?'

Frankie plodded in, her face tripping her. Sarah hugged

the child, but the thin shoulders stayed hunched and stiff.

Mim reached out and touched Frankie's cheek. 'Let's see if Rita can come for lunch on Thursday, shall we?' she said to Sarah. 'Then Frankie can meet little Jamie. And next time we go Manchester you'll be able to see all the things they have ready for the baby, Frankie.'

The girl looked up, a spark of interest in her eyes. 'I've never seen a tiny baby close up.'

'They're delicious,' said Mim. 'I expect Rita'll need a lot of help at first. You and I can be chief babysitters.'

Frankie smiled briefly. 'S'pose. Will Mr West know more about my mum when he comes tonight?'

'I imagine so, but Frankie, I'm going to ask you to let Sarah and me talk to him by ourselves first. If there's anything that's going to be upsetting for you, I want to know about it first, because then I can help you better. Will that be all right?'

Frankie stood tearing little strips from a supermarket receipt that had been on the table. 'S'pose.'

Frankie's mouth was drooping as they walked towards Ward Three, and Sarah could see why. This was the oldest part of the hospital, and there was no natural light along the corridor. Colditz Castle again...

'The décor's not important, Frankie,' she said firmly, hoping to avert tears. 'It's the care that matters.'

Wilma was in a four-bedded room with three other old, old ladies, one of whom was unconscious and breathing loudly and gutturally, and two others who were confused and noisy. None of them had visitors. Frankie took one wide-eyed look round the room and squeezed up close to Sarah, her chin wobbling, but apart from keeping an arm round the girl there was little Sarah could do. Rita had phoned for a chat just before they left, so Mim stayed at home, and Sarah wished with all her heart there was another adult here to talk to. The non-silence was too much for her to fill alone.

Wilma was drifting in and out of consciousness. Once she appeared to recognise Frankie and stretched a shaking hand towards her, but a few minutes later she glared at the child and roared something unintelligible, making Frankie shrink even closer to Sarah.

'Time to go,' said Sarah. 'She doesn't know what she's doing, Frankie love. Maybe things'll be better tomorrow.'

She was gathering her jacket and handbag when Nick's face looked round the door.

'Hello, you two. I had to bring a patient to a clinic here – thought I'd look in on Wilma.'

He stood for a moment beside the bed, but Wilma kept her eyes closed. It was impossible to know what Nick was thinking behind his neutral nurse-expression.

'Why did she get worse?' Frankie sounded very young and very unhappy.

Nick turned away from the bed. 'She had another big stroke. A bleed into her brain. It happens sometimes with very old people, Frankie, and unfortunately there's not much we can do.'

Frankie nodded, and Nick glanced at Sarah. 'There's a Red Cross tea bar further along here. Coffee and gingerbread?'

'Okay,' said Frankie, before Sarah could speak. 'Why

do old people's brains bleed?'

Nick led the way along the dingy corridor, telling Frankie about weakened blood vessels and clots, and Sarah saw how the girl was lapping it up. This was good – something that could be explained, even though it was something bad.

The tea bar ladies evidently knew Nick, and supplied them with large chunks of gingerbread. Sarah accepted hers, feeling uncomfortable. Had Nick really brought a patient to a clinic this afternoon? Or had he come to see her, knowing she'd most likely bring Frankie to afternoon visiting? If he had anything to do with Wilma's money and Petra's death, he'd want to know what was going on with the police investigation, wouldn't he? And behind the reassuring nurse-chat to Frankie, Nick was on edge – his brow was shiny and his feet were tapping up and down under the table.

'Will Gran be going back to your ward?' said Frankie, licking her fingers.

Nick shook his head. 'Probably not. We'll miss her. Evan and Vicky and I were saying this morning what a cheerful lady she was.'

Frankie sniffed. 'Evan's always cross.'

Nick stirred in his chair, grimacing at Sarah, who had no idea what to reply. 'Evan's had problems with his parents. He's not really cross, and he's a good nurse.'

Sarah looked at her watch. 'We should go, the police are coming soon. Thank you for helping Frankie.' She added the last sentence in a low voice as the girl was taking their tray to the bar.

Nick stared for a moment, then smiled. 'Pleasure. I

hope I'll see you again soon.'

He clapped her shoulder and Sarah shivered. She took Frankie's hand on the way back to the car. At least Nick had given the girl a good explanation of what was happening to Wilma, but oh, God – the sooner Petra's killer was found, the better she'd feel.

By half past four Sarah was back in the kitchen, preparing a tea tray for the police visit. She glanced outside and saw Caitlyn coming out of her garden shed with a tin of paint. An idea struck Sarah and she beckoned the other woman over, grinning when Caitlyn vaulted neatly over the fence and strode towards the back door, still clutching her paint.

'Mim's living for the day when she's fit enough to do things like that again,' said Sarah, and Caitlyn pulled a face.

'I bet. Mim'll get there, don't worry. I'm taking her to physio again tomorrow, did she say? I've got some things to research at the hospital.'

'She told me,' said Sarah. 'I wanted to ask if you could entertain Frankie for a while. The police are coming at five and it would be better if she was out the house for the first fifteen minutes at least.'

'Sure,' said Caitlyn. 'She can come and help me paint upstairs. Call me when you want her back.'

To Sarah's relief, Frankie was enthusiastic about the idea. The front door banged behind her and Caitlyn, and Sarah went back to her tea tray.

Harry West and DI Summers drove up at five past five.

Sarah opened the front door and stood back as the two police officers went through to the living room.

'Mrs Dunbar. I hope you're recovering well?' DI Summers sat down heavily in what had been Pop's chair and accepted a mug of tea.

'No complaints so far,' said Mim, and Sarah gave her a quick hug.

'Right,' said Harry. 'We've had the initial post mortem results. The cause of death was a blow to the forehead. There were at least two blows but the first was almost certainly fatal. She was killed at some time late Saturday morning, and as far as we can tell she wasn't raped or otherwise assaulted. The body was put in the canal some hours after death occurred. We still have no information as to where she was between leaving the rehab unit and being found in the canal, and I'm afraid there were no clues about her killer on her body.'

Aghast, Sarah's eyes met Mim's. It didn't sound as if there would ever be any definite answers. Were the police really doing enough? There was nobody left who cared about Petra, apart from Frankie.

'So what happens now?' said Sarah. 'This is going to be dreadful for Frankie. She doesn't know her mother was murdered yet. When we tell her I think it's important we give her some kind of hope that Petra's killer will be found.'

The sergeant's next words would have been more encouraging if he hadn't sounded so downcast. 'We'll get a break sometime. The killer will make a mistake, or someone will remember something. The majority of killers are caught and brought to justice. Tell her that.'

'Frankie's next door. Do you want to see her?'

'Not unless she wants to ask something. We'll be back later in the week, and hopefully the investigation will have moved forward by that time.'

Sarah swallowed miserably. If Petra was here she'd be pushing and chivvying the police to find out about the missing money. 'He killed her because of the money, didn't he?' She blurted it out before thinking about it, and both officers stared. 'I mean – she must have known something, right? And the killer couldn't risk her telling anyone about it.'

DI Summers leaned forward with his forearms on his knees. 'Not necessarily,' he said. 'It could be that she was killed to stop her finding something out.'

'Do you think it could be someone who visited her? Or a member of staff? Maybe even someone Frankie and Wilma know?'

'At the moment anything's possible, but believe me, we're working to solve this case and I think we will.' He stood up.

Sarah accompanied the two officers to the door. That was it, then. There were no clues as to who had murdered Petra; he – or she – was still out there somewhere. What a truly horrible thought.

Chapter Nine

Wednesday, 12th July

Sarah crossed the High Street and turned into Warren Road, where Señorita, her favourite boutique was. This was the pedestrian area of the town centre, and even on Wednesday afternoon it was busy with a good mixture of shoppers, though the majority were women, many pushing baby buggies. Sarah paused outside the bookshop, watching the crowds. It was good to be back. And yet loneliness surged through her, surprising her with its intensity.

She wasn't really 'back' in the same place, was she? Most of her old friends had relocated now, and Brockburn town centre hadn't been standing still either. There were new shops here and there, and the big Deli had closed, and oh, heck – so had Señorita. It was called Bubble now and was full of the trendy, inexpensive clothes youngsters liked. Sarah grimaced. Where else could she go for some new stuff? She was okay for tomorrow's date with Jack, thanks to an early summer sale in Zürich, but if they went out again she'd be stuck. She'd expected to spend this holiday tramping round Yorkshire with Mim, not going out to elegant restaurants with handsome men. Not to mention memorial services.

Sighing, she trailed into another boutique, conscious that most people here were shopping in pairs. What was she going to do with her life? Her mobile buzzed in her pocket – a text from Caitlyn. *Still on for 4pm?* Cheered, Sarah replied *CU then* ☺ and pulled a pair of black linen trousers from the rail. These looked great – and she did have friends here.

It was exactly four o'clock when she rang Caitlyn's doorbell.

'Come in, it's open!'

Sarah went through to the kitchen. 'How did you know it was me? You could have been inviting a double-glazing salesman, or some religious weirdo into your house. You should be more careful.'

Caitlyn shrugged. 'I knew you were coming, so it wasn't likely someone else would ring the bell bang on four, is it?'

Sarah lowered herself into a kitchen chair and propped her elbows on the table. 'I suppose not. Sorry, Caitlyn – I'm jumpy about this business with Petra.'

'Does Frankie know how she died yet?' said Caitlyn.

'Not really and it's horrible – how do you break news like that to a child? Mim told her Petra died after a bang on the head but we're not sure about the details. She reckons it'll be time enough to say the word murder when the police find out more. Personally, I'd have told the kid her mum was killed. Frankie isn't stupid.'

Caitlyn put a coffee in front of Sarah and set the machine again for her own. 'So how did you get on?'

Sarah told her about interviewing Wilma's visitors and Ralph Bailey. Caitlyn listened, frowning, and when the story was finished she pushed the biscuits across the table.

'Have a biccy. I didn't have much luck today either. I wandered about at the rehab unit while Mim was at physio, but no-one I spoke to saw anything. I asked in the cafeteria, and chatted to a couple of cleaners, and I went up to the old ward, too, and spoke to one of the nurses there. Dark-haired guy called Evan – that's not the one who asked you out, is it? He was a bit short when I started about Wilma. He said the police had questioned all the staff, but still no joy.'

'Evan always seems jumpy. And – Nick came to the new ward when I was there with Frankie,' said Sarah. 'I thought when he appeared it was a bit odd; I'd told him I was seeing someone and I doubt if he really was just visiting Wilma. But he was great with Frankie.'

'He would be, if he wanted to put you off your guard. Be careful, Sarah. So we have two dodgy nurses in Ward Five. But there doesn't seem to be anything to connect either of them to Wilma's money.'

'Another dead end,' said Sarah, dunking her biscuit in her coffee and trying to get her head round one of the nurses being a swindler and a murderer. *Surely* not... But Nick had been as nervous as Ralph Bailey, what was that about?

'Not necessarily. Let's think. The money disappeared the same day Wilma got it. She'd have shouted the place down if it had been swiped, so... she must have given it to someone.'

'Or she posted it to someone,' said Sarah, and Caitlyn sat up straight.

'That's an idea. She'd need a padded bag or something, but it's not impossible – there's a post box at the entrance to the cafeteria.' She stopped and thought. 'But even if she did, it was still to someone who swindled her into it, so it wouldn't change anything.'

Sarah scowled into her mug. 'Posting it's a bit far-fetched. I think either she had a visitor we don't know about, or –'

'Or she gave it to a member of staff. We always come back to that, don't we? And that could be Nick, or Evan the bad-tempered – or several hundred other people who could wander in and out.'

Sarah bit into another biscuit. 'Nick and Evan would've had most opportunity to take the money.'

'Or our swindler could be someone from outside, pretending to be a junior doctor from another department, or a secretary clutching an armful of files.'

'Heck. And I suppose it's not impossible that Wilma gave it to another patient. So what do we do now?'

Caitlyn sat up straight, her eyes shining. 'Sarah, I've just had the best idea ever. I'll get onto some of my journalist contacts, not to mention the hospital contacts I have now I'm in the middle of this wastage project, and we'll try to find out if anything like this has happened before.'

Sarah banged the table. 'Yes! It could have happened before, couldn't it? Stealing money from old ladies... it could be the kind of scam someone could milk for ages. I'll see what Jack can contribute when we're out tomorrow night. Oh, and we're having a memorial service for Petra on Friday at two. Mim's hoping it'll help Frankie, and it could be ages before the body's released for a proper funeral. We're going to the Royal Hotel for afternoon tea afterwards. Can you come?'

'Of course. Poor Frankie. I'll drive you all, shall I? And Sarah, maybe Frankie would like to help again with my redecorating? She enjoyed it yesterday. That might help her too.'

'Great. The more she has to think about, the better. Talk to Mim about it.' Sarah stood to leave.

Caitlyn winked. 'Good luck with your research with Jack tomorrow.'

Sarah grinned at her. 'Oh, it won't all be hard work.'

Netta Chisholm closed the front door behind her and switched on the hall light. Brr, it was chilly in here. People were always going on about global warming, but it didn't stop the weather turning cold when you least expected it.

She slid out of the camel hair jacket she'd found in the Oxfam shop last week and went through to the old-fashioned kitchen at the back of the house. They'd had a good evening in the church hall. It was years since she'd played snakes and ladders; such a good idea, this twice monthly games evening.

And it was something else that got her out of the house. She had the Woman's Guild every Monday, and the games night every other Wednesday. And the Wednesdays in between she and Ma Baker and Wilma sometimes had TV nights, or tea and gossip, three old women together. Except it looked like it would only be her and Ma Baker from now on. Poor old Wilma.

The kettle boiled, and Netta carried her tea through to the living room and sank into the sofa, looking at the armchair where Wilma always sat. Growing old was tough. You never knew when a stroke or a heart attack was going to pounce and rob you of everything you held dear. And poor Petra, what a terrible business. All they could hope was the police would catch the killer, but there had been nothing about it on the news today. An old woman robbed and her granddaughter killed, and it was newsworthy for five minutes. What a sick world they lived in.

Tears rose in Netta's eyes and she blinked them back. There was no point blubbing over what couldn't be changed – and some folk *did* care; she shouldn't paint the world blacker than it was. Look at that nice young woman where poor Frankie was staying, kind enough to phone and tell everyone about Wilma's new ward.

Netta reached for the remote and switched on the late night news, pressing the mute button when she saw the commercials were still running. She frowned. After that phone call she'd realised there *was* someone else she'd heard Wilma talk about. It was a week or two ago when Wilma was still doing well. But who had it been? Netta sighed. She hadn't been listening, that was the trouble. They were in the cafeteria and she'd had such a good piece of Madeira cake, just like her granny used to make. She'd been enjoying the treat and remembering the old days instead of paying attention to her friend. It was someone Wilma'd been speaking to on the ward – or was it in physio or OT? A man, anyway, and Wilma'd been all giggly about him. But instead of asking more, Netta had changed the subject to grandmothers and cake. Ah well. Maybe it would come back to her.

When the news ended she lifted the evening paper. What a load of junk they printed nowadays – who cared what politicians did in their free time? She turned to the page listing Hatches, Matches and Dispatches. Not that she knew many of the Hatches and Matches these days, but she had come to the age where people she knew appeared in the Dispatches with depressing regularity.

More tears came to her eyes when she saw the notice – a memorial service for Petra, on Friday afternoon. She would go, for Wilma's sake. Ma Baker would come too. Netta raised a hand to her face, blinking hard to keep the tears in. Dear Lord. A memorial for Petra, and the way things were looking it would be Wilma's turn next.

'Come on, Netta love,' she said aloud, taking her tea cup back to the kitchen. 'One day at a time, that's all you need to do.'

Slowly, she went through to the bedroom and started to prepare for bed. Tomorrow she would tell Ma Baker about the memorial, and the others at church who'd visited Wilma, and...

Who *was* the man Wilma'd been talking about?

Chapter Ten

Thursday 13th July

Rita's car vanished round the corner, and Sarah fled upstairs. The visit had lasted longer than she'd expected – she'd have to hurry to be ready in time for her date. But how well Rita was looking – not a sign of the exhaustion you were supposed to have during the last weeks of pregnancy.

The new silk tunic she'd bought in a summer sale shortly before leaving Zürich was hanging in her room, grey-toned blobs merging gradually into each other, and it was perfect with the new black linen trousers. Anticipation warmed its way through Sarah as she dressed. Her first date on British soil for years – how exciting was that?

Mim and Frankie were poring over the menu from the Indian takeaway when Sarah went down to collect her phone, which was charging in the kitchen.

'You look very nice,' said Mim approvingly, and Sarah laughed.

'Funny, isn't it – at my age that's a compliment, and at Frankie's too, but in between there's the age when your mum thinking you look 'very nice' is enough to have you change every garment you have on,' she said, noticing how this remark touched Mim.

It was true, though. She remembered almost nothing of her own parents, and Gran had been so much older – Mim was the mother figure in her life. It would be different for Frankie. At eleven, her memories of Petra were clear, good memories and bad ones too. Maybe they should talk about that sometime.

The restaurant was in the town centre, not far from the canal. Sarah stepped inside, looking round curiously as Jack swung the door shut behind them. This place used to be a fish and chip shop, but you'd never know it now.

'I wonder how long it took them to get the chip-fat smell out,' she said, while they were waiting for the menus.

For a moment Jack didn't speak, an uncertain expression crossing his face. 'Smells good enough now, doesn't it?' he said, sniffing as a waiter swept past with a basket of garlic bread.

Jack was looking very smart, thought Sarah, in his dark grey suit and grey shirt and tie. They had co-ordinated their outfits rather well. The menus arrived, and she opened hers, aware of an awkward pause. Jack was different tonight. He was tugging at his collar, scanning the menu with a frown on his face. He looked nervous, which was rather sweet. Time for some serious confidence-boosting.

'This is my kind of place, well done you for suggesting

it!' she said, smiling over the top of her menu. 'I'm going to have the Mediterranean veggie anti-pasto, and Penne alla Milano for my main course. And a side salad.'

Jack closed his menu, relief on his face. 'That sounds perfect. I'll have the same. I haven't had much experience of Italian food, so I'm glad to have an expert to guide me.'

Surprised and amused, Sarah picked up the wine list. It seemed unusual to not know much about Italian food. She ordered the meal, and a carafe of house red to go with it, and sat back.

Jack seemed to be waiting for her to start the conversation, and Sarah cast round in her head for something to say. What had happened to the rapport they had before? Seeing him in the hospital in his role as porter had her heart beating faster every time. But now she couldn't think what to say to the man, and he was obviously having problems too. And he'd grilled her so thoroughly about Switzerland at the farm, she could hardly start with that again. But this was bordering on embarrassing...

'It's Petra's memorial tomorrow afternoon,' she said wildly.

It wasn't a very cheerful topic for a dinner table, but Jack nodded. 'Yes, I heard. Some of the nurses from Wilma's rehab ward are going. I'm going too, if you don't mind – for Wilma, really.'

Sarah felt warmed. They were talking, and it wasn't platitudes. 'Thank you so much. It makes a difference to know that people care enough to come – for Frankie more than anything. Petra doesn't seem to have had many real friends. Mim and I were worried we'd be the only ones there.'

'Would you like a lift? I could pick you all up.'

Sarah touched his hand quickly. 'Thanks. A neighbour has already offered to drive us. I'll see you there.'

The starters arrived, and for the next few minutes the conversation was culinary. Sarah swallowed her last bite of aubergine and wiped her mouth. She caught Jack's eye as he laid down his fork, and he smiled, but oh, Lord, there it was again, the awkward pause. Yet she fancied the pants off this guy – what on earth was wrong that they weren't finding anything to say to each other?

'Have you been to the new cinema complex yet?' she said.

'No... no, not yet.' He was pulling at his collar again, and Sarah despaired. The hospital and the horror of Petra's family seemed to be the only point of contact tonight. Oh, well, she'd wanted to ask him about Wilma anyway. But it wasn't very romantic that it was their sole topic of conversation, was it?

'We visited Wilma on Tuesday but she was pretty out of it. When did her confusion start, do you know?'

Jack looked taken aback and Sarah cringed. Another horrible topic for the table, and he was obviously wondering how to answer her.

'A couple of weeks ago, I think. She would get mixed up about whether it was morning or afternoon, and who had been to see her. That kind of thing.' Jack took a sip of water. 'Did you go to Italy while you lived in Zürich?'

They were back in Central Europe. Jack would soon be able to write a book about her two years in Zürich. But at least they were talking about something interesting again. Sarah told him about trips to Tuscany and Rome, then asked about his favourite city.

'Oh – um – the best holiday I ever had was in Edinburgh when I was a lad. You know, the castle – and we went to the Tattoo as well – and there are some very pretty villages round the coast not far away.' He ducked back into his penne.

Sarah stabbed at her own pasta, squinting across the table. Jack's hands were shaking, and Sarah was suddenly touched. This was all nerves. He was such a private person, and this date with her was obviously important to him. She should make more effort here, after all, he was kind as well as good-looking, and they had the connection of a shared past, too – but with his shyness it was going to be down to her to make sure they got to know each other well enough to make this work. And she wanted it to work.

She poured them both more wine and started to talk about Mim and Pop. The subject of growing up kept the conversation going for the rest of the meal, what with school and teenage years and career choices. But it was all so one-sided. No matter how she tried, Sarah couldn't get Jack to open up, and she finished her coffee still not knowing what made him tick. This was harder than she'd thought; the man was cripplingly shy. Either that or he'd decided that going out with her was the worst idea he'd had all year.

He ran her home, and she was glad to have the excuse of Petra's memorial the next day not to ask him in for coffee.

Mim was still up, watching a travel documentary

which she switched off when Sarah came in. 'Well?' she demanded, and Sarah sank down beside her.

'Oh, Mim, he's a lovely bloke, but getting him to talk about himself is like pulling teeth. I don't know if this is going anywhere. But he's coming to the memorial tomorrow so you'll be able to judge for yourself. And some nurses from Wilma's old ward are coming too.'

Mim heaved a sigh. 'I'm glad for Frankie's sake that people are making the effort to go.'

Sarah went up to her room, wondering if, after tomorrow, she should go out with Jack again. He ticked a lot of boxes but they had to be able to talk to each other about more than Swiss cheese and James Bond. Maybe she should end it sooner rather than later.

No, she thought, smoothing cream over her face and neck. She would give him another chance – they could do something next time – go to an exhibition, or walk round the botanic gardens, something that would provide an automatic topic of conversation. Jack might open up more easily when they weren't staring at each other over the dinner table. It had to be worth a try. But it was time to get some sleep.

Tomorrow wouldn't be an easy day.

He pressed the car key to activate the central lock, and turned to open his front door. For once the sight of the freshly-painted hallway didn't warm his heart as he stepped inside. He tossed his jacket over the bannister and slouched into the living room. Home. He was safe here, but was he safe in the outside world too? Wilma wouldn't say anything now because she couldn't. Neither could Petra. Was there anyone else? The other old dears? Surely not.

Sarah. How he wanted to sweep her into his arms and hold her close – it was the way she cared about people. Seeing her with her foster mother, and Petra's daughter... it was an almost-painful pleasure. Mim Dunbar was crazy about Sarah; you could tell by the expression on her face. Humorous. Loving. So obviously happy just to be with Sarah. His mother had never looked at him like that. All her gaze did was suck the life from him; anything he did was only good if she could feel better about herself because of it. *My son passed his exams, see what a good mother I am*. Sarah didn't have to cope with that; she could be her own sweet self with family. And the way she walked close to the girl, shoulders touching, ready to give out a hug... Lucky Frankie, being hugged by Sarah.

It was the stuff of his dreams.

CHAPTER ELEVEN

Friday, 14th July

A thud from Frankie's bedroom woke Sarah, and she lifted her phone to see the time. Oh no. Ten to four. If this was her up for the day she'd be dead by lunchtime – and what a sick thing to think on the day of Petra's memorial. Bad as this was for her and Mim, it was infinitely worse for Frankie. Sarah forced her feet to the floor and grabbed her bathrobe.

Frankie's door was cracked open and Sarah pushed it gently. 'Frankie? You okay?'

'I fell out of bed,' said Frankie, and the despair in her voice prompted Sarah to go right in. The girl was sitting on the floor, clutching the duvet which was half on, half off the bed. Her eyes were huge, staring at Sarah in the dim light from the street lamp outside.

Sarah tucked her in again. 'I guess you were dreaming.'

Frankie scrunched the duvet under her chin, her lips trembling. 'Sarah...' She stopped, and screwed her face up.

Sarah sat down on the bed. 'Out with it. Keeping things to yourself never works. Let me help.'

She had to lean forward to hear Frankie's whisper.

'You and Mim – and the police – you all said Mum died of a blow to the head... Sarah, did someone kill my mum?'

The horror was plain to hear, and Sarah blinked back tears. They'd been wrong to conceal the truth from Frankie. She wasn't a little child, and the life she'd led with Petra must have made her more worldly-wise than most eleven-year-olds. But that was no help to the girl in this nightmare.

'Sweetheart – no-one knows what happened. Someone seems to have hit her with something, but the police don't have any details yet. Mim – we thought it would be better if we didn't say anything to you until we knew more, but perhaps that was wrong. I'm sorry.'

A single tear was tracking down Frankie's left cheek and she brushed it away. 'But why would anyone want to kill my mum?'

'I don't know. It seems incredible,' said Sarah. Not quite true, but in the general scheme of things it *was* incomprehensible that one human being could kill another merely for financial gain. She searched for something to comfort Frankie. 'I think the best thing is to let the police get on with their investigation. Mr West said they solve virtually all these crimes, and he was sure about that. So if someone did kill Petra, they'll be caught.'

And hell, she still hadn't told this poor kiddie the truth. It might have been better to say straight out that Petra had definitely been murdered. But on the morning of the memorial... Sarah stood up. They could talk another time.

'Go back to sleep for a while, and try not to worry. We

can trust the police to find out what happened.'

I hope, she thought, kissing Frankie, who closed her eyes and turned to face the wall. Sarah shivered back to her room. Finding the truth wouldn't help Petra, but it might give Frankie the closure she needed. And at least Petra hadn't suffered for long – or had she? There was no way to know what had gone on before Petra's death.

Sarah shuddered, and rolled back into bed, grasping her duvet in much the same way Frankie had hers. She dozed fitfully until seven o'clock, then went downstairs to find Mim making coffee.

The morning seemed never-ending. Sarah made Frankie a bacon sandwich which the girl toyed with for half an hour before binning it. She took Mim to physio and Frankie to see Wilma, who was either unconscious or asleep, and made a Spanish omelette for lunch. How were she and Mim to help Frankie through the service? The child had barely uttered a word all morning. She'd been all for the memorial a few days ago, but the reality of a service for her dead mother was going to be very hard, especially with others present. A horrible thought came to Sarah and she stood still. What if the killer came to the memorial? He might be hanging around somewhere, watching them all, getting his kicks from the whole sorry pageant.

Mim went to change her clothes, and Sarah joined Frankie, who was at the kitchen window, watching Thomas climb the apple tree outside.

'Frankie. My gran's funeral was the worst day of my life because she was all the family I had and she was gone. I felt terrible for a long time, and I know you feel terrible too. But you're not alone, lovey.'

The shoulder beneath her hand relaxed slightly, and Sarah hugged the girl, relieved when Frankie didn't pull away.

Caitlyn arrived at half past one, looking elegant in a grey trouser suit. 'How are things?' she mouthed, nodding towards the living room.

Sarah made a face and shook her head. 'We're ready.'

It was a short drive to the crematorium, which was macabrely situated just beyond the hospital. Backing on to the geriatric unit, in fact – dear heavens, thought Sarah, who on earth planned these things? She sat in the back of Caitlyn's car, holding Frankie's cold little hand and watching as Brockburn passed by outside. Brilliant sunshine was splitting the skies, and the people going about their daily business were summer-clad – T-shirts and mini-skirts and happy smiles all over the place. And here she was, holding the hand of a child who should have been part of her past, going as one of the chief mourners to the memorial service of a woman she barely knew.

The chapel was in the middle of an old, unkempt graveyard. Caitlyn swung the car into the driveway, and Sarah felt the hand clutching hers shake as they rumbled along the weed-strewn gravel, mossy, overgrown graves on either side.

'This is the old part, Frankie,' said Mim, turning round. 'The chapel's up ahead, and the garden of remembrance is on the other side. It's less wild there, a gardener looks after it regularly.'

A dozen or so people were waiting outside the chapel.

Nick was there with Evan and Vicky, and that must be Mrs Chisholm with the blue hair, and her friend would be Mrs Baker. And the police were here. Four women were grouped to one side; Petra's neighbours, maybe, or workmates. Sarah considered the little group. Could any of them be involved in Petra's death? There was no way to tell, and this wasn't the time to ask Frankie who they were.

And there was Jack, standing by the chapel door.

He hurried over and opened the car door for Mim and then Sarah, smiling briefly at them both. When Frankie came to stand beside Sarah he put a hand on the girl's shoulder and squeezed quickly. 'Remember your mum's found her peace,' he whispered.

Frankie nodded, all eyes, and Sarah shot him a grateful look. That was the right way to help Frankie – brief contact and words of support. Well done, Jack.

The others crowded round as they walked towards the chapel door, Mrs Chisholm murmuring, 'She's in a good place now, lovey, don't forget that,' as she patted Frankie's back.

Frankie gave a gulp and grasped Sarah's arm as they moved inside. There were two wreaths lying at the front where the coffin would normally be; lilies organised by Mim for Frankie, and pink roses from the family in Australia. Sarah put her arm round Frankie as they settled into their pew, and saw that Mim was holding one of the child's hands in both her own. The atmosphere was hushed, anonymous background music filling the silence.

The service was mercifully short. Frankie remained motionless, her eyes fixed on the flowers. Sarah couldn't tell if she was listening as Mr Paul the vicar spoke about life after death, and comfort in heaven. But then he mentioned Petra by name, and Frankie began to sob. All Sarah could do was hold the girl tightly, her own eyes closed to keep the tears in, the memory of Gran's funeral intensifying her pity for Frankie. This shouldn't be happening, it shouldn't... it wasn't fair. Sarah was aware of Jack beside her, his shoulders trembling too.

The 23rd psalm marked the end of the service. Sarah helped Frankie to her feet, wondering if the past half-hour had been any help to the girl at all. Mr Paul approached and invited them to follow him outside, but Frankie shook her head, dropping back onto the pew and pulling Sarah down beside her.

'I'll go out and thank people,' said Mim.

Sarah waited as Mim, Caitlyn and Jack left, followed by the other mourners. 'Take your time,' she said to Frankie.

When the room was empty, the little girl went up to the flowers, touching the lilies with tentative fingers. 'My mum loved flowers.' Two tears ran down her cheeks.

'They'll put these in the garden of remembrance for her. We can go there as often as you like, and take more flowers. You can choose her favourites.'

'Will the proper funeral be here too?'

Sarah rubbed the thin back. 'Yes. It'll be for family only next time, though.'

Frankie stood for a moment before turning to go, her face white as they walked to the door.

The Royal Hotel, opposite the graveyard and probably owing much of its business to funeral parties, was ready for them. The others were milling around in the hallway, and Mim held out her arms to Frankie, crutches dangling.

The girl went for a hug, and Jack put his hand under Sarah's elbow. 'It was a good service for Frankie, wasn't it? She'd take comfort if she was listening, and if she wasn't, it wasn't too long.'

'That's what Mim had in mind,' said Sarah. 'But I don't know. Frankie's terribly pale.' Oh, dear. They'd hoped the memorial service would help the child, but Sarah couldn't tell if they'd been successful or not. How had she felt, immediately after Gran's funeral? It was hard to remember. Mim had been there for her, but it seemed that Sarah was the person Frankie wanted to be close to this afternoon. The girl was back, hanging on Sarah's other arm. In a way it was understandable. Mim with her crutches needed help too.

Afternoon tea was set up in a dining room with a long oval table. Mrs Chisholm came up to talk to Frankie, and the little girl's face brightened for a few seconds. Sarah found herself sitting at one end of the table with Frankie, Mrs Chisholm and Jack. She turned to see what Mim was doing, but Caitlyn was seating her further along with the three nurses. A handful of people from Wilma's church were in between, but the women Sarah had noticed before hadn't come for tea. Harry West and Mandy Craven had left immediately after the service too.

Rather to Sarah's surprise, Jack started the conversation at their end with a story about a funeral his grandmother had wanted to go to on a Scottish island, but only the men were allowed to attend. She glanced at Frankie but the girl was listening avidly. Mrs Chisholm joined in with an anecdote about a graveyard cat, and Frankie actually smiled. Sarah relaxed. Frankie would grieve for a long time, but she had seen that her mother's passing had been noticed and marked.

The little girl wandered across the room to look at an aquarium, and Sarah glanced down the table to Mim, who was listening to Vicky with her usual bright expression.

Jack and Mrs Chisholm started talking about Wilma.

'You must miss her,' said Jack, shaking his head when Mrs Chisholm offered him the sandwiches. 'Do you manage to visit her much?'

'Well, it's a bit of a trek from Burnside Road but we visited regular, nearly every day while she still knew which way was up. We used to have a real laugh. A magnet for gossip, she was, and she didn't believe in keeping it to herself. Such a shame… there's not a word to be had out of her these days.'

Sarah noticed Nick staring down the table at them. He gave her a strained smile as soon as she caught his eye, then turned back to Evan.

Frankie returned, and Jack changed the subject to summer flowers. What a help he was being today, thought Sarah. Maybe she'd judged him too quickly yesterday evening.

'I wish Frankie would let me help her more. Poor Sarah, it isn't her job,' said Mim, her mouth turned down.

Caitlyn glanced up the table, where Sarah and Frankie were listening to some repartee between Jack and Mrs Chisholm. 'I don't think Sarah sees it like that. I wouldn't worry. Once your knee's better you'll be able to do more with Frankie.'

Nick was gazing over too, the expression in his eyes intense. 'Sarah has a huge sense of family, doesn't she?'

Caitlyn saw him jerk in his seat. Vicky was giving him a very significant look – had the other nurse kicked him under the table?

'Nick, don't stare. You'll freak... Frankie out.' Vicky passed him a sandwich, and Caitlyn glanced at Mim, who was obviously fully aware that Nick had the hots for Sarah, because she gave Caitlyn a tiny smile.

'Sorry.' Nick accepted a sandwich and turned to Mim. 'How's the knee?'

Caitlyn glanced at the man opposite her. Evan was staring at Sarah too.

'Young lady, I want you to promise you'll stay in touch,' said Mrs Chisholm, passing Frankie the biscuits. 'Ma Baker and I want to know how you're getting on, and we can't depend on meeting at the hospital while we're visiting Wilma. So you make sure and phone us every now and again.'

Sarah's lips twitched as Jack spoke in a low voice.

'Frankie, if I were you I'd be very careful to do just that. I'm sure Mrs C here is an angel in disguise, but Ma Baker sounds like a dangerous woman. Isn't she the one who's a crack shot and head of a team of gangsters?' He looked meaningfully across at Mrs Baker, who was eating a ham sandwich with a placid expression on her wrinkled old face. Frankie giggled.

Mrs Chisholm poked Jack's arm, and he winked at her.

'Don't worry. I know you're the boss.'

'Away with you! Charm the leaves off the trees, you would.'

Jack chuckled, and turned to Sarah with a remark about how the town council was proposing to do up the old graveyard.

I *was* wrong about him last night, thought Sarah, as he went on to tell them more about it. Well, everyone was allowed an off-night. He was everything a girl could wish for today. Sensitive with Frankie, yet not afraid to talk about death, flirting with the old ladies, interesting talk. Warmth spread through her as she listened – he was doing this for her. Her life had taken an unexpected U-turn and no mistake. She'd arrived here expecting a holiday to cheer her up after Andreas's desertion, and instead she'd found – what? A chaotic home situation that could well put the Geneva job in jeopardy – and Jack.

Sarah looked down the table at Mim, and saw that Nick's shoulders were hunched all the way to his ears. Tense didn't begin to describe his posture. Was that about – was Mim okay? Maybe it was time to break up the party.

Frankie was hugged and kissed by everyone present on their way out, but she bore it very well. Jack kissed her cheek and then Sarah's, saying he would call later, and helped Mim into Caitlyn's car.

'Your Jack seemed delightful today,' said Mim, as Sarah settled into the back seat. 'He was a good help, wasn't he, Frankie?'

'I guess I was a bit harsh last night. Good, huh?'

Frankie looked across the road at the cemetery. 'My

mum would have liked him –' Her voice choked into silence.

Sarah gave her a warm smile. 'She would be proud of you today, Frankie. We'll come back tomorrow with more flowers, shall we?'

Netta Chisholm watched as Frankie drove away from the hotel with her new family, then glanced round for Ma Baker. They were going to get the bus home; their pensions wouldn't stretch to a taxi both ways. Ma was nowhere to be seen, and Netta concluded she'd nipped off to the loo. She sat down on a regency chair opposite the reception desk.

'Waiting for the royal coach, are you?' said a voice beside her, and Netta gazed up at Jack, remembering with a pang that her Pete had been like that too, a real ladies' man.

'A number seventeen bus, more like,' she said, as Ma joined them. 'Well, let's be off, Ma. Goodbye, Jack dearie, if we see you again I hope it'll be in happier circumstances. But poor old Wilma isn't looking so good, is she?'

His eyes shone in sympathy and Netta felt warmed. What a nice young man. She staggered as she rose to her feet. It had been a long day. Jack steadied her arm and Netta beamed at him. Just like her Pete, he was.

'Are you all right, Mrs Chilsholm?' The blond staff nurse from Wilma's old ward hurried over and took Netta's other arm, and she beamed at him too. Goodness, she was surrounded by handsome young men – here was the dark-haired nurse too, the one who barked a lot but he was a sweetie really.

'I'm fine, dearie. My legs had a wobble, that's all.'

'Is someone driving you home?' The dark-haired nurse bent over her.

Jack pulled out his car key. 'I'll do that, shall I? I've plenty of time, and I'll be passing Burnside Road on my way to Leeside Centre.'

'That would be lovely,' said Ma, before Netta could open her mouth. Ma had never been much of a bus fan. She said all the jolting gave her indigestion.

The blond nurse felt her pulse then patted her hand. 'Fit as a fiddle.'

The other nurse didn't look convinced, but Jack turned to the door, crooking his other arm to Ma Baker.

'Come on, ladies, your chariot awaits.'

He ushered them past the nurses and into his car, and Netta relaxed into the passenger seat. Oh, she was tired. It would be good to get home and put her feet up. They drove by the hospital and she winced. Poor old Wilma. But they were nice people, those doctors and nurses. Maybe tomorrow she and Ma could visit Wilma in the new ward, suss out the nurses there.

Jack manoeuvred round the roundabout and Netta straightened up.

'Here we are, Burnside Road. Ma's number ten, and I'm across the road at number fifteen. You can let us out over there, thank you very much indeed.'

He pulled in at an empty bus stop, and opened the doors for them both, back-chatting like mad. Netta and Ma stood waving as he drove away again.

'A thoroughly nice young man,' said Ma.

Netta yawned. 'Isn't he!'

She crossed the road and walked along to her own block. East, west... there was never a truer word said.

Chapter Twelve

Saturday, 15th July

Sarah stretched luxuriously, then rolled on her side and stared at her mobile on the bedside table. Quarter to nine. For the first time in ages she had slept through the night, and she could only hope this meant Frankie had too. The girl had been quiet all evening yesterday after their return from the memorial, but she seemed content, doing a jigsaw with Mim. It was a start, although real closure wouldn't happen until the police investigation was concluded and the killer locked away.

Her phone was flashing when she came out of the shower, and Sarah saw she'd missed a call from Caitlyn. She pressed to connect. 'Hi, Caitlyn.'

'Fancy a coffee? There's something I need to run by you.'

'Coffee sounds good – I have news too. Harry West phoned last night. Shall I come now?'

Ten minutes later she was pulling out a chair in the kitchen next door.

Caitlyn opened a packet of ginger nuts. 'So what's the latest from the police?'

'Harry said they'd been talking to Ralph Bailey about Wilma's signature, and how it was still being investigated. That made me think there must be some kind of uncertainty about it. But surely, as an ill woman her signature might be different. I'm a bit worried the police are clutching at straws here.'

'Interesting,' said Caitlyn. 'And it needn't be clutching at straws. It could be the police are wondering if Ralph forged the signature.'

'I thought about that too, but I'm sure an expert would be able to take Wilma's condition into account. And Caitlyn, he's such a wimp. I can't picture him battering someone to death.'

'People are capable of more than you think. Ralph could have a dark side we know nothing about. But if they haven't arrested him it must mean there's no proof.'

'Or he's innocent,' said Sarah darkly.

Caitlyn leaned across the table. 'We might be closer to finding that out. Big news. Sarah, we were right. It *has* happened before.'

Sarah jerked upright. 'You mean someone else had their money swindled away?'

'Yes. I spent yesterday evening on the phone to various journalist contacts – and I struck lucky. A couple of months ago an elderly lady in Manchester lent her son-in-law three thousand. She was in a Manchester hospital recovering from a hip replacement at the time, and apparently the son-in-law phoned and said he needed cash to pay for a surprise holiday for her daughter. She had the money brought to the ward, he sent someone to collect it, and a day or two later she went away to one of those convalescent places. Then this week when her bank statement came she got onto the son-in-law about why he hadn't paid her back yet, and he didn't know the first thing about it. He informed the police straightaway but they couldn't do anything.'

Sarah sat straighter. 'But why didn't this woman realise it wasn't her son-in-law on the phone?'

'She said the voice sounded like her son-in-law. And he mentioned the daughter's name, and a couple of other little details that were correct – she didn't suspect a thing. And you know what phones can do to voices... It's a clever scam, isn't it?'

'Cruel, too. What are the police doing about it?'

'Investigating with no success, my friend said.'

Sarah drummed her fingers on the table. 'Caitlyn, do you think we could go and see this woman? She might be able to tell us something we don't know.'

'I hoped you'd say that – I've got her address. Are you doing anything this afternoon?'

'Looks like I'm going to Manchester, doesn't it? Give me a minute and I'll see if Mim and Frankie want to come too, and visit Rita. I'll call you.'

She rushed off. Mim was all in favour of a trip to Rita's, and Sarah pulled up Caitlyn's number, excitement making her fingers slide on the screen.

'Caitlyn? We're all going. We can drop Mim and Frankie off, visit Mrs Brady, and collect them again at Rita's. Is it okay if we leave at half one? Rita said we're to be back at hers for cream tea at four-ish.'

'Brilliant. I'll drive again, shall I? My car's more comfortable for Mim.'

'Okay, but for heaven's sake don't say that to her. She's so impatient to get back to normal. Thanks, Caitlyn.'

Early afternoon saw them unloading Mim and Frankie outside Rita's suburban semi. Sarah moved into the front passenger seat and watched as Caitlyn set the satnav.

'Does this lady know we're coming? What's her name, anyway?'

'Glynis Brady. No, I thought we could take the chance. My journalist friend said she was very upset and angry about it all – I was afraid she might refuse to speak to us if I phoned and asked first.'

Mrs Brady lived in a small terraced house west of the city centre. Caitlyn backed into a space twenty metres up the road, and Sarah undid her seat belt, frowning.

'How shall we do this? You've got more experience interviewing people – do you want to take the lead?'

'I think you should do that – you're more involved than I am. Cross your fingers she's at home.'

Traffic buzzed along the busy road as they walked to Mrs Brady's door and rang the bell. For a long moment there was nothing, and Sarah had begun to think they'd had a wasted journey when shuffling footsteps approached the door and it opened ten centimetres on a chain. Two chains, actually.

Sarah launched into her speech. 'Mrs Brady? I'm Sarah Martin and this is Caitlyn Mackie, and we're wondering if you could help us. An elderly friend of ours was swindled out of a lot of money in hospital recently and I know you had a similar experience. Can we talk?'

The woman behind the door stared at them without speaking. She could have been anywhere between seventy and eighty, and her eyes were sharp in a thin, lined face that looked as if it had forgotten how to smile.

Sarah's heart sank. 'Please,' she said quietly. 'All we want is to find whoever tricked our friend.'

Mrs Brady sighed, but she clicked the chains down and opened the door. Sarah smiled warmly as they entered, but the older woman's face remained sombre. Walking with two sticks, Mrs Brady led the way into the living room. It was clean, and painfully neat, but the furnishings were old and the carpet was thin and worn.

'How's your hip?' said Sarah, sitting on one end of the sofa while Caitlyn went to an armchair beside a dark, polished Welsh dresser.

Mrs Brady lowered herself into the other end of the sofa. 'The hip's fine, but when I heard the news about my money I fell and twisted my ankle. What happened to your friend?' The flatness in her voice made Sarah wince. Poor soul, the loss of her money must have been a huge blow.

Sarah injected as much warmth and compassion as she could into her voice, and gave a brief account of Wilma's money disappearing in the hospital. They had agreed not to mention Petra's murder – that would be terrifying to a woman who was old and infirm and had already been robbed.

Mrs Brady listened without interrupting, her face pale. 'I don't see how I can help. I want to forget it ever happened. It's made me afraid to open the door in my own home in case he's come back for more. I don't have more.'

Sarah didn't know what to say. There was no reason Mrs Brady should cooperate with them; they'd have to earn her trust. Maybe some personal details would help. 'Wilma's only relative is an eleven-year-old girl, Frankie, and she's been placed in foster care in my – family. Mrs Brady, do you have any idea who could have done this to you?'

The older woman shook her head. 'None at all. I told the police that. You don't know it was the same person both times, do you?'

'No, but I feel it must be.' Sarah reached out and touched Mrs Brady's arm. 'Could you maybe think back again to when you were in hospital, think of all the people you met there, people who were strangers before. Who did you talk to about your family? Who could have learned your daughter's name?'

'I'm sure no-one did.' Mrs Brady picked at her cardigan sleeve. She clearly wasn't enjoying the conversation, and Sarah's heart sank.

'They wouldn't have asked directly. It would be in the course of general chit-chat.'

Mrs Brady shook her head. 'I really can't say. There were so many people. Nurses, doctors, medical students, physiotherapists, cleaners, lab people – I could go on and on. And you know how you do chat in hospitals...'

Sarah exchanged a glance with Caitlyn. It was true. And they were talking about a bigger hospital than Brockburn General, with many more members of staff and patients. Sarah inched towards Mrs Brady. 'Are you all right? It must have been a terrible shock. Is your family nearby?'

'Elderlea Park near Birmingham. I don't see them often. I'm fine here, there's lots of things for me to do. Clubs and the like. Except now I've lost my savings.'

A lump rose in Sarah's throat, and she rummaged in her bag for pen and paper. This poor old thing. It didn't sound as if whatever family she had were much support to her. 'Mrs Brady, we're going to do our best to find this person. If you think of anything that might help us, here's my phone number. And if you'd like to phone to see how we're getting on and have a chat about it, that's fine too.'

Mrs Brady took the note and placed it on the coffee table. 'He had a deep voice on the phone,' she said. 'The same as Stuart. You know how some men sound deeper on the phone than they are.'

Sarah stood up. 'That could be very useful. Thank you so much for talking to us, Mrs Brady, and if you remember anything else, all you need to do is lift the phone. It'll be no trouble to come back, will it, Caitlyn?'

Tears welled up in the old woman's eyes. 'Thank you,' was all she said, and two minutes later Sarah and Caitlyn were back in the car.

Caitlyn fumbled the key into the ignition. 'Oh, Sarah, that poor old thing. You were great with her. I think I'll visit the police station, see if I can have a word with Harry West – as a journalist. And I'll see what some of my other colleagues in the media are saying about this, too. You can try to find out how long all the nursey people have been working at Brockburn General.'

Sarah nodded, staring back at the house. There was no sign of Mrs Brady. 'Good idea. Drive on, Caitlyn. If she's looking out we don't want her to think we're sitting here talking about her.'

Caitlyn pulled the car into a U-turn and they drove back past Mrs Brady's house, Sarah waving in case the old lady was watching. But as far as finding new information was concerned, the visit had been a dead loss.

He leaned over his kitchen table, head clutched in both hands. This was dire. The pits. He'd hardly slept all night, and then he'd been rushed off his feet at work because two people were off sick. And all he'd been able to think about was Wilma. Terrible old woman, clacking away about Nurse this and Doctor that, all the stupid, *stupid* gossip – had any of it been about him?

The answer was probably yes – the old girls were always so flattered when he stopped for a chat. He'd remind them of their youth, of course, flirting with the boys – and let's face it, no-one else would be chatting them up nowadays. But the big question was, *did Netta Chisholm know about the money?* If Netta heard about the police looking for someone who'd been asking about Wilma's family, well, there was nothing to stop her putting two and two together and coming up with a completely correct four. And even if she didn't know about the money yet, the investigation was still ongoing. She would find out one of these days.

It was a risk he couldn't take. Stupid old woman or not, she was dangerous.

The good thing was, now he knew about it, he could take action. But oh, Christ – he'd have to shut her up too – and he couldn't do it again, he couldn't. Batter the life out of someone.

But if he didn't...

It was no use. He had to get rid of her, because if he didn't he'd have no peace of mind. Why was this happening to him? All he'd wanted was a bit of extra cash. And a proper home. And to be safe. All he wanted was justice.

Tears trickled down his cheeks, and he sniffed loudly and rubbed his sleeve over his face. If Netta was dangerous, other people could be too. Netta's friends, for instance, the other oldies who visited Wilma.

And – Sarah. Sweat broke out on his forehead. Sarah would know about Wilma's missing money; of course she did. She was in the middle of it, wasn't she, with the girl living in the same house and them all going to visit Wilma. But... there was no reason for Sarah to be suspicious of him, was there? As far as she was concerned, all he needed to do was sit tight.

As for Netta Chisholm...

He pushed his chair back and went out to the garden shed. Here was the packet of surgical gloves he'd swiped from the hospital. They were good for many things, only one of which was gardening. An old lady wouldn't put up much of a fight, and of course she wouldn't think twice about letting him into her house. He would wait for dark; it wouldn't do for anyone to see him on the way over there.

Adrenalin was fizzing through him; his tiredness was gone. He paced up and down between the kitchen and living room – impossible to sit still. He was going to kill Netta Chisholm. Stun her and batter her. He was a murderer.

But no, don't think like that. He was doing it to save his new life. There was no other way forward, but... maybe there was a better way to kill an old woman. His steps slowed as the idea formed in his mind. Yes, of course. He'd seen it in a film a few years ago. No need for a spade to beat Netta's face in – this would look like an accident; the kind of accident an old lady might easily have at home.

At nine o'clock he switched on the TV and watched the news. He had a big, modern, flat-screen TV now. It was nothing like Mum and Dad's pathetic little affair, but he couldn't enjoy his new possession tonight. He was going to kill again. Tears burned behind his eyelids. He'd only wanted happiness. And justice. He *deserved* to be happy.

At quarter to ten he stood up. His dark raincoat would be best, and it might be an idea to take the Taser too. Car key... He was ready. His stomach cramped as he locked the front door behind him, but he ignored it. He only had to do the job, and get back home, and then everything would be all right again.

It was dusk, and the rainclouds gathering to the north were on his side. His knuckles white on the steering wheel, he drove towards the town centre. A nervous pain began to squeeze relentlessly at his gut. It had been the same with Petra.

This time it would be easier, though. He wouldn't even have to dump the body.

He retched as the memory of dead Petra flashed into his head. That lifeless head, flat as a bloody pancake, in a blood-soaked sack, lolling on his shoulder. The car veered towards the middle of the road, and a horn blared. Don't *think* about it...

Burnside Road. At last. It was busy, cars parked bumper to bumper along both sides of the street. He drove past Netta's place and found a space opposite a restaurant further along. It looked as if a party was in progress there, with people coming and going and standing around the front door for a smoke. Dismay chilled through him before he realised he'd be able to hide in the crowd. He pulled on the surgical gloves, snapping the fingers to get them fitting right, then thrusting his hands into his pockets as soon as he left the car. On you go, quick, get this done. He wandered along the uneven pavement and ducked into Netta's doorway.

She was home; he could see a TV screen flickering through the crack in the curtains. It was pretty much of a dump, like Mum and Dad's place had been. He pressed the doorbell firmly, his heart crashing beneath his ribs.

A light went on in the hallway, then Netta Chisholm was standing there. 'Well, hello, dearie. What a surprise. Come on in.'

'I saw your light when I was driving past. Thought I'd ring the bell and say hello.'

'And very welcome you are too.' Her stupid, smiling face danced in front of his eyes. 'Let's go and put the kettle on. Though you should be going out with your friends on a Saturday night, not drinking tea with an old woman.'

She was walking in front of him, along the passageway, good, good, into the kitchen, yes, she was almost at the sink – now! He lunged forwards, bringing her down in a rugby tackle, using his body weight to smash her head into the cupboard door. A horrible, rattling breath rasped from her mouth and she was still.

He scrambled to his feet and stared. She'd hit her head on the metal door handle, slid down the door and was lying in a crumpled heap, her head twisted to one side. Her forehead was a bloody gash; one eye was ripped open, the other dull and empty. Blood was seeping along the powdered old-woman wrinkles, criss-crossing in a terrible red and beige pattern. And the big hole where her eye should be... Oh God, oh Christ, *that face*. But she was dead. He didn't even have to smother her. Had Petra's flat dead face looked anything at all like this?

For a moment he fought to control his gut. He had to finish this and get away, away as fast as he could from dead Netta Chisholm. How pathetic she was, lying there with her skirt hiked up over her knees. Old arthritic knees, like Mum's.

Deep breaths, come on. Now for the clever bit. He opened a couple of cupboards before he found what he was looking for. Here it was, beside the tea bags. Sugar. He tipped a small quantity into his left hand. All he had to do was scatter it round Netta's feet and the scene was set. He worked quickly, rubbing the last pinch into the soles of her slippers. Sugar on a linoleum floor was slippery as ice, he knew that. He left the bowl out beside the kettle. Whoever found her would assume that Netta had spilled some sugar earlier on, then slipped on it. A tragic accident.

He left the house and ran across the road before walking back in the direction of his car. From the outside the house looked no different. Netta's lights were still on and the television was still flickering through the window.

But Netta Chisholm was dead and he was safe.

Chapter Thirteen

Monday, 17th July

'Would you please stop being so tactful! It's infuriating!'

Mim was glaring from the chair beside her bed, halfway into the trainers she wore around the house. Sarah raised her eyebrows. The outburst wasn't like Mim, but they were all feeling the strain at the moment. Frankie hadn't smiled since Saturday's visit to Rita's, and had woken the house with a two a.m. nightmare. And Mim must be aching to run up and downstairs like she used to. Sarah's suggestion that the malls at Leeside Centre would be best for their shopping trip that afternoon hadn't gone down well.

But there was no use pandering to Mim in this mood. 'Who rattled your cage? Frankie prefers Leeside too. Loads more shops to find presents for the baby, and as the baby's something happy for her to think about we should encourage it. And don't worry, come the Christmas shopping you'll be diving about town like the fit young thing you really are.'

'That's what I mean!' cried Mim. 'I'm not – and there's the phone and for goodness sake leave me to answer it!'

She grabbed her stick and stalked out to the hallway, chin in the air. Sarah opened the window, grinning when she heard Mim bark hello into the phone then modulate her tone. It was Harry West.

'Mr West, sorry... Is there any more news?'

Sarah lifted Mim's coffee mug and moved towards the kitchen, stopping short as Mim's voice changed again.

'She's outside with the cat. What is it?'

Sarah wheeled round and stood with one hand under Mim's elbow. She could hear Harry West's voice, but not what he was saying. To Sarah's dismay Mim's face crumpled and she whispered into the phone.

'Oh no.'

Mim's arm was trembling, and Sarah found herself shivering too. Something new had happened; dear God, what could it be?

'Thank you for letting us know.' Mim ended the call and turned to Sarah. 'Oh, Sarah. Netta Chisholm's dead. Mr West said her neighbour found her, and I'm afraid that must have been poor Mrs Baker, after she didn't turn up for the evening meal they'd arranged for last night. By the looks of things, she slipped in the kitchen and banged her head. They say she died instantly, but because there's the slight connection to Petra they're being – he said they were being 'careful' with it.'

Sick to her stomach, Sarah led Mim into the living room, picturing Netta Chisholm's face as she said goodbye to Frankie after the funeral. That poor, funny, kind old woman. And oh, how horrible, another death for Frankie, and this time they didn't even know if it was murder or not. How crap was that?

'The police are coming by later this week, when they know more,' said Mim, her voice dull. She lowered herself down on the sofa and buried her face in her hands, leaning forward over her knees.

Sarah didn't know if she was more angry or upset. 'This is horrible,' she said, passing Mim the tissues. 'I suppose we'd better tell Frankie. I don't think she knew Netta very well, though. She told me after the funeral they'd only met a few times at Wilma's, so hopefully she won't be too upset about it.'

'Oh, Sarah, do think we should tell her? The poor girl's had way too much to deal with this week. I don't want her more upset.'

Sarah perched on the arm of the sofa, one hand on Mim's shoulder. 'Supposing she hears about it somewhere else? When we're visiting Wilma, or even on the local news. She'd never trust us again. Don't forget she still doesn't know the full story about Petra.'

Mim wiped her eyes. 'Oh, you're right. Again. But we'll tell her that Mrs Chisholm's dead, and no more. Unless they find out differently we'll stick to the 'slipped in the kitchen' story, so not a word about the police being careful.'

Frankie came running in from the garden when Sarah called her. Mim patted the sofa, and the little girl plopped down. It was all Sarah could do to keep her expression neutral. An eleven-year-old *should* not have to deal with stuff like this. She watched from the armchair as the expression on Frankie's face changed to apprehension when Mim took her hand.

'Frankie, darling, I'm afraid there's more bad news.

Poor Netta Chisholm died at the weekend after a fall in her kitchen.'

'Oh,' said Frankie blankly, looking from Mim to Sarah. 'That's a pity. She was nice to me. She was old, though, wasn't she?'

'Over eighty, I believe,' said Mim.

Sarah's dark mood gave way to an absurd inclination to laugh at Frankie's calm assumption that old people were practically guaranteed to fall in their kitchens and die. Still, at least the girl wasn't distraught.

She stood up. 'We'll order flowers for Mrs Chisholm when we're getting some for your mum. And we thought we'd go to Leeside after lunch and look for a few little presents for Jamie and the baby. What do you think?'

Frankie twirled her hair round one finger. 'S'pose. Can we get red roses for Mum? They were her favourites.'

'Good idea. We'll take them to the garden of remembrance tomorrow.'

Half an hour later Sarah and Frankie were sitting at Wilma's bedside while Mim was at physio. It wasn't the official visiting time, but the ward staff knew the situation and were very good about Frankie going in at odd times. And let's face it, thought Sarah, it wasn't as if Wilma was doing much except lying in bed or sitting propped up in a geriatric chair. Her treatment seemed to be all passive now, and the occupational therapy had been stopped altogether. The difference today was in Frankie's behaviour. Instead of sitting by the bedside looking as if she didn't want to be there, the girl was leaning on the mattress, Wilma's limp hand clutched in both her own. There was little response from the old woman, and Sarah cursed the fact that Netta Chisholm had died so suddenly. In spite of her casual reaction, Frankie was shaken by the new death. When their fifteen minutes were up they drove back to rehab to collect Mim.

Mim was already walking up the corridor from the physiotherapy department, and Sarah frowned when she saw Nick walking beside her. They all met in the entrance hallway.

'Hello again. Mim's our prize patient, you know,' he said, smiling round them all.

Sarah had to make herself smile back. Had he engineered this? It would be easy enough to find out when Mim had physiotherapy. 'She's aiming for bionic woman,' she said, and he laughed a little too loudly.

'Have the police –?' He was interrupted by a shout.

'Coming upstairs, Nick?'

The voice was behind Sarah, and she wheeled round to see the nurse called Evan holding the lift door open. Frankie jumped, her face solemn as she inched closer to Sarah.

'Yup. Catch you later.' Nick jogged across.

Evan waved to them as the lift door closed, and Mim started for the entrance. 'Come on, girls. Home time for us.'

Frankie was still close to Sarah's side, and she glanced down. 'Okay? Did Evan give you a fright?'

'He's creepy,' said Frankie. 'He reminds me of someone Mum... used to know.'

To Sarah's relief, the trip to the shopping centre after lunch was a big success. Frankie chose a selection of presents for the baby and Jamie, then they went for coffee and cake in a snack bar overlooking the centre's ice rink. The little girl wandered over to the rail to watch the skaters, and Sarah raised her eyebrows at Mim.

'This was a good idea, it's taken her mind right off Netta. And her mother.'

Mim finished her apple pie. 'I rather suspect her relationship with Petra was more like a small girl and her teenage sister. I don't think she depended on Petra for the usual mum-things.'

'Well, she has you now. A child should be able to depend on her mother for mum-things.'

Sarah's mobile buzzed in her bag. It was a text from Caitlyn, inviting her over to discuss things, and Sarah texted back that she'd be there presently. It was nice to be wanted by the folks here at home, but... one of these days she'd get some proper me-time. Now if only she could have a date with Jack, one where he was interesting and funny like he'd been on Friday. Something nice just for her. And how selfish she was, thinking like that.

Less than hour later she was watching Caitlyn drop teabags into a glass teapot.

'Earl Grey,' said Caitlyn. 'I love it.' She held a match to a tea light in a stainless steel stand and placed the teapot on top. 'You look worried – is it Netta Chisholm? I heard when I was at the police station this morning.'

'It's horrible. Everything's so out of control. Did you speak to Mr West?'

'No, but Mandy Craven gave me a few minutes. They're still investigating to see if there've been any other cases of missing money. Sarah, I wish we could think of something constructive to do.'

Sarah frowned. 'Did you tell them we'd been to see Mrs Brady?'

'Yes, and Mandy was a bit sniffy about it in a 'leave it to the professionals' way. They knew about her, of course, but they have no leads yet from the info she gave the Manchester police.'

'We should stay in touch with Mrs B, no matter what the police say. If we can talk to her again in a more relaxed atmosphere, she might remember something. She probably freezes up every time a policeman goes near her.'

'I think you're right, plus she's scared stiff about the blackmailer targeting her again. Thank heavens we didn't tell her about the murder.'

'Oh, Caitlyn, it feels like people are dying like flies. Hopefully Mrs Brady won't be next.'

'I'm sure that's not likely. Even if there is a connection between Petra's death and Netta's – and Mandy Craven said she couldn't confirm that – Mrs Brady still has no idea who the swindler could be.'

Sarah rubbed her forehead. 'He might not know that. Let's think. We should assume that Netta was killed because she knew something. So either Wilma told her that something, or she saw it for herself.'

'Yes. Wilma's the connection. Petra died because she knew about the theft, and for all we know she might have worked out who the swindler was.'

'Exactly. So Netta must have had information that would lead the police to the swindler – and of course he's also Petra's murderer.' Sarah took a deep breath. 'But if Netta knew something, why didn't she go to the police? She'd have loved being the centre of attention. Unless of course she didn't realise what she knew.'

Caitlyn sat back. 'Yes! That must be it. But what on earth could she have known without realising? It's so frustrating we can't talk to Wilma. Is she no better at all?'

'Semi-conscious at best. And confused. Frankie and I were there this morning.' Sarah stared at the candle flickering beneath the teapot. They must be missing something here.

Caitlyn reached out. 'More tea?'

Sarah glanced at the clock. There was no reason to hurry back, and wasn't tea supposed to hold more caffeine than coffee? 'A quick one. I've left Mim and Frankie wrapping baby things.'

Her mobile buzzed in her pocket while Caitlyn was pouring the tea. It was Jack, and Sarah wandered out to the hallway. 'Hi, Jack – can I call you back? I'm visiting a friend at the moment.'

'Ah – a nice girly afternoon?'

'Something like that. Oh, did you hear poor Netta Chisholm died at the weekend? She fell in her kitchen.'

'No! I'm sorry to hear that. She had a great sense of humour, didn't she? And that's more bad news for Frankie. Is she all right?'

'More or less. She didn't really know Netta.'

'Just as well, the way things are. Listen, I wondered if you'd like to come out for another meal sometime soon.

I'm afraid I wasn't at my best last time. I had a migraine and I should have cancelled, but – I wanted to see you.'

Sarah smiled into her phone. So there it was. A perfectly reasonable explanation for Jack's behaviour last Thursday. 'I'd love to. Why don't I call you when I get home and we can make arrangements?'

'Perfect.'

Caitlyn was rummaging in a cupboard, and Sarah watched as she pulled out a box of tea lights and put a new one in the teapot stand. What had Netta been doing when she fell? Making tea? Hurrying to get to the phone? They would never know.

Caitlyn lit the candle, her face thoughtful. 'Sarah – did Netta *know* about the money?'

Sarah scowled into her cup. It was a good question. 'I don't know. Okay, where does that take us?'

'Let's see if we can work it out. Petra is killed because...?'

'She found out about the money. That was the Tuesday, when I met her in the hospital. Her meeting was on Thursday. Did the killer want to stop her before she spoke to the administrator – or was that coincidence? Petra told me she didn't know who took the money.'

'But she was killed, so she must have known something that would lead the police to the killer. But why would he then target Netta? Maybe her death is a coincidence.'

Sarah's mind was racing. 'And maybe it's not. Netta could have known something that would lead the police to the killer too.' She stared at Caitlyn. 'But – she wasn't aware of the importance of what she knew because –'

Caitlyn jerked upright. 'Yes! Because she *didn't* know

about the money!'

'But she could have learned about it any time, so she was killed. That's horrible.'

'It can't be the whole story, though. How – and when – did the killer learn that Netta knew what she knew? Netta must actually have spoken to him – or her – quite recently. Maybe while she was visiting Wilma?'

Sarah gasped. 'Caitlyn, other people might be in danger too. Ma Baker, or someone else Wilma confided in. Or Frankie, even.'

It was as if someone had kicked both her shins. If they were right, anyone close to Wilma and Petra could have the same knowledge. Sarah's gut tightened in fear.

Caitlyn stared out of the window. 'I think you should all be very careful, Sarah. And do you know what would be interesting? A list of staff members for both hospitals for the times the two swindles took place. I think I'll go and have another journalistic chat at the police station.'

Sarah drained her cup and stood up to go. Mim was alone with Frankie, and anyway, she had to phone Jack. 'Good idea.'

And now she was going home to look after Frankie – and Mim – as hard as ever she could.

Chapter Fourteen

Tuesday, 18th July

Sarah spent a restless night, dreams of anonymous men stalking her and Frankie circling round her head and waking her twice. As soon as her breakfast coffee was inside her, she went round to see if Caitlyn had found out more.

Caitlyn came straight to the point. 'I spoke to Harry West last night. He didn't have much time for me, but he was reassuring about one thing – he doesn't think Frankie is in any danger. He said if she was, something would have happened by this time and I suppose that's true.'

'Thank heavens for that,' said Sarah thankfully. 'That must mean Frankie doesn't know whatever Netta knew. So we're no further forward. Did you ask about the lists of hospital workers?'

'Yes, and of course they're already onto that. There are a few people on both lists, mostly junior doctors because they change round more. They're being checked out, but Harry isn't hopeful of finding anything useful. He didn't say as much, but I'm sure he thinks Netta was killed too.'

'And every idea seems to lead straight to a dead end. It would be terrible for Frankie if her mother's killer is never found.' Sarah turned away. 'I'd better get back. I left Mim having her first bath since her op; she's wallowing in litres of bath foam. See you, Caitlyn.'

'Doing anything interesting afterwards?'

'Just family stuff, but I'm going for a Chinese with Jack tonight, so I'll see if he has any more ideas.' And how good it would feel to get away from the whole murder and missing money problem for a while. She hadn't looked forward to a date as much for ages. Sarah hugged herself as she ran round to Mim's front door.

After lunch Sarah took Frankie to do a food shop. It was disorientating. Here she was in the middle of a murder inquiry – a double murder – and she still had to spend time worrying about bread and butter and washing-up liquid. The world was a crazy place.

They walked round, piling the trolley with necessities and little luxuries alike. Mim loved smoked salmon, and Sarah bought some to make a starter for the following evening.

'Let's cook Mim a meal with all her favourites,' she said. 'She deserves it, after all she's been through lately.'

Frankie stood still, her eyes bleak. 'A lot of it was my fault.'

Sarah let go of the trolley to hug the girl. 'Sweetheart, *none* of it was your fault. And the next person we'll cook a 'favourites' meal for can be you. So start thinking about what you like best and we'll do that next week sometime. You can invite a friend from your old school class, if you want to. Now –'

Her mobile buzzed in her handbag, and Sarah scrabbled for it. This might be Jack, wanting to confirm their date tonight. But it was Rita.

'Rita? You okay?'

'No – I'm in labour and Phil's just left London. He'll be hours yet. Can you and Mim come? I didn't want to phone her in case you couldn't and then she'd feel bad, but if you can –'

'Oh gosh – of course we'll come. Will you be able to stay at home till we get there?'

'I think so. My neighbour's with me. Thanks, Sarah.'

'See you very soon.' Her heart racing, Sarah broke the connection and turned to Frankie. Should they take the girl with them? They'd be away for hours. But Rita barely knew Frankie, and having a baby was such an intimate, family thing.

'What is it?' Frankie's face was afraid, and Sarah tried to smile, turning the trolley towards the checkout. 'Sweetie, I have to take Mim to Rita – the baby's coming. We'll see if you can stay with Caitlyn in the meantime. Okay?'

Frankie looked as if she didn't know whether to be thrilled or upset. 'The baby! Oh! Okay. S'pose.'

Sarah phoned Caitlyn from the checkout queue, in case she wasn't able to help, though she couldn't imagine who else she could ask to take Frankie. The thought that Mrs Chisholm would have loved to help did nothing to ease the little knot of stress tightening in Sarah's gut.

'Caitlyn – I'm leaving Leeside with Frankie. Mim and I are going to Rita – the baby's coming and Phil's away. Can you keep Frankie for a few hours? And tell Mim to get ready?'

'Can do. See you soon.'

Mim was waiting on the pavement when they arrived home, and Sarah was pleased to see the old, excited-impetuous expression on her foster mother's face. This was better for Mim than worrying about stolen money and murdered women. Mind you, it wasn't so good for Frankie, being abandoned so abruptly. The girl's face when Mim hugged her goodbye was sombre.

Her fingers tightening round the wheel, Sarah drove as fast as she could towards the motorway.

Mim was edgy too. 'It might be better if Rita called an ambulance to take her to the hospital. We could meet her there.'

'A neighbour's with her. She'll call an ambulance if it's necessary. We'll phone when we're almost there and see what's happening.'

Once on the motorway, Sarah put her foot down. Jack's face swam in front of her eyes as Brockburn vanished behind the car. She hadn't even had time to call him yet. The two of them weren't having much luck with their dates. A brunch she'd had to run away from, one date when he'd had a migraine, and now another that wasn't going to happen. Bad things did seem to come in threes. But oh, how great it would be if the two of them got together properly. He was intelligent, and humorous, and he was interested in her... Plus he was the best-looking bloke she'd ever been out with. Was that shallow? Well, yes – but who wouldn't notice looks like his?

A lump rose in Sarah's throat and she swallowed her tears. Rita's baby was way more important than her dinner date. But oh, how very much she wanted a baby of her own, and here was her younger foster sister about to become a mother for the second time. Sarah pulled out to overtake a frozen food lorry, and shook herself – she was being stupid. But – she wanted something to go right for her too. A normal date, a few days' holiday, a restful home. It didn't sound like much to ask for, but none of it was happening. Tears brimming in her eyes, she drove towards Manchester.

Caitlyn helped Frankie unpack Sarah's shopping, squinting at the girl as they filled the fridge and store cupboards. She wasn't saying much. Caitlyn grimaced. Please God her own kids would never feel the anguish Frankie must be experiencing. But she couldn't spend the day thinking like that – Sarah and Mim would be in Manchester until the baby arrived, and it was up to her to keep Frankie happy for as long as it took.

'Let's make smoothies,' she said, leading the way to her own kitchen. 'Are you hungry?'

Chopping and liquidising fruit kept Frankie occupied for quite a while, and Caitlyn congratulated herself. Eventually they sat down with tall glasses in front of them. Frankie stirred hers with the straw. 'Sarah won't be able to go for dinner with Jack tonight.'

'I expect she'll phone him from Manchester,' said Caitlyn. 'They'll make another date, don't worry.' As if

Jack was likely to let a little thing like a cancelled dinner put him off.

'Is Jack Sarah's boyfriend?'

Caitlyn sipped her smoothie. 'They've only been out a couple of times. Maybe he will be soon.'

'My mum had lots of boyfriends. She said it was important to have fun while you were still young.'

Caitlyn sipped her drink again to give herself time to think. Frankie was much more precocious than her Tina. 'I guess she was right, up to a point.'

Frankie raised her hands in a pathetically old gesture for an eleven-year-old. 'She might not have died, if she hadn't always wanted to have fun.' The girl's voice trembled.

Caitlyn took a deep breath. 'Frankie. Petra disappeared on the way to a meeting that was going to be no fun at all. I don't think her lifestyle had anything to do with what happened to her. Don't torture yourself thinking about it. Wait until we see what the police find out.'

'I didn't like her boyfriends.'

Caitlyn wished with all her heart that Sarah was here. Had anything happened with one of the 'boyfriends'? *Did* Frankie know something that would help find Petra's killer? Or was there a more sinister reason for the child's dislike? Heaven forbid.

'Did any of them hurt you?' It sounded abrupt but it was the only thing Caitlyn could think of to ask.

Frankie shook her head. 'No, but my mum was different when they were around.' She pressed her lips together.

'Oh dear. Poor sweetie.' Caitlyn felt sweat break out on

her brow. What the heck could she say to that? She was saved from saying anything more by the landline phone ringing on the worktop. 'Look, it's Sarah. You can take it.'

Frankie rushed for the phone, and Caitlyn sat listening to the girl's side of the conversation.

'Sarah... yes... today?... good... okay... yes, she's here.' She handed over the phone.

'Sarah. How's things?'

'We made it. Mim's in with Rita. The midwife said the baby'll be about another hour, so Phil might get here on time. How are you getting on?'

Caitlyn made her voice upbeat. 'Great. We made terrific strawberry smoothies.' A thought struck her. 'Sarah – shall I bring Frankie to visit Rita and the baby later this afternoon? Would that be any help, or is it a bad idea?'

No, it was a brilliant idea. It would give her and Frankie something to do, and while they were in Manchester, she could drop in on Glynis Brady. They'd be driving through her part of town. She and Frankie could ring the bell and ask if Glynis had remembered anything more about her money. The presence of a child might help the old woman feel at ease.

She could almost hear Sarah's brain ticking over. 'It would be great for Frankie if you came, of course, but Caitlyn, I can't ask you to drive all the way here.'

'Heavens, it's not the end of the earth. We'll see you later.'

She replaced the receiver and turned to Frankie, who was staring, a hopeful expression on her face. 'Get your kit. We're going to Manchester. We can race the baby to see who gets there first.'

Caitlyn pulled out to overtake a blue Ford Escort, and glanced at the child in the passenger seat. Frankie wasn't saying much, but her face was excited. At least she'd stopped thinking about her mother's murder and whatever had gone on with those boyfriends. Poor kiddy.

On the outskirts of Manchester, Caitlyn suggested phoning Sarah to see how things were progressing. 'Say we're ten minutes away, and ask when they want us. No point rushing to the hospital just to wait around. We could do something else in the meantime.' Like visit Glynis Brady.

Frankie pulled out her mobile. She relayed the question, said 'okay' about four times and clicked off. 'She said the baby's still not here but it shouldn't be long. We can go when we want.'

'Excellent. There's an old lady I'd like to visit for a few minutes, if she's at home. Then we could grab a quick coffee somewhere, and go on to the hospital. Okay?'

'Who's the old lady?'

And what could she say to that? But if Frankie was coming to see Glynis Brady, all Caitlyn could tell her was the absolute truth. 'Her name's Glynis Brady. She had some money stolen while she was in hospital a few months ago. What happened to her was very similar to what happened with Wilma's money, so Mrs Brady's helping us by trying to work out who could have taken her cash. I want to see if she's had any ideas.'

She parked outside Mrs Brady's house and rang the

bell. This time she didn't have to wait so long before the door opened to the extent of the two chains.

Mrs Brady's face peered out. 'Oh, it's you again. And who's your friend?'

'This is Frankie. You remember we told you she's staying with Sarah now?'

Caitlyn could tell that Mrs Brady realised exactly who Frankie was, but dear Lord – what the old woman still didn't know was that Petra had been murdered. This might be difficult.

Mrs Brady undid the chains and stood aside, and Caitlyn followed Frankie inside. 'We won't stay long. We're on our way to the hospital to visit a brand new baby,' she said, smiling at Frankie, pleased when the girl smiled back. 'I wanted to ask if you'd had any more thoughts about the theft of your money.'

Mrs Brady led the way into the living room. 'Sit down a moment. I've made a list of everyone I could remember speaking to. When you'd gone I thought I'd been a bit wishy-washy, saying it was impossible to remember everyone. I can't guarantee it is everyone, of course, and I don't have all the names, but I've remembered a lot more than I thought I would.'

She was rummaging in a drawer as she spoke, and pulled out a twice-folded sheet of paper with three handwritten columns on each side, and handed it to Caitlyn. 'I was wondering if I should give it to the police – what do you think?'

'I'll do that for you, if you like.' Caitlyn reached for her phone. 'This is great, you've remembered a lot. I'll take photos, and you can keep the original. You might think of more people to add on.'

Mrs Brady looked doubtful. 'Maybe. One thing that did come to mind – I'm quite sure I didn't talk about my family on the phone to anyone I didn't know. So whoever it was must have been there with me. Whether that happened in the hospital, or before I was admitted, I don't know.'

Caitlyn was impressed. Glynis Brady might have been fooled, but she wasn't stupid and she wasn't helpless, either. 'Those are very good points. Look, I'll leave you my number in case you remember anyone else, and I'll call you in a day or two anyway. And now we'd better get on our way.'

Mrs Brady smiled at Frankie. 'How exciting, going to see a new baby.'

Frankie looked at her shyly. 'It's my – my foster sister's baby. It wasn't born ten minutes ago but it might be now. I hope it's a girl because she's got a little boy already.'

'Oh, you'll be thrilled with whatever it is.' Mrs Brady turned to Caitlyn. 'Thank you for coming by, both times. You and your friend jolted me out of my depression over losing the money. I saw that I *could* do something to help, and that's why I started the list.'

'Good for you,' said Caitlyn warmly.

This time it was Frankie who waved as they drove off, and Mrs Brady stood in her doorway and waved back. Caitlyn tooted her horn. Mrs B. did look a lot more confident today. At least their investigation had achieved that much.

'Will the list help?' said Frankie, as they sat at a sticky table eating iced buns.

Caitlyn shrugged. 'I don't know. The police already have a list of everyone who worked at both hospitals. But I'm sure making it helped Mrs Brady, and that's important too. And hey – we won, didn't we?'

'Won what?' said Frankie, her face blank.

'The race to Manchester, of course. Come on. Let's go and see this baby.'

Sarah stared up and down the maternity department, a long corridor with rooms on both sides. Chairs were placed every few metres, and she was sitting outside Rita's room, wriggling on the hard plastic. Mim was in with Rita. Sarah knew she'd be no good when they got to the messy stage – much better to wait here until the baby was safely born. She watched as a group of young doctors gathered round an older woman outside one room, hanging on her every word. Medical students, maybe. This was a larger place than Brockburn General. More patients, more staff. Nurses, doctors, technicians, porters, and many others whose function wasn't immediately obvious were striding about the place, even here in maternity where the patients weren't actually ill. This was the hospital where Glynis Brady had lost her money – no wonder she hadn't sounded hopeful about remembering everyone she'd spoken to. And talking about speaking to people, she should call Jack and tell him their dinner was off.

She hurried downstairs and went outside, taking a thankful breath of city air. Anything was better than hospital smells. For a moment self-pity almost overcame her. It seemed like every blessed thing she looked forward to nowadays ended in disaster. She gave herself a shake. A postponed dinner was hardly the end of the world. Maybe Jack could manage tomorrow, or the weekend. She made the connection.

'He – llo.' His voice was upbeat.

'Oh, Jack, I'm glad I've caught you. I didn't want to send a text.'

'Is everything okay? All right for tonight?'

'I'm afraid not. I'm so sorry. But my sister went into labour, and her husband's in London so I had to take Mim to Manchester and that's where we are now.'

There was a tiny pause before he spoke. Sarah could almost feel his disappointment, and in a way it was flattering, but oh, how she wished she was at home ironing her outfit right.

'Gosh, that's exciting! Is she all right?'

'Doing well, apparently. They say the baby'll be here soon. It's such a pity about our meal out, though – I don't like cancelling at the last minute.'

'Not to worry, babies take precedence. How about if we make another date for Thursday? I'll phone you around midday to confirm?'

The world was suddenly a much brighter place. 'Perfect. See you soon!'

Sarah clicked her mobile off and ran back upstairs. The corridor was still busy, and the door of Rita's room was still closed. She sank down on her chair again.

Jack had been very understanding about cancelling – no, postponing their meal, but still, it was too bad. And what a cow she was to even think that. Get a grip, Sarah.

The meal out would happen next time. The thought of sitting opposite Jack again made her shiver with anticipation.

Her mind turned to Frankie. The best way for the girl to make a fresh start was to know that her mother's killer had been found and imprisoned. A chill of a different kind passed through Sarah in spite of the warmth in the hospital. She felt a peculiar urgency, and a stomach-churning sense of impending doom. Golly, someone had just walked over her grave and no mistake. The police had been definite that Frankie was in no danger, but the murderer was still out there and Sarah's gut instinct was shouting that he couldn't be far away.

Footsteps running along the corridor broke into her thoughts, and she jumped up to see Phil charging towards her.

'Is it – where –?' he panted.

Sarah pulled him over to Rita's room. She knocked, then put her head round the door. Rita was huddled up on the bed, Mim on a chair beside her.

'Visitor for you!' Sarah pushed Phil into the room.

'And none too soon!' said the midwife. 'Go and wash your hands, Daddy. Baby'll be here any minute!'

Sarah left them to it.

He opened the fridge and stared at the contents. A bottle of white wine he'd picked up last week was waiting, green glass glinting invitingly. A nice glass of wine with... he could make an omelette. Or no – he could spoil himself a little. He would go round the corner to the Indian takeaway and get some dal and a couple of chapattis.

It was a beautiful evening and in spite of his aching shoulders his spirits rose as he strolled along to the corner, lifting his face to the sun as he turned into George Street. Work had been tiring today. He'd been on his feet nonstop, and then he'd been stuck in a traffic jam for nearly half an hour on the way home.

But home was worth the wait now. It was so great to see Mum and Dad's disaster of a place develop into somewhere he could feel happy and secure. Stupid Wilma, getting in the way of his plan. Petra Walker's body as it sunk into the canal flashed into his mind and he shuddered. Nothing like that must ever happen again. It might be better to stop his renovations for a bit... but it would be silly to stop so close to the finishing line. He only needed one more cash injection for the house, and then he'd wait until next year with the garden.

Decision made, he strode along the road, his stomach rumbling. Maybe he could invite lovely Sarah to his home for an Indian meal. A shiver ran down his spine at the thought. But tonight he was alone, so he'd have his meal in front of the television, then he'd have a hot bath in the terrible avocado tub – probably the last bath he'd have in it; the new suite was coming next week – and an early night.

The takeaway was busy. He put in his order and sat on a bamboo chair to wait.

'Hot in here, isn't it?' A woman sat down beside him, fanning herself with a flyer from the rack by the window.

She was about his age or a little older, and she was looking at him with ill-concealed interest. He closed his eyes briefly. The last thing he needed was some sad hopeful chatting him up. He smiled without speaking, but the woman wasn't put off. She was obviously a talker and he resigned himself to listening for the duration.

'I'm in for something to have with my mum. I was all ready to do chops when she said she'd prefer Indian. I only visit once a week, on a Tuesday, so the least I can do is get her what she wants.'

A thought shimmered in his head, and he gave the woman his full attention. 'That's very kind of you. Does she live alone?'

'Yes. She's seventy and very fit, but she's been lonely since Dad left. He went off with one of the neighbours, would you believe. I don't know what he was thinking of, at his age.'

He pricked his ears even further. This wasn't his usual scenario, but maybe he could still use it. 'Bet she appreciates you! That wouldn't be Alec Davies, would it – I heard a bit of gossip about him a while back. I'm John Murray, by the way.'

She fluttered her eyelashes at him. 'Sheena Cameron. No, he's Tom Bruce – do you know him?'

He shook his head, making a mental note of the names. 'You don't live locally, then?'

On she prattled, and he listened, smiling attentively and storing away all the details. She was divorced, living a few miles this side of Manchester with her ten-year-old son, and she worked in a travel agency, which seemed to be a bit of an uncertain job nowadays. Apart from Sheena, her son Tim and her mother, the rest of the family lived in London. She was getting Chicken Tikka with spicy rice for their meal although her own favourite was the veggie and cashew biryani. She didn't mention a partner, and the way she was squinting up at him and giggling was enough to convince him there was no-one special in her life at the moment.

'Do you have far to go?' he asked, when the boy brought out their bags of food.

A look of regret crossed her face and he sniggered inwardly. What fools some women were.

'No, Mum's across the road at number forty-three.'

He held the door open for her and she stood on the pavement swinging her bag; he could tell she was reluctant to end the conversation.

'Have a good evening with your mum.' He gave her his most charming smile and left, hurrying along the busy pavement with his bag of food clutched in one hand. What an interesting fifteen minutes that had been. And maybe he wouldn't have to wait long to get more money. If he changed his tactics a little, Tom Bruce's wife could provide him with the necessary cash for very little effort.

Sarah sat clasping and unclasping her hands. 'Any minute,' the midwife had said, but that was a quarter of an hour ago. And the last moan to escape under the door had been a shocker. The arrival of Frankie and Caitlyn interrupted her thoughts.

'Is it born yet?' said Frankie.

Sarah patted the chair beside her. 'No, but Phil's here and the midwife said any time, now. Thanks, Caitlyn.'

'No problem. We went by Mrs Brady's, and she's made

a list of people she chatted to while she was in hospital. I took a photo so we can go through it sometime. She's remembered dozens.'

Sarah wrenched her attention towards Mrs Brady, but a thin baby wail came from Rita's room, and Frankie clutched her arm. 'That's it! It's born!'

Relief swept over Sarah and she laughed at the expression on Frankie's face. Thrilled didn't come into it, and it was the first one hundred per cent positive emotion they'd had from the child, who was on the edge of her seat. When the midwife looked out a few minutes later the little girl leapt up. 'What is it, what is it?'

The midwife held the door open. 'Come and see!'

Sarah followed Frankie into the room, where Rita was cradling a bundle wrapped in a towel. Another midwife covered Rita with a larger towel and pulled the sheet up, but not before Sarah had seen the bloodstains. Yikes. She tiptoed forward to see the baby.

Rita's face was red and damp with sweat, but pride and love were shining from her eyes. 'It's a girl,' she said, and the expression on Frankie's face as she gazed down at the baby brought tears to Sarah's eyes. This more than anything was going to help the child through the weeks ahead.

'Congratulations,' said Caitlyn behind her.

Sarah hugged Rita and Phil. 'Well done, both. She's gorgeous.'

Caitlyn touched her arm. 'I'll leave you to it, shall I?'

'Thanks so much, Caitlyn,' said Sarah. She sat beside Mim and watched as Rita cuddled the baby, Frankie hovering at her elbow and Phil up beside her with his arm round her, gazing besottedly at his baby. This was her family, right here, and how lucky she was to have them. Wistful thoughts of her own parents drifted through Sarah's head. One day, oh please one day, she'd be the one on a bed in a labour room, but it would be Mim who'd be waiting for another 'grandchild', not her birth mother. How strange life was. And who would be the father? Jack's face swam in front of her eyes.

Chapter Fifteen

Wednesday, 19th July

Caitlyn awoke the next morning with a king-sized hangover, and stood under the shower letting piping hot water massage her shoulders. She shouldn't have had that third glass of wine last night, but seeing Rita with her baby had reminded her how far away her own kids were.

She dragged herself down to the kitchen. Coffee first up, then something to keep her busy. There was Mrs Brady's list to decipher, and she should send it to Harry West. Mug in hand, she printed out the first photo and stared at it. Help, this wasn't going to be easy. Mrs B's old-fashioned spidery handwriting didn't make for quick reading. The sooner this was on a word document the more useful it would be. She sat down to transcribe the list.

At the top were nurses and doctors, but while the first few were mentioned by their full names, others were identified as 'Nurse Livia' and 'Dr W'. Mrs Brady, evidently, wasn't a names person. And it got worse, too. Soon Caitlyn was reading 'Young doctor with short red hair' and 'plump student nurse, dyed blonde'. The last person on the list was described as the Friday lady, and as well as the nursing and medical staff there were cleaners, various therapists, porters, an electrician, library book ladies, serving ladies in the Red Cross tea bar, a gardener, 'six or seven medical students', two secretaries, and a knitting lady, whatever that might be.

Caitlyn slumped in her chair. There could well be people here who weren't on the official police list – medical students weren't hospital employees, for instance, and the library ladies could be volunteers. Were they looking for a man or a woman? Murder always seemed more of a male, aggressive thing, but – did they actually know? And how on earth could anyone find half these people without names?

The doorbell rang while she was printing out the first page, and Caitlyn jogged to the door. Sarah stood there, her face cheerful.

'Mim and I would like to invite you for dinner tonight,' she said, following Caitlyn through to the dining room where the laptop and printer were. 'Frankie and I are cooking – we're doing a Mim-meal with all her favourites, but she doesn't know that yet.'

Caitlyn beamed. 'That would be great. What time?'

'Six. Thanks again for yesterday, by the way – yes, I *know* you don't want to be thanked, but no-one likes being taken for granted. Oh, is this the list?'

'Half of it. I'm redoing it. Here's the original printout.'

Sarah examined the original, then squinted sideways at Caitlyn and they both burst out laughing. 'You deserve about ten meals for that.'

'It took me a while, I must admit. But apart from the medical students and maybe the library, knitting and Friday ladies, I'm sure Harry West'll have all these names.'

Sarah studied the list more closely. 'There are a lot more women than men here. You know, it could be two swindlers working together. She gets to know the family details, then he phones and pretends to be the son-in-law. A lot of women talk more readily to another woman than to a man.'

'Good point. I'll email this to Harry West when I've finished it.'

Sarah was frowning. 'Caitlyn – what's to stop our swindler being completely unconnected to the hospitals? Someone who wanders in looking for old ladies who might be gullible enough to part with their money?'

Caitlyn stared, her brain racing. It was a point. 'Nothing – but I'm sure the police will be on to that, too.'

'That reminds me. Mim phoned Harry West this morning, and they've got Ralph Bailey at the station again for questioning.'

Caitlyn was astonished. 'Do they think it was him?'

'I don't know. He seemed too much of a wimp to me to do anything violent, but he was definitely with Wilma and the money, and he's nervous about it. And they wouldn't have pulled him in for no reason.'

Caitlyn bent over the laptop. 'I'll get this finished and send you a copy, shall I?'

'Good. I should go. Physio today.'

'Aren't you going to see Rita?'

'Phil's folks are going today, and Mim's always tired out after her physio. We'll go tomorrow when she's back home, in the morning if I have anything to do with it because in the evening I'm having dinner with Jack and I'm not going to cancel at the last minute this time.'

Caitlyn smiled. 'You're a lucky lady – a Mim-meal tonight, and your date tomorrow.'

Sarah's face brightened. 'Aren't I? Maybe our luck's changing.'

Chapter Sixteen

Thursday, 20th July

'Am I allowed to say again you look very nice?' said Mim, standing in the kitchen doorway.

Sarah slid her phone into her bag and checked her reflection in the long hall mirror. Her black tunic fell to her ankles, and on top she was wearing a blue blouse, open at the front and knotted round her waist. It was dressy but comfortable, and her black sandals went well with it. She had to admit to being excited about this evening – curious, too. At long last she and Jack would have a chance to get to know each other properly. Would it work out? It would be so good to be one of a pair again.

'You don't think it's too formal?'

Mim walked carefully towards her. 'You're allowed to be dressy once in a while. It's lovely – that blue really suits you.'

'Aw, thanks, Mim. Call me if you need me, okay?'

Mim gave her a little push. 'We'll be fine. Enjoy your meal. If it's half as good as the one you made me last night, you'll be in heaven.'

Jack's car pulled up outside, and Sarah blew kisses to

Mim and Frankie, who was sitting with the iPad swiping through the photos they'd taken of baby Ailsa that morning. Rita had allowed Frankie to hold the baby, and the little girl had been one big grin all the way home.

Jack smiled across at Sarah as they drew away from the house. She settled into the passenger seat, happiness warm in her gut. This was it, me-time at last. Mim was recovering, Frankie was looking a bit happier, and Rita's baby was safely here. She was starting the next chapter of her life. Who knew where tonight would lead?

A burst water main at the end of the High Street was causing congestion all through town, and they made slow progress for a while. Jack was serious, concentrating on his driving, and Sarah sat thinking about last night's Mim-meal. Frankie decorated the dining room table, and they served smoked salmon and cream cheese for the starter, then lamb chops with potato gratin and sugar snap peas, and sticky toffee pudding to finish off with. It was a very successful evening, and Sarah had been well satisfied at the expression on Mim's face.

Jack parked in the restaurant car park and turned to grin at her. 'Made it. Now I can give you my undivided attention. You're much nicer to look at than heavy traffic and diversion signs.'

Sarah laughed, noticing for the first time that he was wearing the same suit and the same shirt and tie as last time. He'd worn them to the funeral too. A couple of times she'd had the impression he wasn't well off – Ceres Road wasn't in an affluent area, and maybe he was paying for his parents' care home? Or maybe he just wasn't a 'clothes person'. There was so much about him to find out. She took his arm as they walked towards the restaurant.

The waiter showed them to their table, in a little alcove.

Jack sat down opposite her. 'Here we are at last. I was afraid you'd rush off again and we'd have to hope for fourth time lucky.'

He wasn't smiling and Sarah glanced at him uncertainly. Was that a joke? She gave him the benefit of the doubt, and complimented him on his choice of restaurant. The opulent maroon and gold décor gave the place a real Oriental feel, while huge windows overlooking the canal kept it bright and airy.

The waiter brought menus, and this time Jack ordered very confidently, checking to make sure she liked prawns before choosing one of the meals for two, which was fine with her.

'Tell me the news from your world,' he said, leaning towards her when the menus had been removed.

Sarah launched into a humorous account of the dash to Manchester and the birth of Rita's baby. He listened attentively, his eyes shining at her, laughing in all the right places, and Sarah relaxed. She'd been right to give him another chance.

The waiter arrived with their starters, and Jack began to talk about the plans for his garden. Sarah had always helped Pop with the garden, and they chatted away about vegetable beds and soft fruit all the way through the baby spring rolls.

When she'd finished hers Sarah sat back. 'I should try to get Frankie interested in the garden. It'd be a good hobby if she's keen.'

'Ah. The first flush of enthusiasm – you want to harness that,' said Jack.

He talked on about formal gardens while they ate sweet and sour prawns and chicken foo yung, and Sarah was glad to see no sign of nerves tonight. He knew a lot about the parks she'd visited as a child. Hearing about the 1995 exhibition in Victoria Park brought childhood memories flooding back, and she told him about a similar event she'd visited in Switzerland.

'Dessert?' he asked, when the plates had been cleared away.

Sarah was full, but she could tell he wanted his pud. 'Lovely.'

He signalled to the waiter, who took the order and returned very promptly with their banana fritters.

'How's Frankie getting on? Are the police any further forward?' asked Jack, starting out on the sticky balls on his plate. 'Hey, these are fantastic. Try one.'

Sarah stabbed up a small forkful. 'They've questioned the bank clerk a few times, but I don't think he had anything to do with it. Caitlyn Mackie – my neighbour, you met her at the memorial – she's a journalist, and she's very interested in the stolen money part. You'll have heard about that?'

He nodded at her seriously, and she went on. 'Anyway, we've been talking to another old lady who had money taken while she was in hospital in Manchester. There might be a connection.'

He was staring at her in complete fascination, and Sarah couldn't help feeling flattered. Maybe they really were going places, her and Jack. It was a heady thought.

He leaned across the table. 'Gosh, that sounds hopeful. But Wilma can't help anymore, can she? Do the police know about this other woman?'

'Yes, her son-in-law reported it, but unfortunately they didn't realise what had happened until weeks after the actual theft. The police seem to be tapping about in the dark.'

'Oh dear.' He tutted. 'You know sometimes I think the police aren't all they're cracked up to be. They still haven't found out who killed Petra, have they? Or who took Wilma's money. Of course it might not be the same person who targeted Glynis.'

Sarah was chewing slowly. The banana fritters hadn't been a good idea. They were delicious for about two seconds, and then you realised how oily and heavy they were. Her stomach was protesting like mad. She forced her mouthful down and took a sip of water before answering Jack.

'She has no idea who took it.' Sarah pushed her plate away. If she ate another bite she would be sick, and what kind of ending would that be to their lovely date? She took a couple of careful breaths. 'Jack, these are beyond me, I'm afraid. Would you like them?'

'I'm full too, thanks,' he said, gazing intently into her eyes. 'Tell you what, though – come back to my place and I'll make you a Tia Maria coffee.'

Sarah thought swiftly. Did he want anything more than coffee? Did she? Her gut knew the answer straightaway – after that meal, not tonight. But it was their first proper date; he wouldn't be expecting more than coffee and a chat.

'Sounds good,' she said. 'I love Tia Maria coffee.'

She didn't miss the look of utter relief that came over his face, though it was gone again almost immediately. Was he so afraid of rejection that her acceptance of his invitation was such a big deal? That was rather sweet. But she should still set some boundaries. She reached over the table and tapped his hand.

'Jack – I'm coming for Tia Maria coffee only. First proper date and all that.'

'Well, if you insist, but I do have some nice little biscuity things as well. It's up to you, though.' He signalled to the waiter.

Sarah giggled, relieved. She went on talking about coffee liqueurs as they walked arm in arm to the car. It was great to be out with an attractive man, going for a meal, feeling good about the blossoming relationship.

She settled into the car, cradling her handbag as Jack pushed the key into the ignition and drove off, silent as he always was in the car. Sarah watched as he steered round the Leeway roundabout. He had strong, workman's hands. He glanced across at her, and all at once she shivered, a chilly little shiver that surprised her. In spite of all the almost-dates she didn't know much about him yet – he always spoke of things, not feelings. But what guy didn't?

It's a cup of coffee, she told herself. And this is Jack, for heaven's sake. You've known him since primary school, Mim has met him, and Netta Chisholm thought he was the bee's knees, God rest her soul.

The sun had long since set, and Jack was concentrating

on the road, looking calm and confident. Sarah relaxed again. He was a bit of an enigma – sometimes so insecure, and sometimes confident. I guess that's what makes him interesting, she thought, smiling at her own nervousness.

The burst water main seemed to have affected the electricity across part of the town. The area they were driving through was dim, the streetlights standing tall and dark. Gathering clouds were promising rain and making the scene even more gloomy. Sarah swallowed, memories of uncomfortable teenage decisions coming to mind. But she wasn't a teenager any longer; she was in charge of her life and she was fine. This was first-date nerves, that was all.

The car came to a halt beside some low buildings and Sarah peered out. It looked like some kind of factory on her side. 'Are we there?'

'This is my lock-up. The house is round the back, but we'll leave the car here – I think after liqueur coffees we'd better send you home in a taxi. I'll just get the lock-up key.'

He leaned past her and opened the glove compartment. Sarah shrank into her seat, then moved to get out of the car to give him more space. His free hand grasped her arm in a painful squeeze, and shock leapt through her.

What the hell – oh God, his face – what was happening? His lips were pressed into a thin line – a cruel line, and the normally smooth forehead was furrowed. And his eyes – they were horribly different eyes and she didn't know them. Sarah's stomach twisted, and she pulled in vain against his grasp. 'Jack! What are you –'

And that wasn't a key – no – *no* – he was going to –

A pulsing pain zapped through her body, and she slumped in the passenger seat, panic scorching her gut. All she could do was watch as he pulled half a brick from below his seat and raised it.

And everything went black.

He stared at her, panting. She was unconscious – wasn't she? He gave her shoulder a little shake and her head dropped towards her shoulder. Blood was oozing through her lovely blonde hair on one side, making it stick to the side of her head. Sarah, Sarah – what had he done? He held his breath to hear hers, panic flooding through him when he couldn't, but then he saw the rapid rise and fall of her chest. It was all right. She wasn't dead. Oh fuck – that meant he still had to kill her.

He leaned back in the driving seat, hands clutching his head. What a mess. He was going to have to kill the woman who should have become Mrs Jack Morrison. How had it come to this? For a moment he gave way to the sobs that were shaking his body, then a distant bike light further along the lane galvanised him into action. He jumped out to open the lock-up, and drove straight in.

It was like Petra all over again, except this time he had nothing ready. Where were the cable binders? He rummaged in the toolbox, swearing when all he found were short binders. It was too bloody dark in here to do this. He should keep a torch in the car. Inspiration struck and he hurried to turn on the headlights. That was better. Now – there was plenty of that cord left. He seized the spool of cord and a Stanley knife and cut a couple of lengths. She was moaning gently, flopped over towards the driving seat. He bound her ankles together and dragged her from the car, dumping her in the spot where Petra had lain.

Now for her hands... He laid her arms across her middle, then wound the cord round her wrists, good and tight, twisting until the knot was at the back where she couldn't get at it. That was better – her arms wouldn't flap about like Petra's had. It looked more comfortable, too. But he only had filthy rags to gag her with. Poor lovely Sarah, except she was anything but lovely now. Her eye make-up was smudged and blood was trickling down a white cheek and he was going to have to kill her and he couldn't... not Sarah...

Sobbing again, he pulled a sack over her head and fled, gunning the car round to the side of the house, stalling three times in his panic to get there, to be home, to be safe. This was a hundred times worse than Petra or Netta.

Jack paced up and down in his new kitchen, his hands clasped and pressed under his chin. He'd never felt so trapped, so afraid. The only way to get through this was to switch his emotions off. It was his own fault things had ended so disastrously – stupid bugger he was, mentioning Glynis by name. What a good thing they'd had those fritters, they'd kept Sarah occupied, but she'd have realised the significance of what he'd said as soon as she started to think about it. He couldn't let that happen. Nausea spread through his gut and he forced it down.

So he had to silence Sarah too. He should have done it straightaway, wielded the spade while she was still unconscious and got it over with. But it would be like killing a member of his own family. Like killing his mum. He'd wanted to do that so many times.

But now it was him – or Sarah. Maybe he could give her another tap on the head, and dump her in the canal? Didn't people say that death by drowning was pleasant? It would all be over in a moment, and the body would be gone. Yes, that should work...

But 'should' was no use; he needed certainty. He might not have the same luck again – suppose someone saw him? Think, think. Sarah had to die, that was clear. And he couldn't trust himself to kill her the same way he'd managed with Petra, or even Netta, that was clear too.

An overdose? He'd need to get hold of something stronger than sleeping pills, and someone might get suspicious if he tried to buy a load of medication. The same applied if he tried to steal drugs from the hospital. Of course, he could always go to every chemist's in town and buy a little in each. But if he hadn't managed to get pills into Petra, he'd never be able to with Sarah. So anything she had to swallow was out.

Set fire to the lock-up? The wooden roof would go up straightaway, and there was oil and petrol in there so it would all burn like hellfire – he could leave the car in there; it would explode. But there was a lot of concrete too, and there would inevitably be something left of the body. A DNA test would tell the police it was Sarah, and how could he explain away her presence in his lock-up when it suddenly caught fire for some strange reason? So that was out too.

Starvation? How long could anyone live with no food or water? Four days? Five days? Six? He didn't know, and leaving her to die in the lock-up would be dangerous. Tomorrow morning people would be walking past on their way to the station.

Unless... suppose he were to take her somewhere, somewhere nobody ever went, where no-one would dream of looking? Somewhere he could dump her and forget about her? That might work. He'd need to be careful to leave no trace of himself on the way there or back, but he had access to sterile hospital garb so that didn't have to be a problem.

Hospital garb...

Of course, of course. He punched the air with both fists. Everything was going to be all right. Sarah could die in peace after all.

He knew just where to hide her.

It was black dark, and something was pressing hard against her head. She couldn't think what it could be, in fact she could hardly think at all. It felt like a too-small metal band around her skull, squeezing, squeezing. No... No, it was pain. A searing, jagged pain was winding round from the back of her neck to right above her eyes. This was by far the worst headache she'd ever had. And... what was in her mouth? She couldn't close her lips, and something was pressing on her palate. Was it a breathing tube, oh no, was she in hospital? She couldn't see, and the pain, dear Lord, she felt so sick. And she could barely move.

She must be in hospital. Please let her go back to sleep... She had never felt this weak.

Mim... Gran... Mama... Who could help? Somewhere in the back of her head a tune was playing, a tinny nursery rhyme. Her lamp with the stars that made pictures on the bedroom wall. She sank into the memory.

Jack's hands were clammy inside the surgical gloves. He glanced at the dashboard clock – quarter to midnight. He should do this quickly. There was no need to hang around. He backed the car into the road and drove round the block to the lock-up.

There was complete silence when he swung the door up. Was she still unconscious? No – the effects of the stun gun didn't last longer than a few moments, and the blow on her head hadn't been a hard one. She'd be playing dead, terrified he was going to batter her face in like he'd done with Petra.

He deliberately didn't speak to her. If she started to moan, he didn't know if he'd be able to stand it. So – a quick zap to her leg with the stun gun, another little bash on her head with the same instrument, and she was blessedly unconscious again. It was the only way he could do this. Moving swiftly, he drove the car into the lock-up and closed the door on the night.

She was still, and his heart raced when he heard the slow, rhythmic breathing. Maybe he'd hit her too hard. But come *on*, Jack. You're going to leave her to die;

it made no difference if she had brain damage or not. He stared at the body slumped on the floor. Just like Petra, except Sarah's head wasn't flat and she hadn't bled enough for it to be seeping through the sack. So not much like Petra, and all the better for that. Grasping Sarah's shoulders, he pulled, and up she came to lean against his legs, all floppy and uncooperative, good. Grab under her knees now, Jack... she was lighter than Petra. He staggered towards the car, her perfume assaulting his senses quite horribly, and manoeuvred her into the back seat, covering her with the blanket that had covered Petra last time. At least her face wasn't flat...

Swallowing the panic, he drove away from the lock-ups and towards the main road, the night sky dark above him. No-one was around to see.

He drove this way nearly every day. It was his working world, the hospital, and it was a huge, rambling old place, a rabbit warren of corridors and cellars. Some of the older parts had rooms tucked away whose existence most people had long forgotten, if they'd ever known in the first place. No-one would find Sarah where he was taking her.

He steered through the main gate and drove towards the porter's HQ at the back of the admin block. Who was on call tonight? Ted, yes, and he'd be asleep unless he was out on a shout. Either way he wouldn't worry Jack and Sarah. Tears sprang into Jack's eyes. Jack and Sarah. It could have been. It should have been. He wasn't a bad person, he wasn't... Panic fluttered back into his throat.

Sarah was beginning to stir as he parked in his usual workday space. Jack zapped her with the stun gun again and ran inside. He burst into the storeroom and seized a set of green overalls, almost overbalancing in his hurry to put them on. He pulled one of those ridiculous shower-cap affairs over his head; it would prevent him dropping DNA-loaded hair all over the place. Hell – what if he'd already dropped hairs on Sarah? But they'd had dinner together, and who was to say they hadn't cuddled in the car park? Everything would be all right, as long as no trace of him was found at the scene of her death. His hand hovered over the box of face masks, but no – that wasn't necessary. Back to the car now, quick, quick.

He drove to the far end of the hospital, keeping well within the slow speed limit. It would never do to make himself conspicuous. Sarah was taking funny little throaty breaths in the back of the car. She would come round soon; she would be afraid, but she wouldn't suffer long, he was sure.

The building he was heading for was psycho-geriatrics, right at the back of the complex beside the rehab block and maternity. It wasn't psycho-geriatrics these days, of course, that was an old fashioned term they'd conjured up at the time of the Second World War. Nowadays it was home to ordinary geriatrics, but a lot of them were psycho anyway, poor sods. The in-joke at the hospital was there'd been a huge red cross painted on the psycho-geri roof during the war, but the Luftwaffe hadn't bombed it. So the same building still stood today, half-wooden, probably half-rotten, old, old, old – with cellars. It was a piece of hospital history down there, a forgotten corner where spiders and cockroaches reigned undisturbed.

And best of all, the psycho-geri cellar wasn't linked

to the tunnel system under the hospital. It was quiet, secluded, and never used. The perfect place to hide and die...

Oh, Sarah.

Jack parked on the far side of the building, as close to the back doorway as he could get. But no-one would be around to see him so there was no need to worry. He unlocked the door with his pass key, propping it open with a chunk of stone that lay nearby. Then he pulled Sarah from the car, arranging her floppiness over his shoulder in a kind of fireman's lift this time. Breathing heavily, he slid inside and down the stairs. It was dark as the grave down here. Rather appropriate. Round the corner he went, through the first cellar door into a narrow hallway, and thank goodness, he could put a light on now. He clicked the switch down. It was a nice dim bulb, good.

There were four rooms down here, and he unlocked one of them. It was used to store unwanted equipment – he'd brought a couple of machines down last autumn. Stacks of old mattresses were propped in one corner, relics from the Second World War too, by the looks of them, but at least Sarah could lie there and die in relative comfort.

He lowered her to the floor and pressed the light switch, but this time nothing happened. Well, maybe that was better. There was enough light from the hallway for what he had to do. He pulled four mattresses into a pile, lifted Sarah again and almost flung her down there. Thank God he was strong. She made a little moaning sound, so he pulled up the sack and tightened the gag a little. Her eyelids were fluttering and she was sheet-white. Quickly, he pulled the sack back over her face and tucked it into the gag at the back of her neck, twisting it to make it hold. Sorted. He could go now; no-one upstairs would hear Sarah even if she did moan. The walls were thick and the geriatrics were yowling all the time anyway. Moans echoed round this old building like something from a horror film. He checked the cords round her wrists and ankles, then covered her completely with a drape from one of the machines. There! She looked like a proper corpse now, and soon she'd be one. Dead on her hospital bed. Regret washed through him. Goodbye, Sarah. Blinking back tears, he locked both doors behind him, and hurried round to the car.

The main thoroughfare was deserted as he drove to the hospital gates, and even in the town centre there wasn't much traffic, thanks to the burst main. Jack turned into the High Street. All he wanted was to go home, go to bed, and sleep. He had to be fresh for tomorrow when the terrible news that Sarah was missing would reach him as one of the first. But there were a couple of things he had to take care of first.

Slowly, he drove along the High Street until he came to the travel agent's opposite the bank, and parked. There was a bus stop about twenty metres away where a handful of late pub-crawlers were waiting for the last bus out to Bellside. They were a bit of a raucous crowd – one of them was being sick into the gutter. They might notice the car, but they wouldn't be able to tell how many people were in it, and they certainly wouldn't be able to describe him.

Sarah's handbag was on the floor by the passenger seat, and he rummaged until he found her mobile. Good, it was on. The surgical gloves were thin; it was easy to punch in the number of the biggest taxi company in town.

He listened as the ringing tone trilled in his ear. Careful, Jack. You've got one chance to get this right.

'B.B. Taxis.' It was a man's voice.

'Oh, please, help me, come and get me! I'm in the High Street and there's a man here and I think he's following me!'

Jack paused, pleased. He'd always been good at theatricals, and although he hadn't done a female voice for a long time it had worked perfectly. He'd convinced the taxi operator, anyway.

'Where are you, love?'

'Opposite the bank. Oh God, he's crossing the road – he's coming!'

'Walk up towards the bus stop, love, there'll be other people there. Taxi'll be with you in two minutes.'

'Oh, please hurry, plea-' Jack broke the connection, noticing happily that a bus was pulling away from the stop. His timing couldn't have been better. He leaned over to open the passenger seat door and tossed Sarah's bag into the gutter, where it landed beside an empty cigarette packet and some greasy old chip paper.

Nice one, Jack. You're safe; it's all right. He pulled the car into a U-turn in the now-deserted High Street. Fifty metres further on he passed a taxi cruising along, obviously looking for a distraught female in need of a lift.

Chapter Seventeen

Friday, 21st July – morning

The doorbell rang, loud and insistent, and then again. Caitlyn tutted in irritation. If that was someone selling something at this time in the morning she'd tell them where to go. She glanced in the bathroom mirror to check she didn't have toothpaste on her chin, ran downstairs, and yanked the front door open.

'Come quick! We can't find Sarah and Mim's scared!' Frankie was already on her way back next door.

Head reeling, Caitlyn looked round for her bag then followed the child across the front wall and into Mim's hallway. What on earth? 'We can't find Sarah' – what was that supposed to mean? She hurried through to the kitchen where Mim was sitting with her hands twisted against her chest.

Caitlyn saw at a glance how afraid the other woman was, and her stomach lurched. 'Mim? What's going on?'

'Sarah didn't come home last night and I can't get in touch with her.' The words were stark and Mim's voice unrecognisable.

Caitlyn dropped into the chair opposite Mim and tried

Sarah's number on her own phone. Nothing. 'She was going out with Jack, wasn't she? To a restaurant? And then –?'

'And then she didn't come home.' Mim's voice was shrill with panic. 'I was up till after twelve watching *Dances with Wolves*, and I checked my mobile before I went to bed but she hadn't texted. I know she's a grown woman and she can do as she likes, but Caitlyn, it's not like her. I hardly slept a wink.'

'And she definitely hasn't been home?'

'Her bed hasn't been slept in and the outfit she was wearing last night isn't in her room.'

Dread dropped into Caitlyn's stomach as her eyes met Mim's over the table. Something was wrong here, very wrong. Standing in the doorway, Frankie began to cry. Mim beckoned the girl to the chair beside her and stroked her head.

Caitlyn tried to think. 'Have you called Jack?'

Mim rocked back and forth on her chair. 'I don't have the number and I can't remember his surname! Sarah must have mentioned it but –'

'It's Morrison.' Caitlyn picked up her phone again and went into the online directory. And of course, Jack Morrison wasn't listed. She swore under her breath and Frankie buried her face in her arms on the kitchen table.

Caitlyn touched the girl's head. 'Try not to worry, Frankie. We'll find her. It's probably just her phone battery conking out.'

Mim patted Frankie too. 'She could be on her way home right now.'

It was clear to Caitlyn that Mim thought nothing of the

sort, but the words seemed to comfort Frankie. The poor kiddie had probably been used to her mother staying out overnight and limping home the following morning with a hangover, but hell – Sarah would not do that to Mim.

Caitlyn rubbed her face. 'Jack was driving, was he?'

'Yes. So she might have stayed with him. But look at the time, Caitlyn – why isn't she home yet?'

Caitlyn didn't know what to say. Mim was right. If Sarah had stayed at Jack's he'd have brought her home on his way to work. And he would start at eight in the morning and it was after that now. Of course, he could be on an evening shift today, or maybe he'd arranged a day off, to be with Sarah? But that came back to the same thing – Sarah would have let Mim know.

Caitlyn's stomach was churning now, and she lifted her phone again. 'I'll try phoning Jack at the hospital.'

Mim gave a little sob. 'Oh Caitlyn, he'll be portering about all over the place, they won't find him.'

'They will. Even if he doesn't have a bleep, someone will know which department he's gone to.' She listened as the number connected and rang out, two, three, four times before a woman's voice spoke.

'Brockburn General Hospital.'

'I need to speak to Jack Morrison, one of your porters, as soon as possible. It's an urgent family matter.'

A moment later Caitlyn was put through to someone in the porter's office. She gave her own mobile number and Mim's landline, stressing the urgency of the situation without divulging any details.

'We'll give him ten minutes,' she said, handing Mim the landline phone. 'I think you should call Harry West.'

Mim's knuckles on the phone were white, and her voice was a mere whisper. 'Caitlyn – she's a grown woman.'

Caitlyn reached for Mim's free hand, not wanting to say how afraid she was. Frankie was silent on her chair beside Mim, shoulders high and eyes wary. Mim pressed out the number. She stumbled over the words, telling them that Sarah was missing, then listened for a few seconds before breaking the connection and staring first at Caitlyn and then at Frankie.

Caitlyn swallowed bile. 'Mim?'

'Harry West is already on his way to see us. He'll be here in a few minutes.'

Caitlyn's ears buzzed and she gripped the edge of the table hard. *Sarah?* Mim's face was a sickly grey colour and Frankie was shivering.

'Has Sarah disappeared like my mum?' she said, tears choking her voice.

'I don't know, lovey,' said Mim bleakly.

Caitlyn fought to stay calm. Sarah *had* disappeared, and whatever had happened, it must have been hours ago now. Caitlyn leaned back, both hands pressed against her mouth and oblivious to the chair-back digging into her shoulder blades. Her thoughts spiralled round, dark and fearsome. Petra. Netta Chisholm. And now Sarah. Everything happens in threes, they say. And what were the police doing? All this time had passed since Petra had disappeared, why wasn't her murderer languishing in a prison cell? And why hadn't Jack kept Sarah safe?

Her phone on the table buzzed, making them all jump. It was a mobile number; this must be Jack. Caitlyn and

Mim exchanged wide-eyed looks, then Caitlyn swung her chair round beside Mim's to allow them both to hear what was being said.

'Jack?'

'Yes. Who is this?'

'Caitlyn Mackie. I'm phoning from Mim's. Sarah didn't come home last night. Do you know where she is? We're worried.'

'She didn't... Oh God. Oh my God, oh no... She – oh *shit*...'

'What is it? What happened? Where is she?'

Jack was hyperventilating down the phone. Panic filled Caitlyn as seconds passed without him speaking. When he did his voice was a mere whisper.

'It was late... and there were traffic delays from the burst water main. She wouldn't let me bring her all the way across town... there was a bus coming and she made me leave her in the High Street, near the bus stop. No, oh no – where is she?'

He sounded distraught, but Caitlyn felt no sympathy for the man. Mim was crumpled in her chair, and Frankie's eyes were wild. She hadn't heard Jack's story.

'The police are on their way here,' said Caitlyn brusquely. 'We'll let you know what happens.' She clicked the phone off and put her arm round Mim. 'Jack dropped Sarah at the bus stop on the High Street last night,' she told Frankie.

The doorbell rang before the girl could answer, and Frankie ran to let Harry West and Mandy Craven in. Caitlyn kept a tight hold of Mim. What was Harry going to tell them, hell on earth, was Sarah *dead?* Maybe they had found her body, beaten and crumpled, dumped and cold in a ditch somewhere? Caitlyn could feel Mim's shoulders shaking. But Harry gave them a brief nod when he entered the kitchen, and Mandy Craven smiled quickly. It wasn't the worst news.

Harry West spoke first. 'Mrs Dunbar, we need to speak to you –' His gaze shifted to include Caitlyn '– alone. Mandy.'

Mandy Craven turned to Frankie. 'You can come to the other room with me, Frankie.'

The girl was standing hands on hips, and quickly, Caitlyn reached across and touched Frankie's arm. They didn't have time for arguments this morning.

'Please, Frankie. It's quickest if we do what they say.'

Frankie glared at Mandy Craven and flounced out of the room. The policewoman followed.

Harry West cleared his throat. 'Last night, a taxi company received a call at about half past eleven, from a woman who said a man was following her. When the taxi got there he couldn't find the woman, and the company contacted us. We sent a car round but there was no sign of anything untoward.'

Mim gave a slight moan, and Caitlyn hugged her again.

Harry West wasn't finished. 'This morning, a bag was found in a shop doorway round the corner from the bank in the High Street. I'm afraid it's Sarah's bag. The woman who found it brought it in. There was no purse or phone, but there's a membership card for a Swiss sports centre, in Sarah's name.'

A dull headache starting behind her eyes, Caitlyn told Harry West about Sarah's date the previous evening and Jack's phone call a few minutes ago. Harry rapped out several questions about Sarah's friends and her relationship with Jack, and Caitlyn and Mim answered as well as they could. Harry's face became grimmer with every question.

'Okay. We'll interview Jack Morrison, and see what witnesses we can find. Someone at the bus stop could have noticed something. I'll need a photo of Sarah. And a description of what she was wearing last night.'

'Caitlyn, can you fetch the photo on top of the television, please.'

Stifling a sob, Caitlyn left the room as Mim started to describe Sarah's outfit. Sarah had dressed up to go out with Jack. She'd been anticipating a happy evening. Caitlyn rubbed her eyes with her sleeve.

Frankie jumped up from the sofa, but Caitlyn shook her head. 'We'll fill you in soon, Frankie, I promise.'

She hurried back with the photo – Sarah in the garden, wearing a big happy smile. A thought struck Caitlyn as she handed the photo to Harry. 'Ralph Bailey?'

Harry shook his head. 'He'll be checked, but there's no reason to think he has anything to do with this. And the signature on Wilma's withdrawal was ninety-nine per cent certainly hers. Thanks. We'll see ourselves out.'

Frankie flew back to the kitchen before the officers had closed the front door. 'What did he say?'

Caitlyn saw that Mim was fighting for control, and gave the girl a brief summary of what was happening. There was no point in hiding the truth.

Frankie began to shake, curling into a ball on the floor beside the kitchen table.

'I want my mum, and I want Sarah, I want my mum, I want my *mum*,' she moaned, her voice rising hysterically.

Caitlyn seized the child's forearm and gave it a little shake. 'I know you do. But this isn't helping, Frankie,' she said firmly, trying to jerk the girl back into control.

Frankie leapt up and ran upstairs, slamming every door she passed through.

Caitlyn turned back to Mim. 'Shall I go after her?'

Mim was pale, but her eyes were determined. She was tough, was Mim.

'Leave her be, Caitlyn. She hasn't had a real crying jag since her mother's memorial, it'll do her good. We've got to think. We've got to find Sarah before it's too late.'

'It might be too late already.' Caitlyn could hardly get the words out.

To her surprise Mim turned on her. 'If you talk like that then it is too late! So don't! Think what we can do to find Sarah.'

Caitlyn rubbed her face on her sleeve. 'Okay. Someone must have been watching Sarah, following her and Jack, waiting to get her on her own. Because she knew something, but we don't know what. So who could this person be?'

They looked at each other. There was no way to know.

Caitlyn stood up and put the kettle on. Tea was good for shock and it might help them think. 'Let's go further back. This is the same person who took Petra. She disappeared in the hospital grounds, so presumably she got into someone's car. Whose car would she get into?'

'It was a terrible day,' said Mim, frowning as she remembered. 'She'd have been pleased to get a lift.'

'Yes. But it's still unlikely she'd get into a car with a complete stranger. So either it was someone she knew personally, or else it was someone she knew from the hospital.'

'You're right,' said Mim, staring. 'She didn't necessarily know him well. Assuming it was a him. So it could be a neighbour, a friend, someone she worked with – or someone from the hospital.'

'And now this same person must have picked Sarah up in the High Street. Mim, if it's someone from the hospital, we'll find them. Let's get Frankie back down here because we need her input. I'll fetch Glynis's list and we'll see if anyone there strikes either of you.'

Mim pulled herself to her feet, and Caitlyn raced back home for the list. They must find Sarah in time, they must.

Her whole body hurt. Lie still, Sarah advised herself. A nurse'll come soon. It'll get better. She lay there, forcing herself to breathe evenly, slowly becoming aware that something was very wrong. She was on a bed but she couldn't move and she couldn't see, either. The smell was tinged with hospitals, but it was old and musty too. What had happened?

Jack's car, yes. She'd been in the car with Jack. They were going back to his house for coffee. She could remember turning left at the lights into Albion Street, but after that her mind was blank. There must be more to remember – had they crashed? And why was it so dark? Oh no – shit, shit, was she trapped in the car? Her heartbeat clattered in her ears; it was difficult not to panic. Pain crashed through her head every time she tried to move. Her body was heavy and limp, oh God — was she paralysed? Breathe, Sarah. Just breathe for now.

Her thoughts cleared gradually. She wasn't in the car, but it didn't seem to be a hospital either. The smell was too stale. She was lying flat, and her feet... She couldn't move her legs much because... because her feet were stuck together... and her hands...

Setting her teeth against the pain, Sarah spread her fingers, but — her hands were stuck; she couldn't pull them apart. She tried to lift her arms — oh no. Christ no. Her hands were tied at the wrists, and a sheet or something was covering her. Horror swamped down; she could feel her lips tingling. *Had she been buried alive?* Panting, she moved her hands upwards and as far as she could to the side; oh thank God — there was space round about her. She ran her fingers over the rough cloth that was covering her head. Sackcloth. That was where the smell was coming from. But the sheet — she could feel it with the back of her hands and it was right up over her head. Like a dead body. The horror chilled back. She wasn't in a coffin, but someone had tied her up and gagged her and left her here.

Where was Jack? They'd been in the car... and then they'd stopped, hadn't they — but where had they been? She couldn't remember, and her head hurt so terribly. Who had done this to her? Was she going to die, like Petra? Jack, Mim, help me...

The panic was unstoppable now and she moaned, sweat breaking out on her brow, her back, between her legs as she tried frantically to pull the ill-smelling sack away. But the cloth moved centimetres at most, it was tied on round the back or something, and everything was pitch black. She couldn't even scream; the only sounds she was able to make were choking, throaty moans. Blackness rose inside her and she felt her thoughts slide away as the pain in her head took over.

It's a nightmare, Sarah decided. You're having a nightmare. Go back to sleep. Everything will be all right in the morning.

She lay still, and after a while a strange kind of peace seeped through her. She dozed, half-waking every now and then as a stab of pain sliced through her head. Someone would come soon and help her. Jack would have gone for help; it would be all right...

It was still black dark when she awoke properly, but the throbbing in her head was no longer crushing. Sarah listened, but there was nothing to be heard except the sound of her own breathing, shuddering and irregular. Eyes closed against the darkness, she tried to work things out.

Someone had brought her here. The last thing she remembered was... arriving at Jack's lock-up. After that there was nothing. Had someone been waiting at the lock-up? It seemed the most logical explanation. And what had happened to Jack? They were both in grave danger; she had to get away. She had no idea what time it was, but if it was still night, Mim wouldn't have realised yet that she was gone.

Shuddering, Sarah rolled onto her right side and stretched her tied hands forwards. She couldn't move them enough to grip anything, but she could feel the edge of the mattress. She was on some kind of bed, and the sheet covering her was loose – she could pull it off. For a moment she concentrated on this, and the cloth slid away. Okay. She should try to sit up.

It took a couple of goes, but eventually she managed to push up into a sitting position, her head swirling. Her feet touched the floor – oh – she had lost a sandal. She kicked the remaining one off and took a shaky breath. Sitting up, she didn't feel so helpless. But it was very disorientating, surrounded by blackness and no idea where she was.

Slowly, Sarah pulled at the sacking covering her head, and by bending her face down over her knees and pulling with both hands, she managed to free her head of the cloth. Christ, that was better.

It was still almost completely dark. Sarah waited, blinking, giving her eyes time to adjust. She could make out dim shadows to her left, as if there was a tiny window over there. There might be people on the other side. Hope flared and she tried to cry out, but she could hardly make a sound. The gag was disgusting – foul-tasting and much too tight; it was breaking the skin at the corners of her mouth. She pulled at it with her fingers, but it hardly budged and her efforts only broke more skin round her mouth. And there was no way she could get the cords off her hands or feet, either. It was too painful, and her skin was already torn and raw under the bonds.

Sarah sat still, trying to think logically. Every minute or two a sick wave of pain surged through her head, but she knew she had to stay conscious and think. There might not be much time left. If she'd been brought here by the same person who killed Petra, then he was going to come back and kill her too. But *why?* She didn't even know who he was. But that was beside the point; the important thing was to get out of here. She turned her head towards the small patch of dim light – she should try to get over there. If it was a window she might be able to attract someone's attention.

Taking care not to lose her balance, she stood up, wincing as the bonds round her ankles rubbed over broken skin. She tried to take little shuffling steps, but the cords tore cruelly at her skin, and warm blood trickled down her ankles. This was no use. If she fell and broke a leg here she'd be done for. She sank to her knees, and found that by pushing with her bound arms on the floor she was able to slide on her knees towards the dim light. Her dress tore and her back ached, but she carried on, and on. The floor was wooden and very dusty, and she kept bumping into things she couldn't see and then having to make a detour round them.

It seemed to take hours, but at last she arrived at the dim light. Something was blocking it, though, a box, or a carton. Right. Now to stand up again. Slowly, Sarah, you can do this.

Moaning aloud as cramped muscles and torn skin protested, she pushed herself to her feet and stood, supported by the wall. Okay, she was standing beside something big here, and the dim light was directly behind it. She reached out again and felt cardboard. It was a pile of boxes, and it moved when she pushed it. Straining, she leant against it and pushed with all her might. Two boxes tumbled to the floor, revealing a tiny window, much too high and too small to climb out. It was covered in the dust of years, and a bush was pressing against it on the other side in ground that was at window level. So she was in a cellar.

Panting, Sarah felt tears well up in her eyes. Wherever this cellar was, it didn't seem to be the kind of place that was often used. Standing precariously on tiptoe, she managed to touch the window, rubbing it with her fingers, trying to clean the glass and let more light in.

It was daylight outside, but not sunny. Sarah squinted at her watch – it was partially under the cords round her wrists but a couple of good wriggles against her chin had the face visible, and she made out it was after eight o'clock. Mim would soon realise she was missing, if she hadn't already. She would be worried, poor Mim; she would phone the police and get Caitlyn to help and they would look for her, look for Jack. Where was Jack? He couldn't be in this room or she'd have heard him breathing. He'd been in the car with her when it stopped, hadn't he? Yes, she had asked where they were and he said this was his lock-up… And then… Sweat broke out on Sarah's forehead as she strained to remember. She'd been so afraid – but why? Something had happened, something terrible. Maybe they'd been attacked; maybe she'd seen her kidnapper. Who was also Petra's murderer. This was dire; why couldn't she remember? Her head, her head. The pain was crashing back and she couldn't think straight. Had she seen Jack killed? Was that why she couldn't remember – was it the shock? Oh, no, no. What should she do?

Rest, her head insisted as the pain swirled round in

nauseous waves. Sit down, lie down.

Sarah slid to the floor, her back to the wall and head rolling sideways, tasting salt as tears trickled down her cheeks and into her mouth, held half-open by the gag. Was she going to die here today?

Jack stood motionless, his phone still in his hand. He was in the porters' office, the cubbyhole where they hung up their jackets and had their coffee, and where the all-important duty plan was pinned on the institutional green wall. Okay – he had received the horrendous news that his – his girlfriend? – his new girlfriend – was missing. He had to react immediately, and it had to be absolutely right. What would a normal reaction be in those circumstances? Ideas tumbled into his brain, replacing the exhaustion after a sleepless night. He could do this.

He needed to be upset. Frantic. Phone the boss and demand time off. Go home? Go to Mim Dunbar's? Phone the boss first, anyway.

'Darren? It's Jack Morrison. I've had bad news. My girlfriend's gone missing, she disappeared from the High Street late last night. Nobody knows where she is. I was on the phone to her mum two minutes ago and she's in a terrible state. I'm sorry, I have to go.'

'Jesus, man, yes, of course. What happened?'

'I don't know. The police are on their way. Thanks, Darren.' He allowed his voice to break, and sobbed down the phone before replacing the receiver and grabbing his jacket.

Right. Home first, then he'd phone Mim Dunbar and see what was happening there. When would Sarah die? Possibly not until next week… Oh Sarah.

He jogged from the building, exhaustion washing back over him and turning his legs to lead. What an awful, awful thing this was. How he wished he'd never targeted old Wilma. All he'd wanted was some cash to do up his house, and look where it had landed him. No, no, don't look, Jack, don't think about it. React. Your girlfriend is missing. Now go.

He flung himself into the driving seat and reversed out of the parking space. It was heart-breaking – he'd been dreaming of Sarah being Mrs Jack Morrison one day. That wasn't going to happen now, so he could be genuinely grief-stricken. He *was* grief-stricken. Or he would be if he wasn't so bloody tired, and so angry that his glorious plan had all gone wrong. For once in his life you'd think he could get a bloody break, but no. Home, Jack. Just go home.

The lights at the top of the High Street were red, and Jack tapped the steering wheel with impatient fingers. Across the road was the place he'd chucked Sarah's bag out. Had anyone found it? And if they had, what had they done with it? He glanced down on the floor where the bag had been and saw something black and shiny sticking out from under the seat. No no *no* – it was Sarah's sandal. Stomach churning, he leaned over and picked it up. Why the fuck hadn't he noticed she'd lost it? It had been dark, and she was wearing a long dress… He would have to get rid of this right now. The police would be contacting him very soon; he'd been the last person to see Sarah before she disappeared so he'd be right at the top of their list of people to interview.

The driver behind him gave a strident blast on his horn, and Jack jumped in fright. Hell, the lights had changed. He pulled away from the intersection, turned left into the first little side street he came to, then took first right. It was a dingy little alley, parallel to the High Street but drab and uninteresting, showing the backs of the High Street shops. Only delivery lorries would come down here, and this morning it was almost deserted. Not stopping, Jack pressed the window control, dropped the sandal into the gutter, and drove away as fast as he dared.

Home again, he allowed himself a brandy. His girl had disappeared; he was supposed to be upset. And shit, he was exhausted. Should he phone Mim before he had a lie down? It might look suspicious not to.

She answered on the first ring. She'd be sitting on the phone, of course, waiting for news of Sarah. He put the fear back into his voice.

'Mim? It's Jack. I'm at home, they sent me off work. Is there any news?'

'No. The police are putting out appeals on the TV and radio. We're waiting to hear something. It's all we can do.' Her voice was dreary; he could hear no warmth towards him. He'd need to change that.

His voice was trembling very convincingly, and it wasn't an act. 'Will you let me know when there's any news? I'll stay at home too and wait and – and pray.'

That was rather good. Mim must have thought so too, because she definitely sounded kinder when she said goodbye. Jack poured another brandy and settled down in front of the TV. He wanted to see the police appeal. There would be time for sleep later. He lifted the remote and leaned back, swinging his feet up on the coffee table. His shoes were still dusty from that cellar; he should clean them.

Clean his shoes... Jack's head swam and he groaned aloud – he had made a terrible mistake.

Sarah's sandal was shiny black leather. And he had touched it – his fingerprints would be all over it. Why, why, why hadn't he thought to wipe it before he chucked it out for God knows who to find? What a stupid, elementary mistake. The police were putting out appeals, a lot of people would know a woman was missing, and a single, almost-new sandal might arouse suspicion, if it was found. He had to find a reason why he had touched Sarah's sandal... Maybe the strap broke? It did have a strap, didn't it? Fresh sweat ran down the side of his face when he realised he couldn't remember; it was just a woman's sandal. And even if it had a strap, the cops would take one look and see it hadn't broken. Hell, no. He had dug his own grave now – should he go back for it? But if anyone saw him... Jack buried his face in a cushion and sobbed.

Caitlyn charged into the dining room and grabbed her printout of Glynis Brady's list from the table. It was a mess; she'd spilled coffee on it last night and the ink had run. They wouldn't be able to read half of it. Better run off a new one. She switched on the laptop, seething with impatience. It was such a pity she and Sarah hadn't had time to go through the list together. She had no idea if any of these names meant anything to Sarah.

The printer was whirring when Caitlyn's phone buzzed in her pocket. It was a number she didn't recognise, and for a moment she thought about leaving it. But then it might be important. The kids... She connected, walking down her hallway with the new list and holding the phone to her ear.

'Miss – Caitlyn, isn't it? It's Glynis Brady. I wanted to ask if you've had any thoughts about my list, and I remembered too I'd forgotten the hospital chaplain.'

Caitlyn almost burst into tears. She sank down on the bottom stair, clutching the phone to her ear. Mrs Brady might help them find Sarah, but how awful – the only person to turn to was an old, old lady... The moment she opened her mouth to speak, her throat closed and her voice disappeared almost completely. 'Oh, Mrs Brady –'

She stopped, fighting for control.

'Is anything wrong? What is it?' Mrs Brady's voice was inquiring but not upset, and her calmness helped Caitlyn find her own.

'Very wrong. Sarah's missing. She disappeared in the High Street late last night and oh, we didn't tell you but...'

Glynis Brady was completely silent during Caitlyn's explanation.

'... so it's likely the same person who killed Petra Walker has taken Sarah too, so please keep thinking very hard. There might not be much time left to save Sarah.'

'Oh my Lord. I'm so sorry. I wish I could help you but... I'll make a new list...' Her voice tailed away.

Caitlyn nodded, brushing tears from her cheeks, then

realised she had to speak. 'Thank you. Maybe – maybe if you make a diagram this time – you know, with different times of day for each day you were in hospital, and write down who you spoke to at all the separate times. If you make your list in a different way, different names might crop up.'

'I'll do my best, but... that poor girl.'

'I'll call you in an hour or so,' said Caitlyn dully, and rang off.

Still shaking, she went to the bathroom to rinse her face before running back next door.

Mim and Frankie were at the kitchen table, a large piece of paper in front of them. Frankie's face was tear-stained but she was calm. Caitlyn sat down opposite, reading upside down. About ten names were printed there in Frankie's round handwriting.

'We're thinking of all the people from the hospital Petra would have accepted a lift from,' said Mim.

Caitlyn leaned her head in both hands. This was so hard, thinking about Petra when all the time Sarah was missing.

'It doesn't have to be anyone she liked particularly, or even knew well,' she said to Frankie. 'Just someone she'd have got into a car with on a filthy wet afternoon. If Sarah knows any of these people too it might help find her.'

'Uh-huh.' Frankie sat chewing her pen.

Caitlyn pushed Glynis Brady's list over to Mim. 'The odds are nothing's going to jump out at you, but have a look anyway. I think I'll go over to the hospital – I might get an idea if I walk over the same ground that Petra did.'

Mim caught her hand. 'Come back here when you've

finished, Caitlyn,' she said. 'It's not a time to be alone.'

Caitlyn drove to the hospital on automatic pilot. The more time that passed, the less likely it was that Sarah was alive. According to the police, Petra'd been killed the day after she disappeared. It was ten o'clock, so Sarah had been missing for nearly twelve hours. And to all those people out there on the street, this was a normal Friday morning. Friday, the day of pleasurable anticipation, of making plans for the weekend.

And Jack. What had he been thinking, leaving Sarah in the middle of town at that time of night? He'd been the last person to see Sarah; the police would ask him all sorts of questions about what Sarah intended doing, what she'd said, which direction she'd walked off in. And most importantly, if Jack had noticed anyone watching them. But of course he couldn't have, or he wouldn't have left her.

Caitlyn drove to the far end of the hospital, parked in front of the rehab building and went inside. There was nothing here today that didn't look perfectly normal. She saw the sign for the physiotherapy department and wondered if Mim had cancelled her appointment for that day. Briefly, Caitlyn considered going along to do it for her, but – what would she say? That Mim's daughter had disappeared? That she was ill? But that would involve speaking calmly, no, no. Explanations could come later.

Caitlyn wandered round the ground floor, forcing her journalist's mind to take over. Petra had left Frankie in the TV room, and gone to do her hair. That was the last place she'd been seen. Then she'd gone back through these doors out to the car park, turned left and walked towards the admin block, which was right at the front of the hospital complex. Caitlyn zipped up her jacket and walked in Petra's footsteps. It was one of those dull but dry days, very different to the day Petra had disappeared. She came to the edge of the rehab car park and stared down the main hospital avenue, as straight and wide as the High Street. The buildings were set back from the road, and there weren't many people walking around outside. The hospital was too large and spread out for that – it was the kind of place you drove or biked if you were going from top to bottom.

She arrived at the admin block eight minutes later, having met only two people on the way – a nurse wrapped up in an old fashioned cloak, and a woman pushing a buggy. The woman asked if Caitlyn knew where dermatology was. She didn't, but was able to point out the information board by the outpatient building.

So what had all this told her? That even on a dry day, people didn't walk about in the hospital grounds. Which brought her no nearer to finding out who had killed Petra and abducted Sarah. It was yet another dead end, and Sarah might be dead too.

Caitlyn sank down on a chilly bench in front of the admin building and closed her eyes. It wasn't very long since Mim had lost her husband. Would she cope with losing Sarah too – especially under such God-awful circumstances? Hardly, but what mother would?

Pushing cold dread to the back of her mind, Caitlyn jogged back the way she had come.

Sarah jerked awake, the scream in her throat ending almost silently in her gagged mouth. Heart pounding, she stared into the darkness of the room. She had fallen asleep under the window – or had she been unconscious? What time was it? She peered at her watch, but here on the floor it was too dim to see the hands. Her legs were shaking and her right foot had gone numb, but she'd have to stand up or she'd never get out of here.

A couple of deep breaths helped. The headache was bearable now, but the cords round her ankles were biting into her flesh. She touched them with her fingers. It was impossible – the knot was viciously tight and round the back, and with tied hands there was nothing she could do to slacken it. Determination flooded through her. She was going to get up and help herself, because nobody else could. She had to get out of here, back to Mim and Frankie. And Jack.

So the first thing was to stand up and have another look at the window. She was lucky there was a window. Perhaps her captor hadn't noticed it, hidden behind the cardboard box.

Every muscle in her body screamed as she forced her legs to straighten and bear her weight. A sob welled up deep in her chest, but Sarah choked it back. The gag was preventing her from swallowing properly; her throat painful enough without the addition of tear-lumps. Upright at last, she leaned against the wall. Okay. It was after ten already. She reached up to give the glass another rub to let more light in, and winced as her fingers touched something sharp on the narrow window ledge.

A sliver of glass. The window must have been broken

and replaced at some point. She lifted the sliver carefully and examined it. It was only about three centimetres long, but maybe, oh please, maybe she could use it to free her hands and feet.

She slid to the floor again and started to work on the cords round her ankles. It was slow, painful work, but she gritted her teeth and kept going, making little saw-like movements, over and over again, trying to cut through the cord.

What was happening at home? They'd be looking for her by this time. Mim would have phoned the police. Tears burned in Sarah's eyes. Would she ever see Mim again? The killer must be planning to come back and batter her head in like he'd done with Petra. And what had happened to Jack? He was most likely tied up somewhere too, but it wasn't here, or she'd hear him breathing. She was alone in this awful place. The tears overflowed as she moaned into the gag, still sawing at the cords. When was the last time she'd told Mim she loved her?

The cord around her ankles snapped with a jerk and the tension lessened. She had done it. Sarah put the glass shard on the floor where she would find it again in the dark and started to unwind the cord from her feet. It was excruciating, the nylon had cut deep into her skin in several places, but she set her teeth and carried on. At last her feet were free, though she was bleeding again.

She made a brief attempt to saw through the cord round her wrists, but gave up almost immediately. There was no way she could hold the piece of glass in a position where she could saw at the cord. She didn't even try to get the gag off; she didn't want a cut face or neck.

Stepping cautiously on bare feet, she started to explore the cellar. The light didn't work, and the door was locked. No easy escape, then. The things she'd crawled round on the floor were machines of some kind, and there were parts of what seemed to be bed frames too. So although she was in the hospital, it was horrifyingly obvious that no-one ever came here. A metal pole on one of the beds fell to the ground with a clatter when she squeezed past. Sarah picked it up, an idea forming in her mind. Still clutching the pole, she looked round for the sack she'd pulled off her head. There it was on the floor beside the mattresses she'd been lying on. She swept it up it and hurried back to the window. The pole had a kind of prong where one of those handles people could grab hold of and hoist themselves up the bed could be attached. Using this, she speared the sack on the pole, and there it was – a makeshift flag. Now to break the window.

The other end of the pole made short work of the dirty glass, and Sarah whacked the last few shards out, glad when most of them fell on the outside. She hoisted her makeshift flag out the window and waved it frantically. Would anyone see it? Christ, they must.

Waving the flag was hard work with tied hands. Sarah's arms were trembling within minutes, and when she began to feel sick she left the flag hanging out the window and stood back. It was bad luck the bush was there; the flag was stuck half behind it. But she would have a rest, and wave some more later. If only she could shout, too.

She sat for a moment by the window, then went back to her exploration of the room, finding another door on the far wall leading into a toilet. No water, though, and no window either. Eventually she went back to her pile of mattresses and sat down, leaning her head on her bound hands. There was one way out of this room – through the locked door.

Tears hot in her eyes, Sarah sat wishing with all her heart that Jack was imprisoned here too. Together, they might have a chance of escaping. A sudden thought made her gasp – the killer might have murdered Jack. But no – she was the one who'd done all the investigating Petra's death, so she was the one the killer would find threatening. But if Jack had tried to protect her... Of course maybe he'd run away to fetch help and returned to find her gone. And if Jack *hadn't* been taken prisoner along with her, he'd be helping the police look for her. Hope flared again. Had he recognised the person who'd attacked them? The attacker could have been wearing a mask, though, waiting there by the garages as they pulled up...

Or... No. Oh no.

The scene burst into her head, and she tried to push it away but it insisted on coming back. They were outside the lock-up, and Jack reached past her for the key, but the object he produced hadn't been a key. The mental picture was clear. His hand holding the object had come towards her... oh no. No... Was it *Jack* who had taken her prisoner? But that couldn't be. That would mean Jack had killed Petra and that – couldn't – be.

His face swam before her eyes, but she couldn't see the person behind the features. No feelings, no emotions. A mask. Jack. But she'd known him since she was a child...

Fool that you are, she told herself. You don't know him at all. You even noticed that he always talked about things, not feelings. His conversation last night had been a mixture of travel brochure, twenty questions, and a town and country planning lesson. He'd probably prepared it the night before... Sarah sobbed into the gag. Help me, Mim, Mama, help me, someone. It was Jack. And he was going to come back for her. She had to be ready.

He was half-asleep on the sofa when the police arrived, and the bing-bong of the bell followed by thumps on the door a few moments later dragged him back to full consciousness. He'd expected them to come, of course, but oh God, he was so tired.

Two officers came in and sat on his elegant sofa, a sergeant and a younger man. They were very polite, or at least one of them was. The younger one was silent, frowning at Jack, his mouth tight. Jack sighed. Good cop, bad cop, the oldest trick in the book.

'We need to know exactly what happened when you left Miss Martin last night,' said the older man.

Choking back sobs, Jack told them about the long-anticipated meal out, and the Tia Maria coffee he'd made afterwards. Then on the way back to Sarah's they'd hit the traffic disruption...

Both officers nodded at this, and Jack blessed the burst water pipe and blocked streets. Sarah had insisted on getting the bus back – it was only a couple of stops – so he let her out in the High Street. The last he saw of her she was walking towards the bus stop.

'You didn't think to wait with her until the bus arrived?' The sergeant raised his eyebrows.

Jack wrung his hands. 'She's independent like that. It was due any minute, and she insisted I went home – she knew I was on early duty in the morning.'

'It's a pity you didn't insist too – on driving her home,' said the man, and Jack winced at his tone.

'Like I said – when she gets an idea in her head you can't go against it,' said Jack, allowing himself to sob. And it was a real sob and real anguish. He'd wanted none of this.

The cops asked a lot more questions – what had they talked about, how well had they known each other, who else was on the High Street, and on and on and on – Jack's head was buzzing with all their stupid, stupid questions. But in the end the officers got up to leave.

'There'll be more questions later,' said the older man. 'You'll need to come down to the station to make a statement, unless Miss Martin turns up very soon. We'll let you know.'

Jack watched at the window as the panda car drove off, then he collapsed back on the sofa. Thank God, and actually, that had gone rather well. Mim Dunbar would confirm Sarah was independent, and he was pretty sure he'd been convincing about stopping in the High Street. Telling them about the bus stop with the people waiting and how one of them had been sick was a nice little touch. Something they could check out.

Bloody police.

Glynis Brady gazed at the list in front of her, her pen hovering in the air. She'd thought and thought while she was doing the housework this morning, but no-one that wasn't on this first list was coming to mind. Days spent in a hospital tended to merge into each other. But thinking like that wouldn't help Sarah Martin. This list had ended up much longer than she'd ever have thought possible, so maybe a new one would too. She'd do what Caitlyn Mackie suggested and make a separate page for every day she'd spent in hospital. She got up for more paper.

The day of the operation might be a good place to start. That was a Thursday. They'd taken her upstairs to the operating theatre at about ten; she was woozy already from the pre-med they'd given her. But she'd put everyone she talked to there on the first list... Oh no, she hadn't – the anaesthetist, she'd forgotten all about him. Mind you, she'd only seen him twice and all they talked about was operations and medication. But it just went to show that it was worthwhile making this new list. Now, in the operating theatre she hadn't been talking to anyone, and when it was over she'd been taken to the recovery room. She didn't remember much about that because she'd still been pretty much out of it, but she'd have spoken to people there, and they weren't on the first list either. She wrote 'recovery room staff' on the list under the anaesthetist and carried on. Back at the ward... everyone there was on the other list. Stuart and Ellen had visited that evening, but she'd been feeling pretty tired and sore.

Could someone have heard Stuart and Ellen talking, and got Ellen's name from that? Or – wasn't Ellen's name in her hospital notes as next of kin? So anyone with access to the notes could have read that.

Glynis made a note on the new list to remind her to talk to Caitlyn Mackie about it, and paused. Right. That was the operation day. What had she done the day before, on the Wednesday? The operation was originally scheduled for Wednesday, but there'd been a problem with the operating table in one of the theatres and a couple of unlucky patients, including her, were changed to Thursday's list. So on Wednesday she'd spent the morning in the ward, not eating or drinking and thinking she would have her operation in the afternoon. Then the operating table had broken, and they'd given her lunch at two o'clock, and she'd gone to sit in the day room. A couple of other patients were there with their visitors, and they'd all commiserated with Glynis. More new people for the list. This was an excellent idea. She couldn't be sure she hadn't talked about Stuart and Ellen to these people. And then – then they had left her alone in the room, or not quite alone, because two old ladies were watching television at the other end, repeats of *Keeping Up Appearances*. She'd sat there, half-watching and leafing through a magazine, and... A man had come in...

A cold shiver ran down Glynis's back as she thought about the man. She hadn't remembered anything about him when she'd made the other list. He was young, late twenties, early thirties at a guess. He came into the room and smiled at her.

'I'm looking for my Aunt Violet,' he'd said, attractive green eyes twinkling at Glynis. 'Mrs Cameron. Do you know where she is?'

'No, I'm sorry,' she'd said. 'I've only been here since yesterday.'

He perched on a nearby chair. 'You look as if you could do with a visitor too.'

They'd chatted for a couple of minutes, the kind of friendly chat people have in hospitals, and... she'd told him her name and about the postponed operation, and – yes, about Stuart and Ellen who wouldn't come in till the next evening now because it was a bit of a trail from their home in Elderlea Park... She had definitely talked about her family with this man. Could it be...

She would sit here for another few minutes and think some more, complete the list as well as she could. Maybe there were other people she'd talked to. In fact there were, other people's visitors had chatted to her too. But not alone, like this man had. Dear Lord.

She sat thinking and writing until half past eleven, then considered her efforts. She had seven new people, plus the recovery room staff and other people's visitors. She should phone Caitlyn Mackie. Except she seemed to have lost her phone number... but here was Sarah's. It was a landline, but surely there would be someone there.

Ignoring her sticks, Glynis stood up and walked to the phone. Had she spoken to a murderer that day?

Chapter Eighteen

Friday, 21st July – afternoon

Jack paused in his pacing between the kitchen and living room, and dropped onto the sofa. It was no use. He couldn't hang around waiting for the phone to ring. Mim Dunbar would hardly call to tell him that Sarah hadn't been found. She must really resent him; she'd be thinking if he'd been a bit more careful, Sarah would still be fine – which was correct, but not in the way she'd mean it.

Sweat broke out on his forehead when he thought of Sarah in her cellar room. Were her bonds tight enough to keep her still? His imagination was running riot here... Sarah, waiting to die. And Petra's flat face, and Netta's bloody one, and oh, if only he'd never started this. He was as trapped as Sarah was. Suppose she managed to attract attention? But that was idiotic – she was in one of the oldest buildings in the hospital, right up at the far end of the complex, and the cellar room was at the back of the building. She was behind two doors which he had locked personally, and nobody ever went down there. Nobody would hear her if she screamed, and anyway, she was gagged. But...

Jack thumped the arm of the sofa. It was no use. He'd have no peace of mind until he'd seen her again, dying comfortably on her mattress.

He drove the few miles to the hospital automatically. A curse on old Wilma and her wretched family; this was all their fault. The main hospital thoroughfare was busier than usual and he pondered where to park. He was supposed to be off duty and out of his mind with worry, but if anyone saw the car he could say he'd left his phone. There were spaces in the rehab car park, and he pulled up beside a black van and switched the engine off.

This was actually a pretty good time to come and be unnoticed. Patients' lunches were served about half past eleven so the nurses were busy helping people eat, and the rest of the staff would be having lunch too or doing paperwork. No-one would be watching who was going in and out of the psycho-geriatric building.

Jack pulled his jacket round him, stepped confidently through the psycho-geri front doorway, hurried round the far corner to the stairs and ran down. There! No-one had seen him; no-one had heard him. He was safe in the dark.

He pulled out his chain with master keys for the entire hospital – one of the boons of being a porter, though of course he was supposed to hang it in the office safe when he wasn't working – and unlocked the first cellar door.

In you go, Jack, close the door behind you; it's a nice soundproof one. This building had been built to withstand air raids and act as a bomb shelter. Had they really brought the patients down here during the war? Jack shivered. Imagine being stuck in a dark cellar for hours on end with a crowd of mad geriatrics, listening to bombs going off.

He opened the second door and stepped into Sarah's room, pulling the torch from his pocket, swinging it over the pile of mattresses, and *hell*... His heart thundered into his throat as something hard struck him on the side of his head. He swirled round, arms up to defend himself. Sarah was standing just out of reach, a long metal pole in her hands, staring at him with an indescribable expression on her face. She was nowhere near dying.

He leapt forwards and grabbed the pole, twisting it while she fought against him, kicking out as well as shoving with the pole. But he was stronger and her wrists were still bound. It only took a moment to wrest the pole from her grasp and fling it to the side. The clang of metal on metal rang round the cellar room as the pole slithered over a bed frame. Jack seized Sarah's wrists with one hand and squeezed, and her legs buckled. He had won. He yanked her back to the pile of mattresses and shoved her down again. Her eyes, he had to cover her eyes, they were looking at him so terribly. How had she managed to free herself?

Fear and fury alike gripped him. 'What do you think you're doing? Where's the sack?' he hissed, and saw her flinch. Aha, she thought he was going to kill her right here and now. Well, she was lucky he wasn't. He pushed her flat and she struggled anew, but he won in moments.

'You think you're so clever, don't you?' He spat the words out, he was so angry. Holding her head down on the mattress he played the torch round the room while she tried to kick towards him. That window – hadn't it been blocked up before? The beam of light revealed the cords on the floor by the window and oh, clever Sarah, she'd made a flag and pushed it outside. Bloody poles... He seized her shoulders and shook, and she moaned, jerking away from him. Beside himself, he slapped her cheek as hard as he could then strode to the window.

'Aha. What a good idea,' he sneered, sliding the flag back inside and detaching the sack. 'But you're not so clever really, are you? You had no idea about anything, the whole time. You didn't even notice at the restaurant when I talked about Glynis. So you can lie back down and do as you're told.'

Despite his anger it hurt, speaking to Sarah like that. Ignoring the guilt, Jack strode back to where she was struggling into an upright position, and hauled the sack back over her head, avoiding her feet as she kicked out again. He sat on her legs while he retied her feet, as tightly as he could this time. When he had finished she was still, and he could tell by her breathing she was terrified. He hesitated. Could he kill her now? He was angry enough; he was furious that everything was going so bloody wrong and it wasn't his fault. A few good swipes with that pole would end it all for Sarah.

But no, he couldn't do it. Not Mrs Jack Morrison. He would have to leave her here to die when she was good and ready.

He should restrain her a little better, though, just in case. Jack pulled a mattress from the stack in the corner and dumped it on top of her body, hearing her breath catch as it landed on her chest. They were dusty old things, these mattresses. He stared – he couldn't see her at all now. She wouldn't get up again, but to be safe he added a further mattress.

Right. Everything would be okay. Jack went back to the window and replaced the boxes she'd managed to push down.

He didn't speak on his way out, but he looked back from the doorway, then clicked his torch off. Everything was dark again, pitch black and quiet for Sarah's death. Sarah... but don't think about it anymore. She would die quietly, peacefully. It might be years before they found her.

Relief washed through Jack as he locked the doors behind him and ran back upstairs towards the main door – but shit, no – here was Evan from Wilma's rehab ward, and there was no place to hide.

'Hey, Jack. I'm being porter today,' said Evan, slowing down as they approached each other. He was carrying a small cardboard box.

'Oh?' managed Jack, aware that his voice was higher than usual. Evan couldn't have heard that Sarah was missing, so if he kept things brief and normal there would be no reason for the nurse to wonder about meeting him.

'Mrs Munro was transferred here this morning and I forgot to pack the stuff in her locker drawer,' said Evan, stamping on towards the lift. 'So I'm playing delivery man in my damned lunch hour. See you.'

Back in his car, Jack took a moment to recover. That had very nearly been disastrous. If Evan had been five seconds earlier, he'd have seen Jack coming up from the cellar, and that might have been unusual enough to stick in the nurse's mind.

Fortunately, it had all ended well. But visiting Sarah was too dangerous. Tears burned in his eyes. He would never see her again.

'Yes, she's here... It's Mrs Brady.'

Mim held out the phone and Caitlyn took it, her hand shaking. Mrs Brady wouldn't call unless she'd found something.

'Have you remembered anything?' Her voice came out a breathless whisper. It was unendurable, watching time tick by, knowing that at the very best Sarah was in terrible danger, and at worst already dead.

Mrs Brady sounded breathless too. 'I think I have. There are a couple of hospital people I'd forgotten about, and some visitors, and there was one man in particular who spoke to me when I was alone. He said he was looking for his aunt and we spoke for a few minutes. He definitely asked me about my family and I told him about Stuart and Ellen.'

'Do you know his name?'

'He did say but I can't remember. Steve, I think, or John. An ordinary name. Should I call the police?'

'Let me tell our Sergeant West, and we'll leave him to organise things. I'll call you later.' Caitlyn ended the call and turned to Mim and Frankie.

'She's remembered talking to a man.' At last, at last, it was something positive. Caitlyn punched out Harry West's number.

'Glynis Brady in Manchester called. She remembers talking about her family to a strange man while she was in hospital,' she said baldly, and heard Harry inhale sharply.

'I'll get my colleagues there to help her make an e-fit image of him. Bring Frankie to the station here in half an hour, and we'll see if she can identify it.'

Caitlyn relayed this to Mim, and saw hope replace the calm despair on the older woman's face.

Frankie pulled at Mim's arm. 'Is this the man who killed my mum?'

'I don't know, but Frankie, we'll manage this,' said Mim, stroking the child's hair. 'Oh Caitlyn, if only it isn't a false alarm. If we know who's taken Sarah, that's a big step towards getting her back, isn't it?'

All Caitlyn could do was nod dumbly. Who was she to destroy what might be the last hope of getting Sarah back? But even if Frankie did recognise the picture, even if she took one look and said, 'That's John X,' – there was still no guarantee they would find Sarah, or that she was still alive.

'I'll lock up next door,' she said, and escaped the unbearable brightness in Mim's eyes.

E-fit pictures weren't always accurate, she knew that from her work. Would they be able to take one look at this one and know who it was?

A pain flashed through her head then vanished, leaving light in its place.

John X. No. Jack. It was Jack. It couldn't be, yet it must be. It all fitted. Jack had access to Wilma in the hospital. Jack the porter could easily have offered Petra a lift to the admin building, and she wouldn't have thought twice about accepting. Jack had spoken to Netta at the funeral... and he'd been the last person to see Sarah.

Hands trembling, Caitlyn lifted her phone.

'We're keeping an eye on him, don't worry,' said Harry West heavily. 'But he was pretty convincing about leaving her in the High Street. A couple of things he said about that check out in his favour. The image from Mrs Brady will be through very shortly, and we'll know. Get Frankie to the station, and we'll take it from there.'

Caitlyn lifted her car key from the hall table and turned to see Frankie standing in the doorway.

'You think she's dead, don't you?' she said accusingly.

'Frankie, I don't know. No-one can know that. And don't you dare say anything to upset Mim even more, do you hear?'

The girl nodded, tears in her eyes. Caitlyn hugged her briefly as they went back next door. Suppose they never found Sarah, never found a body... People sometimes disappeared without trace, and no-one ever found out what happened to them. Please, not that for Sarah.

The drive back across town was enough to settle Jack's nerves. Everything was sorted; he could get on with his life. But how empty it seemed without Sarah. All he had left was the house, and he couldn't do much more there until he had more cash. Well, he would get that, and this time from a source unconnected to a hospital. It would distract him from what was going on with Sarah and at Mim Dunbar's. He had to make his life bearable again.

He'd given some thought to the woman he'd met in the Indian Takeaway, Sheena Cameron, and her mother, and concluded they were ideal candidates for his next cash injection. He couldn't use his usual modus operandi, but a new plan would be worth making. He'd swing past on the way home and see if he could find out anything useful.

Thanks to the takeaway, the parking spaces near Mrs Bruce's home were all full, and Jack had to park quite a long way beyond it. He walked back along the narrow pavement, wishing he'd left the car at home. Mrs Bruce lived in a mid-terrace house with a small patch of gravel in front. There was a brass name plate by the bell and he crept up the path. Damn – all it said was E + T Bruce. But maybe he could work this without the woman's first name. Jack returned to his car, playing out the possible phone call in his head. When he arrived home he went straight to the drawer in the kitchen and pulled out the prepaid mobile he used for the scam. Now the phone book – hopefully E + T Bruce were listed... yes, there they were. And now was as good a time as any.

'Mrs Bruce? I'm John Murray, a friend of Sheena's – can I ask you something?'

'Yes?' She sounded suspicious, and Jack began to wonder if this was going to work after all. Oh well, he'd have one good try, and if nothing came of it he wouldn't have lost anything.

'I'm planning a little break for Sheena and Tim and me, a long weekend. Sheena said Tim would be happy whatever I chose, but I'm sure she just didn't want me to book anything I couldn't afford. So I thought I'd ask you the kind of thing Tim would enjoy most.'

Mrs Bruce sniffed. 'Teenage boys ain't hard to please. Rollercoasters, that kind of thing. Like they have in Paris.'

Jack made himself sound uncertain. 'Oh – Euro Disney? I'm afraid that would be a bit too expensive – though Sheena did once say she'd love to go there...' He allowed his voice to trail away. 'I don't suppose you could lend me the deposit?'

It sounded desperate even as he spoke, but she didn't refuse outright. 'Why don't you and Sheena come for tea tomorrow? Tim has a birthday coming up. I'll call Sheena – maybe we could work something out.'

'Excellent. Thank you so much. I'll see you soon.' Jack stammered his goodbyes and flung the mobile back into the drawer. What a disaster. What would Sheena think when her mother talked to her about her friend John Murray? Oh, well – it would only have been a few hundred. Trips to Paris didn't cost the earth these days.

But oh, God – when would Sarah die?

None of them spoke on the way to the police station. Caitlyn parked in one of the visitor spaces at the side of the building, and went round to open Mim's door. The older woman was back on both sticks today, so she must be feeling shaky. Caitlyn gripped Mim's arm as they walked. Should she have said something about her suspicion that Jack was Petra's killer? No – there was no point upsetting Mim even more until they knew for sure, and that would be very soon.

Mandy Craven met them inside the door. 'We're using DI Summers's office. The image should be here very shortly.'

Mandy settled Mim into the one comfortable chair

while Caitlyn and Frankie sat on a broad window ledge overlooking a sports field. DI Summers came in and greeted them briefly, then sat down facing the computer screen, Harry West standing behind him. The silence in the room was oppressive, but Caitlyn couldn't for the life of her think of anything to break it. This was too important for the trite – and there was nothing meaningful she could say, either. Frankie looked up at her, all eyes, and Caitlyn wondered how on earth the girl would cope if Sarah died. First Petra, then Sarah. No child could cope with that.

The minutes ticked by, and Caitlyn squirmed on the hard window ledge. How long did it take to make an e-fit picture? She was about to ask when DI Summers spoke tersely.

'Okay. Here we are.' He gazed at the computer screen, lifting the phone when it started to ring. Caitlyn stared at him, aware that Mim and Frankie were staring too, and none of them were breathing normally. DI Summers clicked then double-clicked the mouse and spoke into the phone.

'Yup. It's here. Hang on.'

He swung the screen round to face the room, and Caitlyn and Frankie stepped forward to lean over the back of Mim's chair. The face on the screen was an unreal-looking caricature with short dark hair, a long nose, high cheekbones and wide-set eyes.

Caitlyn's ears began to buzz and she fought back dizziness. Mim's hands were fluttering towards her throat.

'But that's Jack,' said Frankie, her voice puzzled. 'He's

Sarah's boyfriend.'

Harry West's face was as grim as Caitlyn had seen it. 'I'm afraid people aren't always what they seem.'

Mim was trembling, and her voice shook. 'Why would Jack take Sarah – why – dear heavens, was it Jack who killed...'

Caitlyn leaned over to hold her, then Frankie began to cry, and Caitlyn let Mim go to cuddle the child. 'Mim, we'll find him. We'll make him tell us where Sarah is.' But oh, would they be in time to get her back alive?

DI Summers clattered the phone down. 'They're on their way to bring him in. We'll search his home and his workplace. We'll question the neighbours and his workmates and any other names we come across. If it is humanly possible, Mrs Dunbar, we'll find her. I want you to go home and wait there.'

Caitlyn helped Mim to her feet. How shaky she was, leaning heavily on both sticks. With Mandy on the other side they went back to the car, away from the bustle inside the police station, all the rushing and shouting that was the start of the search for Jack – and Sarah.

'We'll be home in ten minutes, Mim, and get you some tea.' Caitlyn reached across to fasten Mim's seatbelt. As if tea was going to help. Poor Mim. Poor all of them. And thank God in heaven her kids were with their father, well away from this.

Mim was leaning back in the passenger seat, her eyes closed. Caitlyn looked round at Frankie. There was anger as well as sheer misery on the child's face, exactly what Caitlyn was feeling too. No-one could imagine a worse scenario than this. And there was nothing they could do to hurry the search along.

'Miss Mackie! Mrs Dunbar!'

Mandy Craven was running back towards them and Caitlyn stalled the engine, her heart hammering. What had happened? Had they found –

Mandy Craven opened the door and bent to speak to Mim. 'We've just heard – a shoe has been found behind the shops in the High Street, and it matches the description of Sarah's. Could you wait and see if you can identify it? It's being brought here now.'

'Of course,' said Mim faintly.

Caitlyn and Mandy helped her back into the building. This time they were shown into a waiting room close by the front desk. Mim reached for Frankie's hand. Caitlyn saw how the girl held on for dear life, and how Mim choked back a sob. At least they had each other. But if Sarah's shoe had been found then she wasn't wearing it, which meant – what?

A few minutes later they heard people at the front desk. Caitlyn and Mim exchanged apprehensive glances. This was the shoe arriving.

A few minutes later Harry West came into the waiting room, carrying a black strap sandal in a see-through plastic bag, and Mim sat up straighter. Caitlyn leaned forward.

Harry gave Mim the bag with the sandal.

'It looks like hers,' whispered Mim. 'Black leather, silver buckle. And new.'

She turned the sandal over and Caitlyn began to shake. The size was there on the instep, a continental 38 and not the British 5. It was a Swiss shoe.

'It is Sarah's,' said Mim, choking on the words. Frankie burst into tears, and Caitlyn closed her eyes as Harry grabbed the sandal and strode off with it.

Mandy Craven came back in. 'That's all. You can go now. The sandal's off to forensics, and we'll be in touch.'

For the second time Caitlyn helped Mim back to the car.

Jack stood in his lovely kitchen, trying in vain to calm his racing heart. This couldn't be good for him. This was stress; you were supposed to avoid it. Everything would be all right, because it had to be. The Sarah situation was under control. He swallowed painfully. Of course he was sad she would never be Mrs Jack Morrison, but... that wasn't meant to be, and he had to get on with his life. And the best way to do that was to concentrate on the house. One more cash injection, then he'd take a break until next year. He had to forget Sarah and start living normally again.

He would go to the caff for something to eat, yes – the fridge was empty. And he should think about Sheena's mother – maybe he could still turn that round. The woman didn't know he was the one who'd phoned her... maybe the face to face method he used in the hospitals was best. He could plan while he was eating, and go and see Mrs Bruce on the way home. It was quite safe; Sheena only went on Tuesdays.

Forty minutes later, a hamburger and chips digesting in his stomach, he was standing on the other side of the road, looking across to Mrs Bruce's house. The problem was, for some reason his head wasn't cooperating – he couldn't think of an excuse to go and see the woman. He'd have to leave this for another day. And even if she did give him a load of detail about her life, he could hardly phone and pretend to be yet another of Sheena's boyfriends wanting to give her a treat. He licked his lips. He could go and... no, he had to...

It was difficult to think straight. Tears welled up in his eyes and he fumbled for a tissue – was he losing his touch? All those years he'd spent running round doing what Mum and Dad told him, being a puppet. Now was his time, and he couldn't lose that. He needed a lovely home – he hadn't meant anyone to get hurt. Not Petra and not that old woman and oh, not Sarah.

It was all hopeless.

A movement in the window of the house opposite attracted his attention, and to Jack's horror he saw Sheena standing there with – presumably – her mother. His heart almost stopped, so great was the shock. He knew the older woman. That was Liz. He hadn't known her surname, but she was one of the people his mother would meet at the supermarket and chat to, while he was standing there behind her, sweating with a boxful of groceries.

Now Sheena was pointing at him and Liz Bruce was talking, then Sheena held up her phone. Christ no. She'd taken a photo of him, her friend John Murray, the one who'd phoned her mother and wanted to borrow money for a surprise...

Black despair crashed down on Jack. That was it. It was over.

He turned and fled back along the road. Home, home. Back to his refuge.

Caitlyn slumped in the corner of the sofa, clutching the mug of tea Frankie had made. She should call Mrs Brady and thank her for doing the e-fit picture. The lists had worked, and if they got Sarah back it would be largely due to Glynis Brady.

The phone rang, and Frankie rushed to answer it before Caitlyn could move. Mim reached out a hand and Caitlyn gripped it tightly. Every phone call, any moment, might bring the worst news of all. There was nothing she could say to comfort Mim; the poor soul was in hell.

'It's Mr West,' said Frankie. She gave the phone to Mim and leaned on the arm of the sofa, her thin little body tense.

Mim's face was set. She said 'Yes,' and 'I see,' and clicked the phone off. Caitlyn breathed out. Whatever it was, it still wasn't the worst news.

'Anything?' she said, surprised she sounded so calm.

'He's coming round. Jack's fingerprints are on the sandal,' said Mim.

Caitlyn slumped. It brought them no closer to finding Sarah. The police would be searching Jack's house, they'd be fingerprinting things there too, and looking for evidence that Sarah had been there. Other officers were at the hospital talking to Jack's colleagues.

It was after two o'clock. Sarah had been missing for over twelve hours.

The doorbell rang, and Caitlyn rose to answer it.

Frankie immediately took her place and cuddled up beside Mim on the sofa.

Harry West, and one look at him told Caitlyn that there was still no good news.

He sat on the armchair and spoke quickly. 'We're searching the area where the sandal was found, but we haven't found anything else there. Jack Morrison seems to have vanished off the face of the earth, and that's not a good sign. We're speaking to the neighbours and we're pulling the street apart looking in sheds and so on. He has an old lock-up too. There was a, em, a –' he raised his eyebrows at Mim and Caitlyn, then glanced towards the kitchen where Frankie had gone to fetch Mim a glass of water, '– a stained shovel there that we're, um, investigating.'

Caitlyn heard Mim's breath catch, and reached for her hand. It was cold as ice.

'The stains are old ones,' said Harry hurriedly, and Mim's hand shook in Caitlyn's. So the shovel may have been used to kill Petra, but not Sarah.

'What are you doing now?' said Caitlyn, shifting along the sofa as Frankie reclaimed her cuddle position beside Mim.

Harry stood up. 'We're bringing in dogs to use at the hospital and at Morrison's place. We need a couple of things that Sarah has worn, for the scent.'

'Fetch Sarah's blue pullover and her slippers, would you, Frankie?' said Mim. Her voice broke as she continued. 'She was wearing them yesterday, before she went out with – with him.'

'What about an appeal?' said Caitlyn.

Would Jack tell them where Sarah was, if he was caught? There was no way to know what had been going on in his mind all this time. He could act, that was clear.

'We've got Jack's photo out on TV and online,' said Harry. 'There's a recent one on his file at the hospital.'

Mim drew a shuddering breath. 'I don't care if you find him or not,' she said, her voice wobbling dangerously. Caitlyn could hear that in spite of her efforts a storm of tears wasn't far off. 'Find Sarah, that's all I want.'

'I know.' Harry West turned to go.

Caitlyn rose to her feet. 'I'm coming with you. I want to help, and I know Sarah and the hospital too,' she said, and was surprised at the decisiveness in her own voice.

'I wish I could come,' said Mim, putting her hands round her new knee and shaking it.

'You stay here with Frankie. Caitlyn, you can come if you don't get in the way,' said Harry.

Caitlyn picked up the plastic bag with Sarah's clothes and touched Mim's shoulder on the way out. In the car she sat silently as Harry pulled away from the house. She didn't look round; she knew the sight of Frankie standing in the window would have her in tears. And she needed to be strong now for Sarah.

Please God there still was a Sarah.

Chapter Nineteen

Friday, 21st July – evening

Jack scurried along the road, pulling up abruptly when he reached the end of his street. Two police cars were sitting at his garden gate. Outrage crashed over him when he saw movement in the living room window, and he began to pant. What were they doing in his beautiful house?

Think, man, think. The police couldn't possibly have found Sarah. They couldn't know he had taken her. Maybe they simply wanted to ask him more questions... they'd said there would be more later. Had they come to collect him, take him to the station? But why go inside? And why the second car? He should go and see what they wanted – help them with their inquiries. It would be best to appear cooperative.

But no. What was happening at his house was more than a pair of policemen arriving to interview him. A third car had arrived, and four officers were going up the path with a couple of cases. Someone inside opened the door, and the new arrivals vanished into the house. Jack wiped his sweat-streaked face with one hand. Now they were cordoning off the street; a tall policeman was stretching blue and white tape from one side to the other. Mrs Grant across the road came out and spoke to him, and the officer gesticulated towards Jack's house. They must be going to search it, but didn't they need a warrant or something? Or maybe they had one. Well, they wouldn't find anything of Sarah there.

But that would mean they were looking for him, too.

So. It had happened. The worst thing of all. They had somehow found out that he was the mastermind behind – what? Sarah's disappearance? Petra's murder? Swindling a handful of old dears out of their savings? Whichever it was, it was all up for him. He would never be able to finish his perfect house; his glorious dream of building a perfect future in his lovely home was over. His beautiful, brightly-coloured bubble in the sky had burst.

He would go to prison. There would be more humiliation, more pain, more Mummy and Daddy people telling him what to do all the time, forcing him to be subservient, an underdog.

At that moment Mrs Grant saw him and raced back to the policeman, who was attaching his tape to someone's gatepost. The cop yelled over his shoulder and two other officers appeared. They all charged down the street towards Jack.

And he stood there, because there was nowhere to go, and nowhere to hide. If he'd known, he could have gone to the hospital to lie in death with Sarah. He sank to his knees on the grubby pavement and waited for them to reach him.

Her throat hurt so much. She was breathing through her mouth now, because the tears that came when Jack left her had blocked up her nose and nearly choked her. Why had he done this to her? Was he some kind of psychopath? He must be. And if she'd had half her brain switched on back in the restaurant, she'd have realised something was wrong when Jack mentioned Glynis. He was right; she'd been a fool, sitting there worrying about greasy banana fritters. Now she was paying for it.

She thought of the Jack she had first known, way back at primary school. He'd been small then, a mere sliver of a child in a grey school pullover. His uniform was always freshly ironed; he was the only boy in the class with a school cap, and he'd had one of those short back and sides haircuts that were popular in the 50s. And his mum had never let him go to anyone's home to play after school. He was a little comedian, though. He'd made the other kids laugh, and because of that he'd been accepted. All the little girls had secretly fancied him. He could turn on the charm and he could act, even then. He'd been acting with her, all the time. He'd murdered Petra. Lucky Petra – she had her peace.

The silence was absolute. Wherever this was, it was well away from the cheerful camaraderie of the wards. Maybe she was down near the mortuary, some long-forgotten corner in the oldest part of the hospital. This place would have no cheerful river name, no. This was the dead ward. Ward Zero. Oh God, she was going to die here.

The mattresses on top of her were heavy and ill-smelling, even through the sack over her face, and they were pressing hard on her chest. Her head was twisted to the side – it was the only way she could breathe at all. Countless times she'd choked and spluttered, and each time she'd thought she was going to die right then, and it was so painful and so frightening. She didn't want to choke to death. But she would die here unless someone found her very soon, and what hope was there of that? If they'd been going to find her they'd have done it by this time. Oh, Mama. She didn't want to die.

The pain in her ankles had been replaced by blessed numbness. She could hardly feel her feet. Maybe the numbness would creep up and up her body until she was dead. Mim and Rita would be so grieved, and baby Ailsa would never know her Auntie Sarah. Even Jamie wouldn't remember her long. And she'd never know if Frankie stayed with Mim or went to Australia – stay with Mim, Frankie love. She'll need you.

Please let her die soon... Let it be over. She would never have a proper, loving relationship; never have a baby, be a mum... It was too late, and it was all her own fault.

The blackness was frightening. It was hard not to panic, but she knew if she started to cry she would choke again, and that would be such a horrible way to go. Better to wait for the numbness.

Was there life after death? Soon she would find out.

Caitlyn wiped sweating palms on her jeans as the police car sped towards the hospital. Her stomach was churning, but this was better than sitting at Mim's.

'What makes you think Sarah's at the hospital?' she asked, and Harry glanced across.

'We don't know where she is,' he said bluntly. 'But she's not at Morrison's house, and she's not in the lock-up affair he has, which is where Petra Walker was kept before he disposed of her. And apart from the hospital and the place where the sandal was found, there's nowhere else to search.'

Caitlyn swallowed. There was nothing positive about any of that. He didn't think Sarah was alive, Caitlyn could tell. The radio buzzed and a voice croaked into the car. 'We've got Morrison, boss, but he's not talking.'

'Make him talk. Report back as soon as he does.'

Caitlyn clenched her fists. There was hope, wasn't there? But Petra had been killed quite quickly, then dumped in... Her mouth went dry.

'The canal?' she whispered.

'We have teams up in the woods and along the pathway where Mrs Walker was found,' said Harry, turning into the main gate of the hospital. 'If they find anything we'll be the first to know.'

He pulled into a parking space outside admin. Caitlyn got out and stared round the sundry buildings. It was a huge complex, but surely there could only be so many places a missing woman could be hidden. It was a case of searching until everywhere was covered – it wasn't rocket science. Could Sarah really have been secreted away here, where thousands of people were in and out every day? Or were they were looking for a needle in a haystack where no needle was hidden?

Two brown and white dogs, some kind of spaniel, were

waiting with their trainers, and Harry West took them the plastic bag containing Sarah's sweater and slippers. Caitlyn blinked hard. That was the sweater Sarah'd been wearing the day they sat in the supermarket coffee shop, talking about the case for the first time. If they'd left well alone...

'Caitlyn.' Harry West's voice was firm. 'Come on.'

Caitlyn swallowed the tears. 'I'm okay.'

'Right. I want to go over the wards and departments Morrison worked in myself.' He reached into his jacket and produced a plastic folder. 'We've got a list of all the places he went to over the past two weeks. We'll start with maternity, rehab, and geriatrics.'

Caitlyn got back into the car and they drove to the end of the hospital. The rehab car park was distressingly familiar. She'd brought Mim for physio several times now, and she'd asked people here about Petra, too.

Harry West led the way into the nearby maternity block. 'Obstetrics and Gynaecology' was above the door, and Caitlyn winced again. Last week she'd been in another maternity unit, waiting for Rita's baby to be born, and Sarah had been there too, longing for a baby of her own. Caitlyn had seen the expression in her eyes.

This unit was the same vintage as the rehab unit – modern in a retro, 70s way. An administrator was waiting for them at the reception desk inside the main door, a bunch of keys in his hand.

'We'll start at the bottom and work up,' Harry said to the waiting man. 'You can lead the way.'

The administrator led them downstairs and they started to go through the cellar rooms. Caitlyn felt despair creep over her. They were going through the motions here, that was all, eliminating the impossible.

Cellars searched, they went back upstairs and walked through the wards. There were several little rooms to look through, storerooms and cupboards, not to mention offices and treatment rooms. The atmosphere was lively and bright; there were babies here, mums and dads and happy families.

'No attic?' said Harry, staring up at the ceiling when they'd completed the top floor.

'No. It's a flat roof. There's a terrace, if you want to put your head out, but nowhere anyone could hide,' said the administrator, leading them to a tiny stairway leading to the roof.

Harry did put his head out, grunted, and came back inside. 'Let's go over to rehab next.'

Caitlyn followed him, the heaviness back in her middle. She wasn't helping, but she didn't need to because even Harry didn't think they would find anything. She should have stayed with Mim and Frankie.

'What are the dogs doing?' she asked.

'Checking the grounds. If Sarah walked anywhere from a car yesterday, they'd scent her.'

Caitlyn swallowed. That didn't sound likely either.

The cellar in the rehab block was similar to the maternity cellar. Harry and Caitlyn pushed open doors and rummaged round storage rooms while the administrator talked on his phone.

Caitlyn bit down on a trembling lip when they were back on the ground floor. This was where everything started; where Sarah met Petra and Frankie and Wilma.

If that hadn't happened, Sarah would be at home now, helping Mim through Friday afternoon, safe and happy. How cruel life was. There were only a few cupboards to look into here, then they went up to the wards. Caitlyn's head buzzed. This was where Sarah met Jack...

Nick's head appeared out of an office as they passed. His face was drawn. 'Caitlyn. I've heard what's going on. I can't believe it... How's Mim coping?'

Caitlyn had to fight not to burst into tears. The last time she'd spoken to this man was at a memorial service. Please God they wouldn't attend another together. 'Not great,' she managed.

Nick pursed his lips. 'Let me – oh, here's Mr Benson back from getting his shunt cleared. Straight into his room, Evan.' He turned to help manoeuvre the bed through the doorway, speaking over his shoulder. 'I'll catch you up in a moment.'

Caitlyn followed Harry into two more storerooms. Trolleys, wheelchairs, stools, weird machines she had no idea about – everything but clues as to where Sarah might be. This was a waste of time.

Footsteps thudding along the corridor and men's voices shouting had Caitlyn racing to the door. Nick and Evan were hurtling towards them while patients and staff alike scattered out of their path, craning their necks to see what was going on.

Nick was in front. 'Evan saw Jack Morrison in geriatrics at lunchtime!'

'Show me where!' shouted Harry.

Caitlyn was already running for the stairs, her heart in her mouth.

'I was taking some things to a patient and he was walking up to the front door,' said Evan, panting as they thundered downstairs and tore across the car park towards the neighbouring building, the administrator following on. 'Now I think of it he looked a bit wild, but we didn't say much. It was around twelve. Bloody hell – I didn't know, I hadn't heard...'

'Save your breath and run, man,' said Harry, dodging between parked cars.

Hope and suspense were vying for top place in Caitlyn's mind. If Jack had come back here, did that mean Sarah was still alive? Not necessarily, her journalist's logic pointed out. Weren't murderers supposed to revisit the scenes of their crimes?

They clattered through the geriatrics doorway and stopped. Caitlyn was panting, fear mingling with wild hope in her heart.

'He was there,' said Evan, pointing to the floor about five metres from the stairs.

'Up or down?' demanded Harry. 'What's more likely?'

'Down!' Nick charged down the shadowy stairs, the others following more carefully until he switched on a dim light. 'There aren't many rooms here. It's never used. Shit, oh shit, it's locked. Evan, go and –'

'I have a master key,' said the administrator, pulling it from his pocket and unlocking the door.

Caitlyn was trembling. The terrible fear that Sarah was going to be dead on the other side of this door was almost stopping her breathing. They went through the door into a little hallway, and saw footprints in the dust, telling them which room to unlock next. Darkness leapt out as Harry pushed the door open. Nick pressed a switch but nothing happened, and they moved slowly into the room, the administrator holding the door wide open to let some light in.

'Sarah! Are you there?' called Nick, his voice shaking.

Caitlyn stared wildly round the room. Piles of goodness knows what, old beds, mattresses –

'She's here!' Evan was pulling mattresses from a pile. Caitlyn took one look, horror and dizziness washing over her. She crouched to the floor, fighting faintness.

Sarah's head was covered by a sack, which Nick pulled away to reveal a dirty rag tied round her mouth, and dried blood on her chin and neck. She was dusty and white, whiter than Caitlyn had ever seen anyone except bodies on TV, and her eyes were closed. Caitlyn suppressed a scream. Sarah's hands and feet were bloody and tied, and her dress was torn, twisted up past bloody knees. Oh God – had she been raped? Nausea swept over Caitlyn, and she knelt on the floor taking shallow breaths.

Nick and Evan pulled the mattress to the door where the light was better and crouched over Sarah, checking her pulse and her breathing.

'She's alive,' said Nick. He patted Sarah's cheeks, and a faint sound came from her mouth. For a second he leaned his head down to touch hers.

Evan pushed him aside and started to work on the gag with his scissors. 'Nick, get a grip. Undo her hands. Caitlyn, come over here and talk to her.'

Caitlyn crawled over to Sarah's head. 'Sarah. It's okay, we've got you,' she whispered, and saw Sarah's eyelids flicker.

Harry was on his phone in the hallway, and Caitlyn heard him ask for Mim. She put a hand on Sarah's brow. It was hot. 'You're safe now, Sarah, it'll be all right,' she said, and Evan pulled the gag away. Sarah coughed.

Nick was examining the cords round Sarah's wrists. 'This is impossible. Let's get her upstairs into a treatment room. Rob, run on ahead and tell them in Ward One, will you, and see if there's a doctor around.'

The administrator ran up the stairs, and Caitlyn saw Sarah's eyes crack open to look at Nick. Her lips moved but no sound came.

'Don't try to talk,' said Nick, gathering her into his arms, and the expression on his face made Caitlyn want to cry.

Sarah's eyes opened again as they all trailed out. 'It was Jack,' she whispered, her voice cracking.

'We've got him,' said Harry. 'And Mrs Dunbar's on her way in.'

Sarah blinked across at him and nodded before closing her eyes.

Evan clapped Caitlyn's shoulder. 'Come on. Up to Ward One. You can entertain her while we get her sorted.'

Caitlyn didn't know whether to laugh or cry. They were going to sort Sarah.

Sarah's eyes were stuck shut again. They were full of dust, and it was so bright here. She fought the faintness that was threatening to overcome her. Nick was carrying her and she could hear his breathing; they were going up stairs. Caitlyn's voice came from behind, reassuring her again that she was going to be all right. Everything hurt, but she wasn't going to die. She had her life back.

She felt herself being laid on a bed, and new voices were here now, talking to Nick. Someone took hold of her arm and wiped it with something wet and cold.

'Sarah, we're going to put up a drip, give you some pain meds, and get these cords cut. They'll take you across to A&E afterwards and put proper dressings on,' said Nick. 'Sharp scratch coming up.'

She barely felt it. 'My eyes.' It came out in a tiny whisper, but a moment later her eyes were being wiped. Sarah blinked furiously, and saw Evan with a damp cloth in his hand. 'Again,' she whispered, and Evan complied.

Sarah took a deep breath, then another. She could see and she could breathe. It was wonderful.

Her wrists jerked apart and she moaned.

'Sorry,' said Nick. 'The cords are cutting in. We'll cover them with gauze and leave them until the painkillers kick in.'

She blinked up at him and saw concern written all over his face. This man cared about her and all she'd thought was he might have stolen Wilma's money. Or worse. What a fool she'd been.

He settled a blanket over her as two paramedics came in with a trolley. 'An ambulance is here to take you down to A&E. Evan and I have to go now, but I'll come and see you soon. Okay?'

Sarah nodded, blinking as the two men left the room. How lucky she was.

CHAPTER TWENTY

Saturday, 22nd July

It was nine in the morning. The morning she'd thought she'd never see. Sarah moved her shoulders cautiously, then rolled on her side. She was in a single room off A&E, and everything hurt – especially her wrists. And her mouth. She ran her tongue round the inside of her lips, feeling how swollen they were; it was worse than yesterday. But she was alive, and she'd even slept, although it was a restless, dream-filled sleep which left her exhausted.

Now that it was over, her ordeal seemed like a bad dream. She could dimly remember the sudden bangs and shouting, and the frantic tone in Nick's voice when he shouted her name. The sheer, blessed relief that flowed through her at the sound of that voice. Another few hours in the cellar would literally have been the end of her.

A nurse put her head in the door. 'Oh good, you're awake again. You've got a visitor. Just five minutes, then we'll kick him out and I'll help you up.'

Wondering, Sarah pulled the cover up to her chest. Him? Was it Harry West?

It was Nick. He sat down and gazed at her without speaking.

'I was going to bring you chocolates,' he said at last. 'But I thought you might not enjoy them with a bashed mouth so I brought this.' He reached into his pocket and put a paperback – *1001 Hospital Jokes* – on her locker, and sat staring at her again.

Sarah saw the longing in his eyes. What could she say to this man? He wanted to be part of her future, but she had to come to terms with the present and the past before she could begin to think of things to come. A tear glittered in the corner of his eye and he flicked it away.

Sarah reached for the joke book and handed it to him. 'Hey. I know I'm not very beautiful right now, but I hope it's not so bad you have to blub about it. Find us a good joke – I could do with some humour here.'

He gave her an almost-smile. 'You're a sight for sore eyes, that's what you are. Who cares about being beautiful?'

Sarah managed an almost-smile back. 'Ouch. Well, I do. But they say I'll have mended in a week or two.'

He leafed through the book, then glanced up. 'Okay – here's a good one. It can be our joke.'

Sarah settled back in her pillows. 'Our joke' was maybe a good place to start.

Fury was tightening his gut. They'd kept him here all night, in a stupid little cell in the stupid police station and it was disgusting. He'd barely slept a wink on this narrow bench with its inadequate plastic-covered pad, but even if it'd been a king-sized bed, the shouting and swearing from the drunks they kept parading up and down would still have kept him awake. The front desk appeared to be just round the corner. And the smell of vomit and piss hanging in the air wasn't exactly restful, either.

He couldn't go on like this, he couldn't – they had no right to treat him like a common criminal. They'd tried twice to interview him yesterday, growling the same stupid questions over and over, even bringing in some stupid woman to 'represent' him. All she'd done was tell him to cooperate, so he'd refused to say a word.

A key clicked in the door and two men walked in. Ha! It was the DI and that stupid sergeant Sarah'd always been on about. Time to go, Jack, time to go. Bye bye.

He gave the men his broadest smile, and both their faces froze.

'Mr Morrison, we're going to do another interview and this time I strongly recommend you cooperate. Your lawyer will be here shortly and she'll talk to you first. Is there anything you'd like to say before she arrives?' The DI's voice was bored.

Jack slid along the bench and squeezed himself into the corner. 'Is Mummy coming soon?'

Sergeant West cleared his throat. 'No-one is coming because you refused your right to a phone call yesterday. Do you want us to inform your parents?'

Jack began to cry. 'I want my mummy.' He stared at the officers, making no effort to wipe away the tears streaming down his face. 'Mummy!'

Sergeant West leaned towards the DI. 'He's faking, boss.'

The other man turned for the door. 'Faking or not, we need the doc here. He's round the front.'

They left without a word to Jack, and the anger spilled over.

He ran to the door and beat it with his fists, sobbing in a high-pitched voice he'd never heard before. 'Mummy! I want my *mummy*!'

It wasn't long before the little window in the door was slammed open.

'Stop this racket! The doctor's here to see you.'

The cell door opened and Sergeant West came in with a solemn young man in a crumpled suit. He looked like he'd been up for a long time. Jack fled back to the corner of his bench, and the young man sat down about a metre away.

'Jack, I'm Doctor Cassidy and I'm here to help you. What's the problem?'

'I want my mummy.' It was a peevish whine, and Jack blinked at the doctor. He had kind eyes.

'Sergeant West can phone your, ah, mother, if that's what you want. What's her name?'

Jack giggled. 'Mummy.' His voice rose and cracked. 'Mummy, mummy, *mu – ummy*!'

The doctor patted his shoulder and went back to the officer on the door. 'Let's call her. We're getting nowhere here; you're going to need a psych assessment.'

'He's faking – isn't he?' The sergeant sounded less sure now, and Jack began to sob, then laughed loudly as the men left.

He was alone for a long time. Once the door opened, and Jack shouted, 'Mummy?' – but a tray with a plastic cup of tea, and a piece of toast was slid into the room without comment. Jack ate the toast and poured the tea on the floor.

Soon after that he heard her voice in the hallway.

'I can only assume you've got the wrong person here, Detective Inspector. My Jack wouldn't hurt a fly. He's a good boy.'

'He's a grown man, Mrs Morrison, and he's in bad trouble.'

'Nonsense.'

'I'm afraid not.'

The voices stopped a few metres away, and his mother spoke again. He'd heard the same self-satisfied outrage in her voice so many times before.

'Locked in a *cell*? This is ridiculous – Jack, darling! I'm here.'

Footsteps approached the door, and the key turned in the lock. This was it. Crunch time.

Jack began to scream.

The End

If you enjoyed *Ward Zero*, you may like to try Linda Huber's other books. Here's an extract from *Chosen Child*.

Chapter One

Saturday 3rd May

Ella held her breath, squinting at Rick as he inched the Peugeot into the narrow space between a battered Clio and a shiny new BMW. He was nervous – of course he was, she was too – and it didn't make the manoeuvre any easier. The Peugeot crept forward until Rick yanked the handbrake up, and Ella's shoulders sagged in relief. A scrape on anyone's car would have been the worst possible start to their first adoption party.

'I'll need to get out your side,' said Rick, glaring at the Clio. 'What a cattle market. I can't believe we're doing this – we'd be much better waiting for Liz to find us a kid the traditional way.'

Ella opened the passenger seat door. Rick was a planner; he'd never been the kind of person to simply have a go and see how things turned out. She tried to sound encouraging. 'Liz said these parties were a great place for people to find a child they were – attracted to.'

It was the wrong choice of words.

'I don't want to be attracted. You don't get to pick out an attractive baby when you have one of your own, do you? I don't care if he's blonde like you or dark like me, or whatever. All I want is a nice little kid – a boy, preferably, one we can give a good home to and enjoy as he grows up.' He struggled across the passenger seat and emerged beside Ella in the car park, crammed today with a motley selection of vehicles, including a tandem. People attending adoption parties seemed to be a varied lot.

Ella took Rick's arm as they walked towards the entrance. The Majestic was the largest hotel in St Ives, a relic from a slower, more elegant era, its white walls dazzling in the warm spring sunshine. She was conscious of the nervous churning in her stomach – this was the first time they would come face to face with children who were up for adoption. It was the dream of a lifetime for Ella – how very much she wanted to read bedtime stories and mop up tears and be frustrated because they couldn't find a babysitter. And this afternoon could bring them a huge step closer to doing just that. As of last Thursday, they were panel-approved to adopt, so 'all' they needed now was a child.

Ella was astonished when she learned about the adoption party project. It sounded so lightheaded, like going to a salesroom and picking out a new car.

Liz, their adoption society worker, had explained. 'It's organised as a fun afternoon for the kids, with loads of games and activities. People who're panel-approved can meet the children in an informal setting. There've been several successful events around London, though this one's the first in our part of the country.'

Ella wasn't sure she'd understood. 'So we have a look and see if there's a child that might suit us?'

'It can make a difference when you see a child in

person. I've known several instances of a couple saying beforehand they'd only consider a baby, or they must have a girl – and then they go to a party and fall in love with a completely different child. Of course you still need to go through all the normal channels afterwards.'

'Sounds a bit plastic to me,' said Rick, and Ella knew by his tone if he hadn't respected Liz so much he'd have called the idea something a lot worse than plastic.

And now it was party day and Rick was showing his nerves, so Ella had to be the calm one. She took a deep, steadying breath as they joined the other prospective adopters in the dining room. A woman name-badged Kirsty stood up and went on to tell them everything Liz had already gone through. Ella could feel Rick twitching beside her. Why was this so hard for him? It wasn't as if they had to make a decision today.

'And of course, the most important thing about this afternoon is that the children have fun. So on you go and have fun with them,' said Kirsty, gathering her papers at the end of her talk. 'The foster carers will be available for questions, and this room can be used if anyone wants a quiet place.'

Ella squeezed Rick's hand as they joined the general shuffle towards the door. This was it. The search for their child had begun. The sound of excited young voices floated across the garden, and anticipation fizzed through Ella. Any second now they might come face to face with the little boy who'd be their son.

'It's well organised, isn't it?' Her eyes flitted across the garden, where a bouncy castle, a couple of donkeys, and a clown were already in action. A marquee with games was set up to one side, and the smell of coffee came wafting over the grass.

'Hm. So we find a kid and start talking?' said Rick, and Ella gave his arm a shake.

'Yes – and give it a proper chance, please,' she said briskly.

Rick shot her a hunted look, and Ella felt the tension creeping back into her shoulders. She fought against rising resentment. This was supposed to be a fun day and she wanted to enjoy it. But if Rick went on like this he would ruin it for both of them.

After a few minutes the procession of adults dispersed around the garden, and the children became more visible. Some were clinging to foster carers, more were playing independently. A lump rose in Ella's throat – all these children needed a forever home, and all these 'parents' wanted a child. Surely some of them would find what they were looking for.

They stopped by a dark-haired boy of about three and Ella crouched down. 'Having a good time?' she asked, patting the plastic tractor the child was riding.

'I'm a farmer,' said the boy, whose name badge identified him as Joey. He pedalled his tractor over the grass, and Ella smiled as he swung it round and parked beside Rick. This little boy was just what they were looking for – could they have struck gold already?

A woman with a foster carer's badge appeared and handed the child an ice cream.

Ella stepped across and spoke in a low voice. 'Has Joey

been with you long?'

'Eighteen months,' said the woman, taking Ella a few steps to the side. 'Lovely kiddie. He has epilepsy but it's well-controlled.' She turned to smile at another couple who were hovering.

'Oh,' said Rick blankly when Ella told him what Joey's foster carer had said. 'I'd wondered if we might consider him, but now – no way. I wouldn't cope with that.'

Ella nodded. Rick had said right from the start that he didn't want a child with a disability, and she'd accepted it.

They stood for a while with a group watching the clown, then moved inside the marquee to help two small boys build a tower with wooden bricks. Disappointment and frustration were gnawing away inside Ella. She'd been imagining the equivalent of love at first sight bowling both her and Rick over – that they would see a child and know immediately 'that's the one'. And it wasn't happening. The little boys jumped up and down on the wooden marquee floor, and the tower swayed elegantly before crashing to the ground amid shrieks of laughter.

Rick was grinning too as they turned away. 'Fun, but not quite what we're looking for.' He pulled her towards the queue for coffee.

'We'll probably feel this way when they find us a child on paper,' said Ella, when they were sitting at a table overlooking the inside play area. 'It's normal.'

'When they find us a child the usual way, at least we'll know he ticks the important boxes. And we'll be able to get to know him in a quiet place, not in a bloody rabble.' Rick jerked his head to the corner of the marquee where two small boys and a thin little girl were quarrelling over an electric racing car track. The boys weren't letting the girl have a turn, and she wasn't taking it quietly.

Ella sipped slowly. Rick had given up on the afternoon. Why was he being so defeatist?

The racing car dispute came to a sudden end when one of the boys ripped up a piece of track and threw it at the girl before running off with his friend. The girl stared after them, blinking hard and pushing long dark hair behind her ears.

'Oops,' murmured Ella, and went over to the child, who was fitting the track together again, her eyes bleak. 'Want a hand with that?'

The girl looked about six or seven. She wasn't wearing a name badge, which made Ella wonder if she was up for adoption. Not that it mattered; this child ticked none of their boxes. Ella watched as she banged the track into place.

'I can't do it anyway,' she said, her voice trembling. 'But they should have let me try.' She slotted a car into place and lifted the hand control to demonstrate she really couldn't do it.

Rick crouched down and picked up the second control. 'I used to have one of these. Wonder if I can still make it go.'

'Who's that on there?' said the girl, pointing to the medallion round Rick's neck.

Ella laughed. 'St Christopher. He brings good luck to travellers. Just right for this game, isn't he?'

'It's got a bash.'

'That's because Rick dropped it one day and then drove over it. So maybe it's not so lucky after all.' Ella knelt beside the track. 'Let's have a race. You and me on the red car, Rick on the yellow one.'

The girl slid over and together they grasped the red control stick. A whiff of peach shampoo tickled Ella's nose, and tears welled up in her eyes. Why, why couldn't she have a child of her own? Life was cruel, and there would be no happy end for them this afternoon. All Rick wanted was to go home and let Liz get on with the task of finding them a little boy. Swallowing her disappointment, Ella held the girl's hand over the control and tried to keep the car on the track.

'Faster!' cried the child, pressing harder, and inevitably the red car spun off course.

Rick swept past with the yellow one and stopped. 'Have another go. The trick is to slow right down when you go into the curves.'

The girl gave him a suspicious look, then tried again. The red car crept along the bottom curve, accelerated briefly on the straight, then drove sedately round the top bend and into the garage area.

One of the foster carers came into the tent, relief on her face as she hurried towards the girl. 'There you are! Oh – you're playing cars? Where's your name badge?'

'I took it off,' said the girl. 'Kids were being stupid.'

Ella almost laughed. The words were so direct, and the woman clearly hadn't expected to find this child playing cars or anything at all.

The girl waved the handset towards Ella and Rick.

'Then *they* came and *he* told me how to do it and I drove a round by myself!' Her voice was positively triumphant. She gazed from Rick to Ella and beamed suddenly, showing a gap where a bottom front tooth should have been.

Oh my God, thought Ella, her breath catching in her throat. Oh my *God*.

Printed in Great
Britain
by Amazon